Zero Zone

ZERO ZONE

A Novel

SCOTT O'CONNOR

COUNTERPOINT
Berkeley, California

ZERO ZONE

Library of Congress Cataloging-in-Publication Data
Names: O'Connor, Scott, author.
Title: Zero zone : a novel / Scott O'Connor.
Description: First hardcover edition. | Berkeley, California : Counterpoint Press, 2020.
Identifiers: LCCN 2020001930 | ISBN 9781640093737 (hardcover) | ISBN
    9781640093744 (ebook)
Subjects: GSAFD: Fantasy fiction. | Science fiction.
Classification: LCC PS3615.C595 Z47 2020 | DDC 813/.6—dc23
LC record available at https://lccn.loc.gov/2020001930

Jacket design by Jaya Miceli
Book design by Jordan Koluch

COUNTERPOINT
2560 Ninth Street, Suite 318
Berkeley, CA 94710
www.counterpointpress.com

Printed in the United States of America

10 9 8 7 6 5 4 3 2 1

For Jenn and Linda O'Connor,
and for Marion Blow

I have longed for people before, I have loved people before.
Not like this.
It was not this.

Give me a world, you have taken the world I was.

—ANNE CARSON, "This"

Zero Zone

Prologue

WINTER 1954

J ess stood in the crowd on Colorado Boulevard, jumping for a better view, straining to see. She was restless and chilly in the bright, sunny morning, but hopeful, too. Her mother had promised them all something wondrous, a beautiful disruption in the middle of a city street on the first day of the new year.

They had come to Los Angeles for a week after Christmas. Jess's mother had long wanted to see the Rose Parade in person. For years Barb read about it in *Life* magazine, marveling over the colorful photos of the floats, their elaborate designs and ingenious use of flowers and fruit, calling Jess and her brother, Zack, over to the kitchen table, pressing a fingertip to a glossy image: *Kids, look—will you look at what they did with the poppies!*

So they made the trip, and waited shoulder to shoulder in the crowd. Jess grew impatient, feeling a little claustrophobic, surrounded by so many larger bodies. Her legs ached from standing so long. She was about to complain again when she heard the sound of drums, the bass thump deep in her chest, a marching band approaching, and then a giant pinwheel of color appeared, the first tall float coming into view.

Her mother had been right. *Wondrous* was the word. They pointed and clapped, *oohing* and *aahing* for the bands and high-stepping horses and the floats, *the floats*, sprouting colors Jess had never seen before, deep reds and yellows, pale oranges and pinks (Zack knew the names of the colors, of course—coquelicot and mikado, gingerline and lusty gallant—or at least he said he did, and wanted to make sure everyone knew that he knew), a kaleidoscopic spectrum that made Jess feel like Dorothy stepping from her drab farmhouse into the Technicolor world of Oz. They all watched in a kind of manic shock; the sensory experience was overwhelming. At one point, Jess even saw her father crack a smile. Donald leaned down to whisper into her mother's ear, and Barb nodded, delighted, her eyes glued to the floats, whispering something back that added even more color to the scene, a rising blush on Donald's cheeks.

Convincing Donald to lighten up was one of Barb's specialties, so after the parade, when Jess and Zack had the idea of spending the next day at the beach, she began a new campaign. Donald hated the very notion: the frigid water, sand in his socks and shoes. They had an ocean back in Boston, didn't they? And there were so many other unchecked boxes on the travel agent's itinerary—the Walk of Fame, the Chinese Theatre, Griffith Observatory. But Jess and Zack insisted; they pleaded with their mother to plead with him. The thought of going to the beach in January was so implausible and delicious, playing in the sun and sand while their friends back home were encased in ice and snow.

Barb sent the kids ahead, zigzagging along the emptying boulevard, gathering poppies that had fallen from the floats, so Jess didn't hear how her mother made the case, how she insisted or cajoled or bribed, but by the time they returned to the motel the decision had been made.

Early the next morning they drove their rented Plymouth out to Santa Monica. They walked barefoot over the smooth asphalt of the parking lot, past the big wooden *Muscle Beach* sign, where a few brawny, bare-chested men were already lifting dumbbells and swinging from what looked like acrobats' rings. Off in the distance Jess could see the tops of flagpoles and strings of lights from the amusements on the long pier. Her father told them the pier was off-limits. According to his guidebook, it was full of gypsies and juvenile delinquents. Barb rolled her eyes, but cut off Jess's and Zack's protest with a quick look that said, *We're already at the beach—don't press your luck.*

Jess and Zack played down in the wet sand, just within reach of the lapping morning tide. It was still early, and cold, with a thick low-hanging layer of cloud covering the sun, so they wore sweatshirts over their swimsuits as they dug a grid of connecting trenches. As always, Zack led the project. At thirteen, he was two years older than Jess, and obsessed with elaborate design. His school notebooks were filled with pages of branching patterns, mazes, multicolored spirals that bloomed from invisible centers. Supernovas, Jess thought, always awed by what Zack created. Explosions that left no trace of origin, a universe made solely of repercussion and resonance.

Zack worked feverishly on the beach, drawing guidelines with his fingers, instructing Jess to follow behind and dig with her hands. Every time she thought she had completed a passage, she looked up to find he had moved even farther along, pulling his fingers through the wet sand, lengthening and expanding. Frustrated, she called out to him:

"How do you know when it's finished?"

Zack stopped digging and frowned at what they had made so far, his head and one bony hip cocked in opposite directions.

"It's never finished," he said. "But at some point it changes. It becomes something else."

They dug for a few more minutes, and then Zack stood again, heeding that mysterious internal signal. He turned to the water and raised his arms, shouting like Moses for the sea to heed his call. As if on command, the tide rushed in. They scampered back to safety and watched the water pour into the labyrinth. Jess saw what Zack meant. The maze was alive now with the surging, circling water, one stream finding another and then joining into a single flow, something new.

The morning had grown bright despite the cloud cover, and Jess had to shade her eyes when she looked up the beach to her parents' backlit silhouettes—her father sitting thin and rigid in a lawn chair, her mother cross-legged and bundled in a towel, knees to chin. Just beyond, a lifeguard shack stood on wooden stilts. Jess saw a tall, lean teenage boy in short red trunks on the deck, surveying the water, drinking a soda. The bottle glowed dully in the gauzy light. Jess watched him for a while, and then was struck with an impulse to wave. She raised a sandy arm and waited for a response, but the boy only lifted the bottle back to his mouth and took a long pull.

"What do you think? Time to take the plunge?"

Jess's mother stood beside her, squinting up at the sky. She wore a new swimsuit, with a yellow-and-black sunflower print. Jess thought she looked pretty but cold, her pink skin pebbled with goose bumps. Shivering, Barb tried to convince the kids to shed their sweatshirts and head out into the water. Zack flatly refused, but Jess appreciated her mother's determination to make the best of the intemperate morning. She pulled off her sweatshirt, took Barb's hand, and they walked slowly out into the surf.

The water was staggeringly cold. By the time they were up to their hips they were both laughing and gasping with the ridiculousness of the effort. They hobbled across a wide patch of rocky ground, then reached a quick dip. Jess lost her footing but Barb held tight to her hand, keeping her upright. They continued on, until the water cupped Jess's chin and her mother's breasts. They turned and Barb waved at the beach, but there was nothing to see. The sun had finally come out and the surface of the water was nearly blinding in its dappled brilliance. With her free hand Jess waved, too, thinking of the lifeguard at the shack, but then the hand her mother held was also free, and Jess was loose in the water.

A wave hit her from the back, not a giant wave, but big enough, and then the undercurrent pulled her feet off the ground, spinning her around. She heard her mother shout. A shadow fell over her, a sudden dark chill. Straining to keep her head above water, she turned to find an even larger wave cresting, drawing up to its full height, its hooded head blocking the sun.

It held for a moment, poised, terrifying and magnificent, and then fell upon her.

Falling, then floating, suspended in the emptiness. She opened her eyes and saw nothing, just murky black, but after a panicked moment the salt washed them clear and she could see.

Light reached down, dimly, through the surface far above. Orange and yellow streaks, gingerline and mikado, the light swirling with sand, revealing the vast space around her like columns defining a room. Miniature bubbles drifted by, captured moments of her own final breath.

She floated in that space, the bubbles in the light like a thousand stars surrounding.

Her lungs were full, she was dying and scared of dying but there was another feeling, too, surprising, incongruous. Her body was bright with it, her chest tingling, her fingers and toes. This was something she never could have imagined, this unknown she was now within, the terrible beauty of this once hidden place.

Then a hand was on her, pulling hard, her vision blurring, and then her head was above water, she could see the sky, clear now, blue and white, the pier, the curl of coastline to the north. She was dropped onto the sand, she saw a flash of red trunks, and the lifeguard bent over her, his hands on her chest, pushing until she vomited water, then covering her mouth with his, breathing into her. Jess saw her mother standing behind him, her hands up at her cheeks, her mouth open like Jess's mouth. She heard her father yelling her name from somewhere, and then Zack's voice calling, *Is she dead? Is she dead?*

The lifeguard lifted his head, his lips leaving hers. Jess watched him look off into some inner distance, counting, before lowering and breathing into her again. His mouth was warm and sticky sweet from the soda. After another breath the lifeguard turned his head, his ear at her mouth, listening. Jess wanted to whisper something that only he would hear, something about what she had seen underwater, the terrifying, beautiful place she had discovered, but before she could make a sound he nodded and helped her to her feet.

Her mother grabbed her in a tight embrace. Her father placed a hand on her shoulder, squeezing. He tried to tip the lifeguard, pressing a small fold of bills into his hand, but the boy refused, embarrassed by the gesture. Zack had shut up. He watched Jess with a look somewhere between relief and disappointment.

Back in Pasadena at the Hamburger Hamlet, Zack and her parents couldn't stop talking about the incident, telling and retelling it from different angles, disputing details, already starting to mythologize what was certain to become a tentpole story in Shepard family lore. But Jess knew that this wasn't the right story—losing her mother's hand, disappearing beneath the waves, the lifeguard's dramatic rescue. It was *a* story, it was *their* story, but it wasn't hers.

She was quiet in the booth, picking at her fries. What was this feeling? Not what it should have been. Not relief, or gratitude. It was something else. It was loss, it was grief. She felt the weight of it, alone and overcome, remembering the light under the water, the sacred stillness she had floated in, and feeling, against all logic, that she had been taken from it too soon.

THE
WHITE
ROOM

1

JESS

SUMMER 1979

Jess faced the blank wall, holding her paintbrush, looking for any marks she might have missed. It was a chilly seaside morning, gray and damp, but as the fog began to lift the light through the uncovered windows grew brighter and clearer, washing the white room free of seams and corners, the parameters of defined space.

In the brightness her eyes swam with black floaters, flocks of short, dark lines like headless kite strings rising skyward. The floaters made it hard to judge whether the wall was clean. She dabbed at a few, unsure, but they defied erasure.

On the other side of the studio, one of Beethoven's sonatas turned on the record player. The piano's notes climbed, reaching, vivid and glistening. She tried to focus on the music, its promise, but other sounds seeped in from outside: motorcycles rumbling down on Pacific Avenue; gulls screaming over Venice Beach; skateboarders grinding down the sidewalk on their way up to Dogtown, the abandoned amusement park that still clung to the crumbling pier.

A lone runnel of paint slid down the brush handle to her wrist. She wore a sleeveless white T-shirt and her white painter's pants. In the past, her achromatic work clothes made her feel transparent, enabling her to remove herself from the image of her studio and focus on what the space might become. But now when she saw the room in her mind she could not rid herself from it: her dark frizz of hair, the blue bruises on her elbows from cleaning the floor earlier that morning. She was an intruder, a blemish in the clean white space.

The sonata ended, leaving a sudden silence. Jess crossed the studio and turned the record over. Zack had given this set of sonatas to their aunt Ruth for Christmas, that first year in L.A. Jess had inherited the records, or maybe just taken them, she supposed. They hadn't been willed to her; she found them still stacked on the spindle in Ruth's stereo cabinet the morning after her memorial service.

I listen to them when I need to retune.

Jess could still hear Ruth's voice, a steady, wonderfully nasal tone that never shed the open vowels of her New England upbringing. She remembered her aunt standing by the record player in her bedroom, looking out the back window, the piano's notes rising like the sun over the short row of citrus trees behind the bungalow. It was Christmas morning, six months after their parents' accident. Jess watched Ruth close her eyes in the wash of new light, as if waiting for something to arrive.

Jess had never seen sunrises like those, vivid blue to purple to orange, the entire spectrum imprinted along the horizon. And then the other side of those hours, the bookend of the day, the deep rich sunset, bloodred in the west. In the evenings they watched from the front porch, Ruth with a can of Hamm's in one hand, a Pall Mall burning between the fingers of the other. There was no music playing, but Jess still heard the echo of the sonatas, as if the sound had traveled to sink and fade along the sun's arc.

What did you think of that one? Ruth's voice lower now, silvery with smoke. Asking about the sunset, or maybe about the entire day just passed.

In her studio, Jess dipped the long-handled roller into the paint pan and pushed it along the floor. Starting in the far corner, she worked her way out and back. Slow strokes. The paint's sour-sweet smell filled the room. The roller squished in the pan and then there was the sound of the push and spread, *shush-shush*, like a finger to the lips, a secret.

She remembered how they mocked her for this, the ritual, the preparation. All those young men, that club of testosterone-fueled painters and sculptors leaning in the doorway of her big old studio space on Navy Street, smoking and chuckling. Housework, they called it. *Hey, Jess, will you clean my room next?*

Another dark shape slid into the periphery of her vision, like a human shadow lurking. It stood for a long moment, blocking the edge of her sight before moving away.

Most mornings when she left her apartment Jess walked down the stairs, past the locked studio door on the second floor and out onto Pacific Avenue, hurrying through the ever-growing gauntlet of junkies, Jesus freaks, doomsday prophets with their cardboard signs and spit-flecked warnings. But this morning she woke thinking of Ruth, and she wanted to hear the sonatas, not up in her apartment but in an uncluttered space, so she entered the studio for the first time in months. Now here she was, cleaning and repainting. Force of habit, maybe. Once there had been nothing more exciting than the possibility of the white room. This had been the place where she could transform her dreams and ideas and fears into something new. But that was impossible now. She had no new ideas, and her dreams were best swept into the dark corners upon waking. As for her fears, they had all bled free. They walked everywhere with her now, dark shapes floating just out of sight.

Pulling a dropper from her bag, she tilted her head back, prying her left eye wide, staring openmouthed at the ceiling. She squeezed a bead of clear fluid through the dropper's tip, where it hung for a moment, stretching, until it fell and spread, stinging across the surface of her eye. She allowed herself to blink, tears flowing. She repeated with the right eye, then shut them both, willing the drops to do their work, chemical warfare, fighting the floaters, the dark shapes encroaching. Afraid, as she always was now, to open her eyes, terrified of what she was sure would come, the moment when she would be *stricken*—that was the word that looped in her head, the word always used in movies, in the clinical accounts she read obsessively, the word that described the moment when Jess would open her eyes to find so many shapes and floaters that they crowded out all other sight. She would be stricken, and eyes open or shut there would be no difference in the darkness.

From out of the dark, the girl appeared. She was always there, waiting. Isabella was her name, but the proper name conjured even more terror, so she remained, when possible, the girl.

The girl at the gallery in Santa Monica, the girl with the metal canister, the hose, the wand.

It was a hot night in late August, two years before. Jess stood in the gallery beside Anton Stendahl. She was attending his show as a favor. His hand was at the small of her back, heavy, overly familiar. He was full from the attention, smiling for the cameras.

Anton had been very generous to Jess early in her career. He had written the first positive piece about her work—the first piece of any kind about her work—and so even though she didn't think much of his wall sculptures, the garish, fleshy orbs that looked to her like cartoon breasts, Jess agreed to attend the opening. The cameras were there for her, for the recent infamy, she and Anton both knew that, but the publicity would be helpful to him and so Jess believed she was doing the right thing, repaying a long-standing debt.

All she could feel was his hand on her back, pressed against the hard zipper of her dress. She wanted him to stop touching her, but she was afraid that if he did she would float away. In that moment the unwanted pressure was all that made her feel real. It had only been a month since what happened at *Zero Zone* and she was still shaken to the point of numbness. She couldn't move free of the disaster. Every action felt detached, dissociated from her mind and body. She didn't know what she was doing except standing beside Anton and wearing a hollow, idiotic smile.

And then the girl appeared. Jess saw her crossing outside the gallery's front window, then coming in the door. She was a teenager, small and hunched and terribly thin. Her dark hair was cut jaggedly, violently, almost as if it had been torn in places, or bitten off. There was a brown smudge of dirt or ash streaked in a straight line across her left cheekbone. A girl with a dirty face.

The girl looked around, bewildered maybe by the noise and bodies, but she didn't seem lost. She meant to be there. After a moment she moved through the clutch of guests and critics and photographers. She wore a yellow blouse with a beaded multicolor spiral across the front and flared blue jeans. Her clothes were worn, torn, too big. She had the look of someone who had lost weight rapidly—starved, haunted eyes in an overlarge head.

The crowd was like most crowds at an opening—performative, competitive, self-aware—but the girl was small and inelegant, so she moved unnoticed even as she rubbed shoulders and brushed arms. She walked easily through the ranks to stand in the open space between the edge of the crowd and Jess and Anton. With one hand she carried the metal canister by its handle. It was about the size of a large fire extinguisher. A rubber hose ran from its top to the long wand she held in her other hand.

Like Aunt Ruth almost, with her beer can and cigarette on the old front porch. Jess saw a quick flash of the two women, superimposed.

The girl took another deliberate step toward Jess and Anton. Their backs were against a wall. One of Anton's pink-and-white boobs hung just above Jess's shoulder. Jess watched the girl approach—she was possibly the only one who noticed her—and felt a dulled sense of alarm, as if something was wrong but somewhere far away.

The girl looked only at Jess, as if no one else in the gallery existed.

In a corner by the windows, a security guard stirred and glanced their way. He wasn't much older than the girl, his gray uniform hanging from his boyish frame. He seemed hesitant, unsure whether the situation required his attention. Anton stood oblivious, smiling, talking to a critic at the front of the crowd. Someone called out a question about *Zero Zone*. Jess ignored it by widening her smile. A camera flashed again, leaving a bright afterimage, a white punch discoloring Jess's field of vision. Anton's hand on her back held her in place. If his hand hadn't been there she could have broken away or shouted to draw attention to the girl, who stepped toward them quietly, her dark eyes fixed on Jess.

With her thumb, the girl flipped a small lever at the top of the canister. There was the slight hiss of air or gas.

The girl pointed the wand like an accusatory finger. Jess stared at the small black dot of the wand's sharp tip, only a foot from her face. The girl held it steady with what seemed like great strength. When she spoke, her voice was low and clear, trembling with rage. A boiling pot, ready to overflow.

You took this from us, she said. *I'm giving it back.*

The girl's finger jerked on the wand's trigger. A loud blast of air sprayed Jess's face, filling her nose and mouth, burning her eyes. Jess inhaled, she couldn't help but breathe in, stunned. It was like drowning, like falling under the waves once again, reaching for her mother's hand and breathing water. Amid shouts and screams, she stumbled back against the wall. The girl was closer now, her face twisted as she swung the wand, slashing Jess across the face, a searing, white-hot pain. Jess fell to the floor and the girl stood above her, the canister over her head, ready to smash it down onto Jess's face. But then the security guard was there, finally rushing in, tackling the girl to the ground.

Isabella Serrano was only sixteen at the time. A juvenile court judge remanded her to a youth detention facility up by Fresno, a three-year sentence.

The doctors stitched Jess's face, the wound that ran from her right temple halfway down her cheek. They said she was lucky. Her eye wasn't damaged, and the scar would be relatively slight.

They tested the contents of the canister and Jess's lungs and blood and urine and everything came back clean. What Isabella sprayed contained average levels of radiation, normal amounts of particulate matter. There was no explanation for its warmth or taste or any symptoms perceived to be associated with the attack.

It was just air, Miss Shepard, the doctor at the hospital told her. This was repeated by her own doctor at his office after multiple visits and more tests. It was repeated by other doctors, specialists, optometrists and ophthalmologists. She went to see them all, convinced she was being misunderstood or ignored. They thought she was hysterical, psychosomatic. She went to see acupuncturists, herbalists, the spiritual oculist in his alleyway storefront off Market Street who moved the dry pads of his fingertips over her closed eyelids, humming or moaning or chanting, she couldn't tell which. She was willing to hum or moan or chant with him if asked, if that would help, the slight pressure from his fingers creating red-rimmed amoebas sliding behind her eyelids.

It was not just air. There was something more. The breath of the land where she had built *Zero Zone*, or something even worse. Jess could imagine Isabella in that place, planning her attack, pumping her metal canister full of poison.

There, the oculist said, lowering his hands, his breath hot and close, his long hair smelling of sage and patchouli. *What do you see?*

Jess opened her eyes and saw the beaded curtains ringing the room, the oculist's sunburned face, the deep creases in his skin. She saw his mild gray eyes, sanguine, confident in his own power. But that was just background. Here, still, at the front of her vision, black pinpricks appeared, one at a time, and then lengthened, slowly, as if an unseen hand was dragging them, dark scratches across the world's bright face.

She jumped at the sound of Gabe's voice, calling her name from down on the street. She buzzed him up to the studio, blinking, spreading the drops across the surface of her eyes. Then she turned, composing something approximating a smile.

Gabe topped the stairs and leaned in the studio doorway, one tall frame inside another. "I was jogging by and saw you up in the window," he said.

"Quite a coincidence."

"Okay—I was checking up on you. Sue me."

He was still breathing hard, his face shining with sweat. Beads of moisture hung in his mustache. He wore red gym shorts and a gold Sly and the Family Stone T-shirt. A damp band ran along his midsection, right above Sly's Afro.

"It's nice to see you in here." Gabe pulled out a handkerchief and wiped his cheeks and brow.

"I just came to clean up," Jess said.

Still rattled, she crossed the studio to the kitchenette. She pulled a cigarette from her pack on the counter and then offered one to Gabe. He shook his head. She saw his eyes move to the scar, then away. Like everyone else, he tried not to look.

"Don't tell me you quit," she said.

"I quit everything. Smoking, coffee, red meat. We do wheat germ now. Oat bran. David brews a thermos of oolong tea and I sip it all day."

"Nothing in the tea?"

"Just a spoonful of honey."

"Mary Poppins."

"I think that was sugar," Gabe said. "Which I've also given up."

Jess found her matches. "You mind if I continue on unenlightened?"

Gabe smiled. "It's your studio."

She lit her cigarette and shook the match and tossed it into the sink. When she looked back, Gabe was staring into the newly whitewashed space.

"You're thinking about something in here."

"Just housekeeping."

He walked into the studio, as if moving past her response. Not buying it, or not willing to buy it.

"I lectured about *Spectrum* the other day," he said. "I probably rambled for half an hour about the concept and construction, the trial and error, getting it wrong, then getting it right. Trying to describe what it felt like that first night, moving through the rooms. The feeling of, what? *Bathing* in each color. Breathing it in."

He stopped close to the far wall, still in those remembered rooms for a moment before coming back out.

"These are eighteen-year-old kids," he said. "They think they've seen everything. I'm showing slides and sketches, and then I look out at their faces and realize I may as well have kept my mouth shut. It made no sense to them. It wouldn't make sense to anybody who wasn't there. I should have known better."

He closed his eyes, inhaling deeply. "That smell, huh?"

"The cigarettes?"

"The paint. You miss it. That's why you come in here. Don't give me that bullshit about cleaning."

"It's not bullshit."

"Wouldn't it feel good to work again?" Gabe was animated now, unwilling to let it go. His enthusiasm pressed at Jess, boxing her in. "What are you thinking about in here?"

"I'm thinking about painting the fucking walls."

She gathered her brushes in a sheet of newspaper. With her keys she popped open a can of turpentine, dumping the greasy liquid into a bucket. The chemical tang joined them in the room, fumes rising.

Gabe started to respond, then stopped himself. He pulled a breath in through his nose and Jess saw the outer flicker of some internal calming process, another new feature of her old friend. She studied him, feeling a little more in control now that she had been difficult enough to derail his concern. He had lost a significant amount of weight, slimming his previously pear-shaped torso. There was great definition now in the lean muscle of his arms and legs.

"How long have you been running?"

"Half an hour."

He was petulant now, hurt. She softened her tone.

"I mean as a continuing practice."

He bent and pulled a stubborn white sock back up to midcalf. "About a year ago David and I joined a group. The Whole Body Seminar."

Jess winced. "You joined a group."

"It's not like that. Positive energy only. We meet every morning on the beach in Malibu. It's done wonders."

How many times had she seen Gabe in the last year? A handful only, when he stopped by like this to check on her. And in how many of those times had she really paid attention, been able to see past her own fog? He no longer smoked. He was a runner now. He had joined some kind of *group*. She knew next to nothing about his life since *Zero Zone*, his life with David, his teaching. This scared her, this sense of time passing without her, the world moving on while she painted and repainted her white room.

"I heard from Christine," he said.

She had rebuffed him, so now Gabe was jumping to the other reason for the visit, dropping the name on the floor between them like a cat presenting a dead bird.

"She called you?"

"Came out to campus," he said. "I haven't seen her in years. Her son was with her."

"Henry."

"He looks just like Alex. Same crew cut, everything. A serious little man. Three or four, maybe."

"Three."

Jess's cigarette had burned down to the nub. She dropped it into the sink and ran the water for a moment. She wanted another but opening the pack again would feel like an admission of something, weakness or guilt. Instead, she worked the brushes in the bucket and then transferred them to the sink, rinsing their heads clear then flicking the excess, quick sharp whips spattering water around the drain.

"She's looking for photographs," Gabe said, "of the area where you built *Zero Zone*. She said Alex took photos there a year or so before his death. She asked if I knew where they were."

"What did you say?"

"I told her the truth. I'd never seen any photos. I thought she was mixed up—she seemed very mixed up. Like she was confusing your work with his."

Your work. Gabe had always taken pride in their collaboration, his skill in helping build the physical structures Jess designed. *Our* work, he often called it. But not *Zero Zone*, apparently. That was hers alone.

"Are there photographs?" Gabe asked.

An abrupt pop sounded in the room. Jess felt her stomach jump, before realizing that it was the needle rising free of the record. She crossed into the studio and flipped Beethoven over on the turntable.

"There are things he wanted me to have," she said.

"Pictures of the site?"

"Whatever he gave me is none of her business."

"She was his wife, Jess. She probably has some kind of legal claim."

The Fifth Sonata sounded harder this time, percussive, planking notes in the empty room. Jess kept her back to Gabe, facing the white walls, the bright windows, her eyes awash with dark, dancing shapes. Her anger was misplaced. It didn't belong with Gabe. Maybe not even with Christine.

"I'm sorry," she said. "I don't know what's wrong with me."

"Listen," Gabe said. "I know this probably sounds like the last thing you want to do, but one of my students is having a party tonight."

"It does sound like the last thing I want to do."

"We need to get you out of here, just for a few hours. I'll have my tea and you can have a couple of drinks and we'll sit and listen to the kids bullshit about who's hot and who's not, what's in, what's out. Remember those conversations?"

"I hated those conversations."

"So you can hate them again tonight."

"I don't know, Gabe."

"Come on. I can proselytize about health food. Wheatgrass. Spirulina. Say the words. Simply saying the words is the first step."

Jess smiled, feeling herself on the edge of a grudging surrender. Maybe this would be good for her—she could spend some time with Gabe, get out of the apartment, out of her own head for an evening.

"You have to stop blaming yourself." Gabe was behind her now. His size had always felt comforting, supportive, safe. "It's time to move on."

He set his hands on her shoulders and Jess tried not to flinch.

Manifesto

(1965; ink on paper; Venice, California)

D o you need a gallery?
    No.
    A patron?
No.
Someone to choose your work, to endorse it?
No.
To tell you that it's worthwhile?
No.
To tell you what it is?
No.
What it isn't?
No.

The dialogue came from a conversation she and Gabe had over drinks at the Brig after another rejected proposal. They had graduated a few months before. Gabe was in grad school; Jess was working in the secretarial pool at an insurance agency. She had ideas for pieces, she had designs, but no space in which to make them.

The next morning, hungover, Jess wrote down what she could remember of Gabe's questions and her responses on a large sheet of drafting paper. The same answer over and over, but one that evolved, slowly, from dejection to defiance.

A year later she had saved enough to rent her first studio, that drafty old loft on Navy Street across from Duke's Donuts. Duke's had a giant rooftop sign in the shape of a glazed old-fashioned, and the guys in Jess's building spent long, stoned hours up on their roof, passing a BB gun around, trying to shoot bull's-eyes through the sign's wide hole. Jess spent those hours in her studio, dreaming, sketching, building.

A few weeks after moving in, she found the paper with the questions and answers and hung it in the bathroom, over the sink where she had taken down the mirror.

Do you need a champion?

No.

A curator, a critic?

No.

An encouraging word?

No.

Will people ever stop pushing back?

No.

Refusing?

No.

Will there ever be voices, structures, systems not telling you *No?*

No.

Then find something to say *Yes* to.

From *Light + Space*

(1977; 16mm film, sound; 82 minutes;
Laura Lehrer, dir.; unreleased)

Jess sits in the middle of her studio, her wooden chair angled slightly toward the windows, the source of the image's clean white light. She faces the camera, waiting. Then, suddenly self-conscious or aware of a returned gaze, she looks away.

She is thin and pale. Her face is drawn, and her prominent features—the high cheekbones, the bump halfway down the bridge of her nose—appear here as raw vulnerabilities or past injuries newly surfaced. Her hands move restlessly in her lap; the index finger of her right worries at a patch of paint on her left. She wears the sleeveless T-shirt and white painter's pants. Her hair is a dark swoop framing her face. The image would seem black-and-white except for her eyes, flashes of vivid green between anxious blinks.

It is a late summer afternoon, a month after the events at *Zero Zone*, just a few hours before the gallery attack, before the scar that will mark her face with a thin white line.

- To be honest, I'm surprised you agreed to speak with me. I know you're not talking to reporters.

Jess looks toward the voice, the director, Laura Lehrer, speaking off-frame just over the camera's right shoulder. Laura's voice is a surprise in the room, accented, a cool, liquid Australian.

Jess gives a paper-thin smile.

- You're not a reporter. And I think it'll be good to talk about early work, about others' work. When you called you said you were interested in what's been happening in L.A. over the last ten years or so?

- Yes. Artists working with light and space.

- Have you spoken with anyone else?

- Not yet.

Jess takes a deep breath.

- I don't want to talk about anything recent.

- I understand. So let's go back to the beginning. When did you know you wanted to be an artist?

- I was a late bloomer. I was in high school, I think.

- Is that late?

- It felt late. Everyone I met in college made it seem like they had always known, that they had never entertained any other possibilities.

- But you didn't grow up thinking of yourself that way?

- No. My brother was the artist.

- Does he still make art?

Jess shakes her head and closes her eyes, pressing her fingertips to her lids. When she opens them again she seems slightly disoriented, as if she has just returned from some other place. It takes her a moment to refocus, first on the windows, then back on the woman behind the camera.

- That's not entirely true, what I said about not knowing. I did some things early on, I painted on these big sheets of paper my father brought home from work. So maybe I had my suspicions. But it felt like a very private activity, something I shouldn't have been doing.

- How so?

- Zack was the artist. My parents introduced him that way. This is our son, Zachary. He's an artist. And this is our daughter, Jessica.

Jess leans forward, folding at the waist, reaching out of frame. When she sits back up she's holding a pack of Pall Malls, the bold red label another disturbance in the nearly monochromatic image. She taps a cigarette, places it between her lips.

- So your first paintings were made in secret. As acts of rebellion?

- A rebellion against expectations. Or a lack of expectation.

Digging into her pants pocket, she comes up with a silver flip-top lighter. The metal catches the light, a quick glint, and then the small flame appears. She leans in until the cigarette catches.

- I was never told not to paint. It wasn't forbidden. It just wasn't anything that anyone considered.

- What did you paint?

- Dreams, memories. I had discovered Joan Mitchell's paintings, Barnett Newman, Rothko. Zack had a subscription to *ARTnews* and in every issue they printed a few color reproductions. I snuck into his room and turned the pages and stared.

The first hint of a real smile here, at the memory.

- Did you understand then what you were trying to do?

Jess seems about to answer, but then stops herself, reconsiders.

- I was trying to re-create a place. I had this experience once, when I was younger. The world around me disappeared. A new space opened up—a possibility beyond what I thought of as everyday life. Or within everyday life.

She has regained some confidence now. She sits a little taller in the chair.

- I wanted to find that space again. I wanted to share it.

Spectrum

(1968; studio installation; Venice, California)

The idea began to take shape in Alex's darkroom, the cramped, high-ceilinged bathroom he converted at the back of his studio on Pico Boulevard. The studio was wedged between two rehearsal spaces, and on hot nights everybody left their doors open. Alex had just started experimenting with photography and liked working amid noise, at least in the early stages of a project. He and Jess talked and shared a joint and listened to their neighbors play. These were mostly bands they'd never hear from again, but every now and then a recognizable voice or chord drifted over. The 13th Floor Elevators a few times; Morrison and the Doors once for the better part of a week. Alex talked through an idea and dipped photo paper into pans, clipping the developing prints onto wires strung overhead like power lines. The only light in the room came from the painted bulb on the wall, which suffused everything in a deep, dark red. Looking at Alex's face or at her own hands, Jess felt both the imagined heat of the color and a strange remove, as if she were looking at another version of herself, some slightly sinister iteration.

She switched out the red bulb with one she painted blue and felt the room's temperature drop, a wintry chill. A green bulb brought her back to her childhood, a midsummer morning lying in the backyard grass behind their house in Somerville. Yellow transported her to second or third grade, kids holding buttercups beneath each other's chins and looking for the color's reflection on skin, irrefutable playground proof that you were in love with whichever boy or girl held the flower.

"I appreciate that you're on to something," Alex said. "But could you do it someplace where you don't screw up my work?"

He was only half joking. They were on the verge of another breakup. By the time she had an idea for a new space, they hadn't spoken in weeks.

She called Gabe and they built walls subdividing her Navy Street studio: nine rooms of equal size, ten feet by twenty, with a single doorway in the same position on each western-facing wall leading from one room to the next. They covered the windows, hung the doors, installed gelled lights into subtle recesses cut into the ceiling, flooding each slim space with a particular color: violet, indigo, blue, green, yellow, orange, red. The first room was dark; the last was pure white, and led out through the final door, down the stairs to the street.

In the week before opening, they tested the space. Gabe was concerned about injuries. The light in the rooms overwhelmed sight, erasing boundaries and anchors to the solid world. It was difficult to find the doors, to pass from one room to the next. Jess strung a thin cord across the center of each room, waist high, that visitors could follow like a rope line. But the cord felt like a tether, grounding the experience. There was the same problem when they added a coarse-textured strip to the floor, a path to follow. This put too much emphasis on the feel of the studio, the physical structure. They were looking for a solution to a problem that was intrinsic to the work. She wanted the place to disappear.

On the day of the opening, she still didn't have an answer. She considered calling the whole thing off. Work wasted, an idea that didn't fully bloom. She walked down to the boardwalk for some fresh air and a burrito. Waiting for her order, she watched workers remodeling the front of the surf shop across the street. In the middle of reframing, they removed the shop's door and then broke for lunch. Jess stared at the uncovered opening for some time, waiting for the workers to finish the job before realizing she had just finished her own.

She rushed back to her studio and removed all the doors between the rooms. When she turned on the lights, each newly opened doorway framed the glow of the next room, and as she approached each threshold the colors began to mix, creating a bridge from one pure hue to another. Gabe arrived right in time to let the first visitors in.

People called it the *Rainbow Rooms* or *Candyland*. At first this nicknaming angered her. She thought they were trivializing her work. Within a few days, though, she realized that the opposite was true. Visitors were personalizing the space. Not everyone experienced something meaningful or moving, frightening or joyous. Some strode quickly, as if through a hokey sideshow attraction, and left rolling their eyes. But others stayed longer, entering the first dark space alone and moving at their own pace, lingering in certain rooms, pausing in the doorways. A few even sat or lay down, they told her after, fully immersed in each color, feeling it on their faces, in their bodies. The colors filled their lungs, some said, touching their chests. One older woman took Jess's hand and held it to her own flat breast as if somehow Jess could feel what she had felt, as if that touch could convey what she struggled to explain.

Jess planned to keep the studio open for a week, but word spread, and soon when she arrived in the afternoons to clean and prepare, a line had already formed. Kids from the neighborhood, surfers and musicians smoking joints on the sidewalk, but also visitors from tonier parts of the city, little old ladies from Pasadena, Wilshire Boulevard businessmen, Encino housewives, all surprised to find themselves standing around on the seedy edge of town waiting for something they had only heard about.

As the days went on they returned, forming an enthusiastic little community of a line, sharing experiences while waiting for the sun to sink and Gabe to open the front door.

"A year ago, I had a stroke."

Jess overheard the man from where she sat up on the fire escape, letting some paint touch-ups dry. He was about Jess's age, and stood in the line down on the sidewalk, talking to a woman who carried a small boy on her hip.

"I had to quit my job, start my life again," the man said. "My memory was screwed up, my face. My arm, as you can see. My speech. I was angry, embarrassed by how I looked and sounded. I missed my old self. But what I missed most were dreams. I stopped dreaming. My doctor said this was expected, that part of my brain was damaged, like it was burned in a fire. It wasn't coming back. So I'd go to sleep and wake up in the morning and it was like I was dead all of those hours."

It was a warm evening, and the man pinched his shirt collar between his fingers, pulling it away from his neck, letting some air in.

"I go to a pool a couple times a week for rehab," he said. "A girl who works there told me about this place. So I came by last week. Maybe I thought it would give us something to talk about besides my progress in the pool. I didn't know what I was supposed to see here. A different color in each room, so what? I thought it was bullshit, excuse my French."

Still uncomfortable, he unfastened his top button, giving his neck more room, then lowered his hand, smoothing the front of his shirt.

"Then," he said, "that night, I had the most vivid dream. I can't even describe it. It was like when I was a kid. You know the dreams you had when you were a kid?"

He nodded to the boy on the woman's hip.

"Like the dreams he probably has. You can't even describe them, you don't know the words. I woke up crying. I mean, I didn't even cry in the hospital. When all those things were taken, I didn't cry. But that dream was so bright, so real."

Jess heard the front door unlock, and then Gabe's voice, welcoming one of the regulars at the front of the line.

The man below looked toward the door. His body seemed a little taller now. Straighter, stronger, eager.

"I've come back every night since," he said.

2

JESS

SUMMER 1979

Jess stopped her truck at the corner of Beverly and Rossmore, just outside the gates of the Wilshire Country Club. Two women waited for the light at the corner. They were doing their best Chris Evert impressions—short white tennis skirts, matching blond ponytails, terry-cloth wristbands. Jess watched them, impatient. When the light changed they crossed Beverly, revealing what Jess had come to see, the thick old palm with its scaly-skinned trunk and wispy feathered top. It looked like a nodding drunk with a bad wig. Old and tired, the palm was out of place in this landscaped neighborhood of keen young beeches and elms, a hold-over from some earlier concept of topiary glamour.

Maybe it was the conversation with Gabe that had brought her back here, or the news that Christine was looking for her. Maybe it was the drink at the Spotted Gull before leaving Venice. On a stool by the open windows, Jess had watched a group of girls roller-skating on the boardwalk, solos and pairs, long socks and long legs, turning corkscrews and pirouettes. A leering crowd of surfers watched in a loose circle, clapping along to the rhythm from a boom box in a record store window. Anita Ward, "Ring My Bell." Jess knew the song by osmosis. It was everywhere that summer, in bars and supermarkets, all across the radio dial, pumping from the windows of every other passing car. The girls skated an elaborate, ornamental slalom through a long route of empty iced-tea cans, crossing ankles and knees, wrists and elbows, coming together and spinning apart as they glided down the boardwalk.

Jess had ordered a whiskey sour, then another, then spent half an hour waiting for gas at the 76 station on Fairfax Avenue, the shortest line she could find. Gas rationing had been going on for months, with no end in sight. A group of men stood beside their idling cars, hashing through conspiracy theories. The whole thing was an Iranian plot, one said. The ayatollah controlled President Carter, Governor Brown, the oil companies. Some kind of mind voodoo. Khomeini's jacking up prices, the man said, to finance his revolution.

The gas line inched along. Jess didn't mind. She was dragging her feet, feeling both the pull of the street corner a few blocks away and the need to delay her arrival as long as possible.

But now she was here, yet again. Beverly and Rossmore. It sounded like an old movie pairing, a studio romance, names above the title on a marquee. The palm tree's wound was disappearing, the garish gash that seemed like it should have cracked the trunk in two was now covered over with a slab of smooth new skin. The traces of Alex's accident were fading. She didn't know how she felt about that. Whenever she found herself here she wanted the reminder, the proof, but part of her also hoped that the scars had healed.

What didn't disappear: images and memories that still felt immediate. Alex in bed, moving on top of her, below her; Alex behind the wheel of his cobalt Karmann Ghia; Alex sitting in a plain wooden chair in the campus gallery, waiting.

They had met freshman year at Pomona, in a Materials and Methods class. Jess was still painting then, struggling to find something using color and canvas, and here was this boy who had already found his tools, his techniques, the questions for which he wanted answers.

Sitting in that gallery chair for three days, not moving or speaking or eating or drinking. Visitors coming to watch, sitting on the floor before him or standing in the doorway or against the wall. Joking about the audacity of the stunt, the boredom, when and how he went to the bathroom. And then not joking, just watching. The gallery lights burning at all hours. Jess walking by at two in the morning, alone, drawn to the lighted windows and the boy inside, afraid that she would look in and see him devouring a contraband meal, guzzling water, laughing with friends. She didn't even know him then, but his intensity of purpose was magnetic. Standing at the window and finding him still in the chair, motionless and alone, she had felt so relieved by his honesty, and then fearful, wondering how far he was willing to go.

Alex in the chair; Alex stretched out across a bed of nails. Hammering slim spikes into the plywood slab until each tip split through to the other side. Jess watching but unable to help. Understanding what he was trying to do, what he said he was trying to do, but unable or unwilling to facilitate the means of his coming pain. Alex flipping the plywood over to reveal the forest of sharp brown points. Standing before the bed with a gallery full of onlookers. Waiting. An hour, then two, until the gallery began to empty. Grumblings of a hoax, a failure of nerve. And then, finally, when everyone had gone, when even Jess had gone because she knew that she must, Alex setting his body down, stretching his long limbs to the corners, his weight sinking in.

The only proof was the wounds on his back, his neck and arms and legs. Pinprick blood spots appearing through the thin fabric of his T-shirts, Rorschach blottings emerging like points on a map of where he had gone, where no one else was willing to go.

They all talked about the void. Painters, sculptors, writers, performers, they felt it approaching, its ragged edges bleeding in on the nightly news, in the morning paper, images of street protests and napalmed villages, a chaotic war both home and abroad. They tried to fight back. They sat-in and marched. Alex's physical bravery brought out something similar in Jess. She was surprised by her own courage, standing nose to nose with police in riot gear in front of a draft-board office, refusing to move until security guards dragged her from President Johnson's speech at the Century Plaza Hotel. But Alex was the only one, Jess thought, who truly confronted the void beneath the violence. His work made it personal, tearing it from the newspaper page and TV screen, forcing it into the safety and comfort of their lives. He presented the truth, whether anyone liked it or not.

He was celebrated as a visionary; he was dismissed as a stuntman, a sadist. His art was a courageous exploration of the limits of mind and body; his art wasn't art at all, it was a sick plea for attention. But in the days before one of Alex's pieces, and in the days during and after, it was all anyone talked about. It was the lifeblood of the campus, the measure by which the rest of them—whether they admitted it or not—judged their own capacity for risk.

She was drawn to the questions he posed and his willingness to push himself to an edge everyone else refused even to consider. But she was also drawn to the paradox of his personality, his prankster's sense of humor, his grace and kindness. He never played the tortured young artist. He was a sun-kissed child of the beach, tall and muscular and boyishly handsome, with full cheeks and a generous, toothy smile, like the older brother in a white-bread TV comedy. He could have become anyone, with his looks and family pedigree: a captain of industry like his father, a politician, a movie star. He drove a three-thousand-dollar car with the respect that beautiful machine deserved but with none of the ego such a luxury might encourage. Easy, lucrative paths stretched before him in every direction, but he refused them. Jess didn't see this as self-destructive rebellion, or needy exhibitionism. She saw it as integrity and courage.

He questioned everything, including her painting, her intentions, their relationship. They broke up and made up and broke up. She challenged him on methods that seemed showy or hollow or needlessly dangerous. He asked why she wanted to add yet another painting to the world, how she could get at anything meaningful by following in so many well-worn footsteps. When she hit a wall, threatening to throw it all out, screaming at the canvas, he said, *Good, good, this is where you want to be.*

Storms and stillness. She woke in the mornings with his face nestled into her neck, gentle and quiet and warm.

They tried other relationships but always returned to each other. It seemed, at least to Jess, that this would be the pattern of their lives. They would rupture and seal again, they would break off and go out into the world but always find their way back.

Jess gave up painting, and Alex encouraged her abandonment of traditional forms. Her work began to take shape, slowly finding an audience.

He had shows in L.A. and New York. There were plans for Prague, Barcelona, Berlin. Critics said he was a privileged brat looking for attention; they said he was a brave and honest artist making the only reasonable gestures in a world hell-bent on self-destruction.

His father could have maneuvered him out of the draft, but when Alex was called he felt that he needed to go. Not out of a sense of patriotism, but a duty to step into the mouth of the very thing his work had always spoken with.

He spent a year in Vietnam. He returned with a camera given to him by a fellow soldier. He had always played around with photography but was now obsessed. Jess found him harder to reach. He was drinking heavily, chain-smoking. He began taking and showing pictures of disasters, after the fact. Car crashes, crime scenes, protests that devolved into riots. Not the events themselves but the eerily calm spaces that opened when the violence ended. Rubber on the road, police tape, broken signs with half-visible slogans. Children gathering in the wake of adult carnage. Silent witnesses. He traveled to conflict zones: Israel, Angola, Laos, Argentina. Some of his photographs were published in newspapers and magazines, some were acquired by museums. A few became famous, emblematic of a particular struggle or atrocity.

Just after the war ended, Alex returned to Vietnam, and that's where he met Christine, a girl from Ohio working with a small, unchartered relief agency, what Alex would later describe with great affection as an anarchist version of the Red Cross. Six months later they were married in a backyard ceremony in Laurel Canyon. Three months after that, Henry was born.

At the time, Jess felt as if she had missed something, like she had fallen asleep for a year. She and Alex had been apart for a few months, and then he was back in Vietnam, and then a mutual friend told her that Alex was getting married; that he, this friend, had been invited to the ceremony. That the wife-to-be was pregnant. That Alex seemed incredibly happy, as if he had finally found something he had been lacking, some missing piece.

Of course they came back together and broke apart and came together. So now their relationship mutated into a shameful thing, an uncomfortable open secret in their circles, and Jess found herself in a new unasked-for role: mistress, hetaera, potential homewrecker.

None of it could hold. Alex was drinking more, popping Benzedrine like aspirin. He was still obsessed with his work and still, at times, obsessed with Jess. But his guilt was crushing him. The tenor of their arguments changed. He began pushing into places of no return. Art was a lie, he told her. Her art, all art. Art was a distraction from the truth. *What truth?* she shouted back. His truth? Not everyone, Jess said, wanted his truth.

One morning she received a call from the same friend who had told her about the wedding. The night before, Alex had lost control of the Karmann Ghia on Beverly Boulevard. The call seemed like a cruel joke, or part of some elaborate and distasteful new piece Alex had created. She walked from her studio to the newsstand on Abbot Kinney as if in a trance, turning the pages of the morning's paper until she found the photo in the Metro section: the car split nearly in half by the broad trunk of an old roadside palm. The photo was claustrophobically cropped, artlessly composed. Looking at it, feeling its impermanence, the ink already peeling away onto her thumbs, Jess couldn't help but think that Alex would have wanted it that way—the captured moment after a disaster. Cheap, temporary, honest. His only regret, she thought, would have been that he wasn't the one who had taken the picture.

He was driving upward of seventy miles an hour when he hit the tree. He was heartbroken and lonely and high and drunk. He loved Christine, he loved their baby, and he loved Jess, probably, still. He was doing what he did best, staring down pain, pushing into the void. Only this time, he had pushed all the way through.

A breeze moved across the intersection, bending the top of the palm, continuing into the open windows of Jess's truck. An acknowledgment, maybe, of her return to this place. More magical thinking. Her truck was a '69 Harvester Scout, a stout, sturdy bread box on wheels, honey mustard, though faded now from years of sun and salt air. Alex had loved the Scout. It wasn't quite a truck, he said; it wasn't quite a Jeep. It was something else, something hard to define. He always said it was perfect for her.

The morning was heating up, sepia-toned with smog. Jess looked through the windshield grit to the swaying palm. In a children's story, this tree would conceal a portal, a doorway. With the right sequence of words it would swing open and Jess could pass through to join him. But she had run out of words. She went days at a time now without speaking to anyone. Only that single set of Alex's photos remained, the ones Christine was looking for, hidden away in a box under Jess's bed. And even those photos were ruined, corrupted by Jess's need to transform her anger and grief into something new. But she had only managed to create more anger and grief, infecting others with what she made.

Popopopopop. Knuckles banged against her window. A man's face pressed close to the glass, red, damp, his mouth opening from under a mustache overhang.

"Hey, honey, you have a stroke?"

Jess hit the horn to back him away, looking into the rearview mirror to a line of impatient cars. The man approached again, and Jess returned to the horn, a sustained blast to keep him back, to keep all of them back, a wall of sound she carried with her until the man and the tree and the line of cars were far behind.

From *Light + Space*

(1977; 16mm film, sound; 82 minutes;
Laura Lehrer, dir.; unreleased)

T ell me about your early paintings.
    Laura's voice brings her back. Jess looks up from her hands to the camera, then away, toward the windows off-frame.

- There's not much to say. I was painting and not really capturing what I wanted, what I could imagine. Trying everything—oil, gouache, acrylic. All the guys were obsessed with cars, painting cars, so I stole their varnish and layered it on canvas. I started to see reflections in the new surface. Light. Which created a new space. Now there was depth and volume. This was closer to what I imagined, so I built different stretchers for the canvases. My friend Gabe helped. He was studying scenic design at the time, in the theater department.

- How were these stretchers different?

- They were concave. They sank inward so that when you stood in front of the canvas there was an inward pull. At least, that was the idea. It never came off the way I wanted.

She reaches out of frame, comes up with a glass of water, drinks, still thinking, her eyes toward the windows.

- Around that time, my aunt took me to New York. We went to the Guggenheim, and I saw some of Agnes Martin's grids. Those graphite webs of clean, straight lines. There was such power to the work, but I couldn't understand why she was doing this. The grids seemed fearful to me, like fences, barriers against the unknown. That unknown was what I was trying to get to, what we were all trying to get to, and it seemed like she wanted to hold it back.

Jess drinks again, then sets the glass back out of frame.

- My aunt was a voracious reader. She was always searching, opening up to something new. On that trip she was reading a lot of Eastern philosophy. In the hotel that night I came across a passage in one of her books. The next day I went back to the museum, and that time, looking at each of the grids, something happened. I heard a single note, a clear peal, like a bell or a chime. It almost knocked me over. My reaction was that physical. Now I understood. Martin wasn't building a barrier against the unknown—she was pointing, she was showing the way.

- You could hear the drawings.

- It was the most beautiful sound.

Jess reaches for the glass again but stops midmotion. She looks incredulous, still, all these years later.

- I was going about it all wrong. Looking at the grids, I realized that. The painting wasn't important—the layers or concave frames. They were just *stuff*. What was important was the space they created.

- What did you do with your early paintings?

- I threw them away.

- Was that satisfying?

- It was terrifying. That was all the work I'd ever made. But there was freedom in it, too. There was no going back.

- A few of those paintings survived.

- Yes, a few had already sold.

- They sold again recently, for very large sums.

- That's crazy. There's nothing to them.

- What did they sell for originally?

- Nothing. Next to nothing.

- And then they changed hands again and again and ten years later we're discussing five-figure sales. Do you think the paintings are selling now because of what happened at *Zero Zone*?

Jess shakes her head. She looks disgusted, her mouth turned down at the corners.

- I don't see any of that money. That's the secondary market.

- But it increases interest in your future work, doesn't it?

- I thought we weren't going to talk about that.

- About *Zero Zone*?

- Yes. That's what you said when you called.

- But it's all connected, isn't it?

Jess lights another cigarette, stands, moves off-frame. After a moment, there's the sound of the window lifting in two violent jerks, old wood shuddering up along stubborn metal tracks.

Laura speaks again.

- What was the line?

- The line?

- In your aunt's book, that night at the hotel. The line or koan you read, that helped you see Martin's grids differently.

Silence. The empty chair in the middle of the frame. A still life, except for the thin curl of smoke twisting in from the top left corner.

- *When I point my finger at the moon, don't mistake my finger for the moon.*

Breezeway

Fall 1957

There was a threatening charge in the air that night, a prickling current that kept Jess from sleep. She rolled in bed; she sat up, the sheets twisted around her ankles. She listened to Zack's occasional laugh from down in the living room, the TV murmuring, a host's voice and audience applause. *I've Got a Secret.* From her window she stared down at the empty driveway, craning her neck so she could see to the end of the street, waiting for their parents to come home.

They were at least an hour late. This wasn't unusual; her parents were often late returning from dinner with friends. If Barb had her way they would stay for another drink or two. Jess could imagine her father's annoyance, checking his watch, clearing his throat, sending signals to Barb that foundered unheeded. So there was no reason to believe that this night was any different.

Except that it was. Jess could feel a fault line forming in the expected order of events: the headlights appearing, the car pulling into the driveway, her mother's loud whispers as her father opened the front door.

Those things would not happen tonight. Jess knew this. A different ending was in motion. It had already occurred out there, somewhere between her window and the city. She was just waiting for it to roll this way, to crash over her like a wave.

She stood at the window. She waited. She thought about her parents, and her birthday, the party they had planned, just a week away. She was turning fourteen.

Down in the kitchen, the phone rang.

Zack answered. *Shepard residence.* It was the last time Jess would ever hear him say those words. She understood this, somehow. She watched him from the top of the stairs, her toes pressing divots into the nap of the carpeting. Her body tingled, as if every limb was asleep. Zack stared at the TV. His face was blank. She knew what he was being told. Not the details, but the central fact. It was as if she had read ahead in a book, cheating into the final pages.

Zack was so quiet and still, listening. She wanted him to yell or scream or cry out, to tear the phone from the wall. She wanted him to react so she could react. Instead they stayed silent, locked together in the catastrophic moment.

Amazingly, Aunt Ruth was their next of kin. Their grandparents on Barb's side had died a few years earlier, and Donald's father was a bristly recluse who lived alone in the wilds of northern Vermont. Ruth was all Jess and Zack had left.

Ruth was a mystery to her own younger brother, and therefore a mystery to Jess and Zack as well. Donald had always painted her as a reckless figure. When she was eighteen, Ruth left Boston for UCLA and never returned. Over the years, Jess gleaned scant details from tense conversations between her parents and from Barb's phone calls to the West Coast on Ruth's birthday and Christmas Eve. Despite Donald's objections, Barb insisted on maintaining some kind of relationship. Family was family. After a call, Barb would report that Ruth was working as a researcher in a town called Downey, or in an airplane factory in Long Beach. Now she had a job in the admissions office at a college near Pasadena. She was living with a friend, an airplane mechanic, a man; or another friend, a poet, a woman. *Friend?* was a question loaded with impenetrable meaning when Jess's father repeated the word.

According to Donald, Ruth never fit in growing up, had never really tried to fit in, and got the hell out of Boston as soon as she could. He saw this as a character defect. His sister was a bohemian shirker, running from adult responsibilities and expectations. But Jess sensed a furtive admiration on her mother's part. When Donald got going on one of his rants, Barb defended Ruth as someone who at least knew when it was time to make an exit.

One Christmas, they received a card from Los Angeles with a photo of Ruth inside. In the front yard of a small green bungalow, beside a spiny cactus that reached to her shoulders, Ruth stood dressed in full cowgirl regalia: hat, boots, vest, dungarees with chaps. She held a six-shooter in one hand, a lasso in the other. There was no note attached, nothing written on the back. To Donald, the picture was maddeningly nonsensical, further proof of Ruth's immaturity. He crumpled the card and tossed it into the trash, but Barb reclaimed it, smoothed it out, and set it on the fireplace mantel with the other holiday well-wishes. That whole month before Christmas, Jess couldn't pass through the living room without stopping to look at the photo. It was distressed from her father's fist: creases like pale scars cut across the image. This made it seem even stranger, like an unearthed relic. Ruth straight and tall, legs spread wide, chin raised, holding her lasso, her pistol. Jess marveled at the fact that this person was connected to her. Suddenly there was myth in her life, mystery. There was this inscrutable woman somewhere out in California—fierce, defiant, armed and dangerous.

A week after their parents' accident, Jess and Zack arrived at Ruth's house in Eagle Rock, a sleepy, sun-dried neighborhood in L.A.'s far northeastern corner. Two bedrooms were already set aside. Jess's was at the back of the house, facing into the flat, parched yard and its little grove of bedraggled citrus trees. Zack was installed in a converted storage room above the detached garage. This suited him perfectly. Their parents' death had knocked Zack completely into the sullen silence he had been listing toward since the onset of adolescence. For the remainder of that first summer he stayed cloistered in his new sanctuary, shades drawn, door closed. Ruth seemed content to give him his space, either because she thought this was best for a grieving teenage boy or because she didn't know what else to do.

In Jess's dreams she and Zack were in the back seat of their car, their old car, the green Pontiac. Their parents are in the front, Donald driving, Barb leaning toward the rearview mirror, applying a neat line of lipstick. Jess is worried because her clothes and hair smell like smoke—she's just started smoking with some friends after school and the smell in the car's close quarters might give her away. She tries to roll down her window, but the crank is stuck.

Their neighbors' houses pass by, the bakery on the corner, the gas station, her old elementary school, its windows filled with student artwork, paper witches and jack-o'-lanterns and autumn leaves colored like fire. Donald talks back to the radio, arguing with a politician. Barb says, *He can't hear you, dear.*

Every time a car approaches in the opposite lane, Jess flinches. She can see each one swerving into their path, her father jerking the steering wheel, her mother screaming as the windshield fills with another windshield, another face screaming. The violent convergence of lives. With each passing car Jess's terror grows. She turns to Zack in the hope that he understands, that she's not alone in her fear and premonition. But he's opening his door; the car has stopped. He gets out, waiting for her to join him. She realizes then that the crash won't happen, the crash can't happen until their parents are alone in the car. She wants to say something to them—*Don't go* or *Goodbye* or *I love you*—but the car has already pulled away.

Every morning after the dream Jess woke choking, and when she was able to regain her breath she walked from Ruth's house in her pajamas, dazed, up the street and down, gulping air, looking for some place to release what banged around inside her, desperate to get out. It felt like a bomb had gone off in her chest, the blast ringing through her body.

Those mornings she walked for an hour or more, touching things as she passed—cars, mailboxes, the sides of buildings—amazed and disappointed that there was no transfer of energy. A few years before she had found an inexplicable space here, just a few miles away, underwater. She needed a place like that now, somewhere to release what was trapped inside.

She was lonely without Zack. He came down from his room above the garage only for meals or to use the bathroom. When Jess tried to engage he shrugged her off. So she stopped trying, stopped climbing the stairs to his room in the hope that they could talk together, cry, rage, reminisce. Instead, she walked around the backyard, brushing the rough trunks of the tangerine trees with her fingertips, trying to recall every memory of her parents. She was terrified that if she didn't imprint them permanently in her mind they would dissolve in the blinding brightness of this strange new place.

Ruth brought sandwiches and fresh lemonade and kept her distance. Jess unpacked her paints and brushes. Everything was so different here, so turned around, that she no longer felt they needed to be kept secret. But she didn't know what to do with them, either. She didn't want to give form to any of her current dreams.

Ruth built Jess a small easel and set it on the front porch. Jess began sitting there in the afternoons, not painting, just trying to remember everything, to keep it close. When Ruth got home from work she pulled up a chair beside Jess and cracked a Hamm's, smoking and sipping, looking out at the dark ridge of low hills to the north. Jess didn't have the heart to tell Ruth she had never used an easel before, that she wouldn't know where to begin: how to hold her body, where to stand. So instead Jess held a blank pad of paper in her lap and looked at Ruth and sketched what she saw. The sturdy face with its strong bones and tight mouth. The roughened hands, fingertips stained a faint yellow. The cigarette pinched between thumb and index finger, placed between her thin lips and left to burn for a moment, unaccompanied, then lifted away. And Ruth's hair, the wild russet curls that she cut over her eyes into straight, severe bangs, like a steadfast border between warring countries.

"When I was your age," Ruth said, "I thought the sun rose and set on your father's shoulders. I was in awe of him. He was so curious. I wondered what kind of man he'd become. I was excited to see it happen, excited that I'd know that man someday. But I missed my chance."

She lifted the cigarette to her lips again, squinting in the smoke.

"Don't give up on Zachary," she said. "I'll be whatever help I can, but we're not going to let him fade away up there."

One afternoon, Jess heard voices from up in Zack's room, what sounded like adult men. She climbed the stairs and stood outside the door, but couldn't make out what the men were saying. Zack's voice was not part of the conversation. Alarmed, she knocked, and though there was no answer the voices continued. Jess cupped her hands to the dirty window and peered through the narrow gap between curtains. An image glowed on the far wall: three men arguing in the back seat of a car. Jess recognized the actor in the middle—it was Joseph Cotten, looking cramped and worried as the heavy to his left shoved a pistol into his ribs. The image sputtered and leaped, and Jess heard Zack's voice, cursing. She followed the beam of gray light to the other end of the room, where Zack stood beside a movie projector propped on his desk, his hands deep in the machine's guts. The desk was strewn with bolts and gears, light bulbs in various sizes. After a moment Zack stepped back. The image returned to the opposite wall and the conversation again filled the room.

"I have a professor friend who's a real movie nut," Ruth said later. She and Jess were in their chairs on the porch, watching the sunset. "He gave me that projector, said if Zack could get it running he'd help him find some movies to play on it. I figured if Zack's not going to make friends, he at least needs a hobby."

Ruth dug her pack of Pall Malls from the pocket of her dungarees and tapped a cigarette loose. With her eyes still on the rooftops and the horizon beyond, she held the pack out across the span between the chairs. When Jess shook her head, Ruth laughed.

"Who are you trying to fool? I've seen you eyeing these."

Jess took a cigarette and leaned in for a light.

"So I found Zack something to do," Ruth said. "Now we need to find something for you. What might that be, do you think?"

Jess said that she didn't know.

Ruth's voice returned in the twilight. "Then we'll just have to keep looking."

Some days after school, Jess returned to find books on her pillow or bedside table. Museum catalogs and biographies, lean volumes of poetry: Cézanne and Vermeer, Muriel Rukeyser and Elizabeth Bishop. Ruth said that she once dated a poet and the poet left all these books in various places—in Ruth's car, on the front porch, in the bedroom. The poet had a terrible memory, and I never knew, Ruth said, if they were gifts or just things left behind.

Ruth didn't use pronouns when she described the poet, but a picture began to form in Jess's mind, mostly from the poems in the books Ruth loaned her, as if they were written in that absent voice. She imagined a complementary opposite of Ruth, a whirling, impractical woman with a tendency for wide swings of emotion, a hunger for conflict. *The dramatic gesture*, as the artists' biographies called it. Jess didn't ask Ruth about the poet, though the Bishop book contained a slim but tantalizing clue: *S+R*, written in blue ink in the center of the last blank page before the first poem.

It was the pain in the poems that moved her, the fear and uncertainty, the madness always threatening. How these artists turned those raging storms into work to be shared, a space Jess could enter, that could hold some of her grief and confusion while also pointing the way toward the possibility of something beautiful beyond.

Reading in bed, Jess sometimes heard Ruth laughing from out in the kitchen or on the porch. Closing her eyes, she imagined the laugh stemming not from a joke on TV or a particularly galling newspaper article, but from something *S* had said. She could see the two women passing a can of Hamm's back and forth, their bodies shaking with swallowed chortles, their eyes tearing and alive. And then Jess would think of her parents and wonder what they would make of all this. Her father had always presented Ruth as a secretive woman, closed off, unreachable, but that was not how Jess saw her now. It didn't seem that there were any secrets with Ruth. Things were simply left alone. History, memory, emotion. Nothing had been left alone back in Somerville. Her parents overanalyzed every idea and feeling, batting them back and forth like badminton birdies. Here, though, there was room to think and consider. It had nothing to do with secrecy. Jess felt that Ruth would answer any question, if Jess had the courage to ask.

Ruth's professor friend came by with cans of film, and in the evenings he and Zack screened them in the room above the garage. Music and dialogue, gunshots and squealing tires drifted from the open windows, reaching Jess down in the kitchen, where she helped Ruth clean up after dinner.

"I think it's good for him," Ruth said, "to have another man around."

Zack and the professor watched movies or went to see whatever was playing in the theaters or simply walked around the neighborhood, talking. Sometimes, leaving school, Jess saw them sitting on a bench in a baseball field dugout or standing in line at the burger shack. The professor looked like a wizard from a childhood story, tall and gray, his hair and beard shaggy and wild. The first couple of times Jess saw them the wizard was doing the talking, gesturing with his hands, his long fingers splayed as if conjuring some idea from the air. But once, she saw them coming down the sidewalk on the opposite side of the street, and Zack was the one talking, waving his arms to make a point. Jess hadn't seen Zack talk that much since the accident. She wanted to cross the street and join them, inserting herself into the connection they created, but she knew she didn't belong there.

Some evenings a soft ribbon of air unfurled through the neighborhood, east to west, flowing toward the sunset. Whenever Ruth felt it she stood on the patch of concrete between the garage and the house with her eyes closed and her arms spread a little at her sides. One night, Jess found Ruth immersed in that space and wondered how to do that, how to give herself up so fully to a moment.

"We need something here," Ruth said, and Jess realized her aunt's eyes were open again, sizing her up. "A place where we can sit when that breeze passes through."

What she wanted to build, she explained, growing more animated as the idea took shape, was a wooden deck with three tiers. A low eastern tier would face the sunrise, with a step up to a middle tier for midday, and another toward the west for sunsets and stargazing.

Ruth cleared the kitchen table and began sketching plans, running back outside every few minutes to measure, then returning to erase what she had just drawn, impatient with her poor drafting skills. Jess offered to draw so Ruth could stay outside with her flashlight and tape measure, calling numbers in through the kitchen window. When they were finished, Ruth stood over Jess's shoulder and looked at the drawings, nodding. "Something like that," she said, and Jess couldn't help but feel a flush of excitement from the activity, the spontaneous act of creation.

Ruth took the rest of the week off, and the next morning began transferring the plans from the paper to the concrete outside with plumb lines and blue chalk. Jess spent the day at school wishing she was back at the house, wondering how Ruth was going to make this thing, how it would turn from an abstraction on the page to a physical structure, like something carried from a dream into the real world.

After the final bell Jess rushed back. Ruth was waiting with a pair of work gloves and a new pack of Pall Malls.

They talked while they worked. Ruth told Jess about her past jobs, everything from driving a delivery truck to working on a fuselage assembly line. "I suppose I'm something of a dilettante," she said, and Jess was grateful that Ruth didn't define the word for her, as her father would have. But Jess didn't believe Ruth anyway. This was an artificially modest pose, reducing her restless curiosity to something frivolous but acceptable. Jess wanted to tell her aunt that she didn't need to disparage herself when it was just the two of them talking, working together. She wanted to tell Ruth that she understood. Ruth had simply decided not to settle.

Jess told stories in loops, talking about her old friends, her old school, circling the pain at the center, the loss that pulled at her like a drain. Ruth asked questions, opening the stories up further. At first Jess was surprised by Ruth's interest, until she realized that Ruth didn't know any of their family history. She had removed herself from it completely. Jess wondered if Ruth regretted this, or if she accepted the price she had paid for her independence.

One afternoon as they nailed floorboards to the support beams, Jess summoned enough courage to ask.

"I missed out on a lot," Ruth said, holding a nail steady for Jess and her hammer. "But now I get to hear it all from you, right?"

They altered their design as they worked. They adjusted the heights of the tiers, the positions of the benches. Ruth asked Jess's opinion, called her the eyes of the team. *Here*, Jess said, *instead of there*, pointing at two spots on the western tier. The first was where the bench was originally set to be placed, the second a new spot where Jess now stood, looking out to the space between the houses across the street that—from this new angle—framed the swollen sun, giving it focus as it fell.

They finished on a Saturday night, just before Halloween. Ruth brought out a couple of cans of Hamm's and they drank and cleaned up, watching the sky darken, feeling the air move through—tentatively, it seemed, as if exploring the new space for the first time. Ruth stopped sweeping and closed her eyes and held her arms out. After a moment she nodded, satisfied, and said, "We did it," almost in a whisper, and Jess realized how much all of this had upended Ruth's life, too; that Ruth shared her sadness and fear and uncertainty.

Jess took Ruth's hand. She thought the touch would finally release the explosion she had held in since the accident, and it did, but not in the way she had feared. The energy simply transferred, to this place, to this night, opening up and swirling out all around them.

Ruth squeezed her hand and Jess closed her eyes to let the breeze pass through.

3

JESS

SUMMER 1979

The address for Gabe's party was on Broadway, across the street from the Million Dollar Theatre. Jess carried a bottle of wine, looking for the correct number above the gated storefronts. She hardly ever had reason to come downtown, to what seemed like an abandoned city within the larger L.A. sprawl, with its vacant office buildings and desolate streets, newspapers blowing across empty courtyards. But there were occasional pockets of life, where cheap rent attracted artists and quinceañera dress shops, and at least one theater still drawing a Friday-night crowd.

A long line rambled from the Million Dollar's ticket booth, couples in pressed blue jeans and short skirts, cowboy boots and high heels, polished belt buckles and candy-colored vinyl purses reflecting the marquee's cycling incandescents. A coffee vendor wheeled his cart down the line, ringing his bell, chatting with the men, complimenting the ladies, tipping his straw hat before moving on.

RICARDO MONTALBÁN IN BORDER INCIDENT. Jess knew the film. It was one of the few Zack had screened for her during the early days of his movie-collecting mania. She didn't recall much of the plot. It was Zack's disappointment she remembered, his frustration that she didn't appreciate the film the same way he did, or that she appreciated different things, the wrong things. Halfway through, exasperated, he had switched his projector off, so she didn't know how the movie ended.

Turning back to her side of the street, Jess heard shouts and a tambourine keeping a ragged beat. The noise came from a storefront church, its doors open to the warm night. Inside, a crowd swayed in loose rows, men and women, white and Hispanic, clapping along with the tambourine's rhythm. A young white woman stumbled up the center aisle, thrusting her hands toward the low ceiling, shouting in a garbled language. The crowd shouted along with her. She made her way toward the back of the room, where a man in a fringed leather vest stood on a plywood altar. His bare chest gleamed with sweat. He shook the tambourine and the woman moved toward him in time with the sound. He watched her approach with a hunger in his eyes that made Jess recoil.

She turned from the doorway and almost collided with another man blocking her path on the sidewalk. Long-haired and bare-chested, he gave Jess an unsettling smile.

"What do you say, sister? Time to come into the light?"

Jess circled around him. He called out something she couldn't hear, and then she finally found the right address, a locked door between two more gated stores. She pressed the buzzer, looking back to where the man had turned his attention to a young woman, his hand on her shoulder, guiding her toward the gathering inside.

Jess hit the buzzer again and the lock popped open. At the end of a short, dim hallway, she found an open elevator that smelled like mold and minty mouthwash. She pressed the button for the top floor. The doors closed. In fits and starts the small box jerked upward, then shunted to a stop.

A muffled bell chimed and the doors opened again, revealing a large room, an old office, maybe. A string of low windows ran along each side wall. Most of the light came from candles set on tables and crates and the flashing of the Million Dollar's marquee outside. The room was packed and loud and smoky. Everyone was young. There was music playing: howling guitars and an insistent spoken-word monologue—Patti Smith, maybe—from overdriven speakers in a corner of the room.

Jess hoped the doors would close again, taking her back down before anyone noticed, but then a girl turned from a large group and cocked her head, trying to make sense of this new arrival. The girl was tall and pale, all sharp angles and black leather. This was Gabe's student, the hostess. Jess recognized her from the description Gabe had left with the answering service, along with the address.

Hostess, Jesus. Her mother's term just appeared, incongruously, in Jess's brain. That word probably wasn't even in this girl's vocabulary. Or if it was, she would consider it a slight, a word associated with her own mother, maybe, pouring cocktails in a plushly carpeted living room down in Orange or Laguna, entertaining other couples from her bridge group. Hostess as an insult, a cupcake.

Jess couldn't remember the girl's name. Gabe had left it in the message, but her memory was for shit these days.

Stepping from the elevator, Jess smiled and offered her hand.

"I'm a friend of Gabe's."

The girl took Jess's hand and nodded slowly. Her fingers were rough with calluses. She was a guitarist and singer, that was what Gabe had said. Maybe that was her rather than Patti Smith on the stereo.

The girl stared hard at Jess, and then her eyes widened with recognition.

"Holy shit. Jess Shepard."

The other kids in the group stopped talking. They turned to look at Jess. She felt like she was glowing now, radioactive.

"*Zero Zone*," someone said. "Holy shit."

They were all staring at her with a sickening mix of fear and reverence. She wanted to deny it all, her name, her history, to tell them they were mistaken. She wanted to back into the elevator, drop down to the street, but the elevator doors opened again, disgorging another group of kids, and Jess moved forward with the wave, fleeing deeper into the party. She could see Gabe now, a friendly beacon, looking happy and trim in jeans and a tight black T-shirt, talking to a couple of students by the far windows. Jess squeezed toward him, flinching at every barked laugh and drunken stumble, forcing herself into the heart of the crowd.

And then there he was, Anton Stendahl, stepping into her path as if out of a bad dream, tall and thin in a fitted white suit.

"Jess?"

She wondered if she had finally snapped. But no, it was Anton, cocking his head with that familiar smirking smile of whimsical disbelief. With his conspiratorial murmuring and indeterminate accent, Anton had always reminded her of a B-movie character, a slippery underworld informant or the shoddy impresario of a low-rent speakeasy. Jess hadn't seen him since the night of the gallery attack two years ago. He stepped closer, ducking his head to create some privacy between them.

"What are you doing here?" Jess said.

"I'm in town for my show," he said, as if stating the obvious. Then he waved his hand, dismissing the misunderstanding. That wasn't important; it was not why he was here, now, in front of her. Jess could see his concern. She was missing something.

"Didn't you hear?" Anton said. "About her?" The music grew louder, more insistent, but somehow Jess still heard Anton clearly, the urgency in his voice cutting through all the noise.

"Who?" she asked, knowing the answer but trying to delay the inevitable. Her stomach turned liquid with the thought of the name about to be unleashed into the room.

"Isabella Serrano," Anton said. "She's out. She's free. Three years down to two for good behavior."

From *Light + Space*

(1977; 16mm film, sound; 82 minutes;
Laura Lehrer, dir.; unreleased)

I'd like to talk about *Zero Zone*.
- That wasn't part of our agreement.
- But it's impossible to ignore. It's part of your work.
- There's nothing left to say.
- You haven't said anything publicly.
- It was all in the news.
- But I'm interested in your thoughts on the piece. About what happened.

Jess is back in the chair. She takes a breath and holds it, lifting her chin as if attempting to make herself larger, puffing up in defense.

Laura sounds like a narrator now, reciting facts:
- *Zero Zone* was a concrete room you constructed in the New Mexico desert near an abandoned military base.

Jess looks toward Laura, then into the lens, defiant, a criminal hearing the charges against her.

- There was a small group of visitors to the room who refused to leave. Danny Aguado, Tanner Helm, Martha Reed, Isabella Serrano. They said that they saw something in there. And then they began to keep others out.

Jess nods and looks away.

- That's when I first heard what was happening.

- From the man who owns the ranch?

- Yes.

- What did he say?

- He asked me what to do. These people didn't have much food or water. They wouldn't accept anything. It was incredibly hot in there. It wasn't designed for—no one was supposed to stay inside that long.

- Eight days.

- Yes.

Off-frame, somewhere down below, a car's engine growls, rolling by.

- The rancher called the authorities.

Jess looks toward the camera, defiant again.

- I told him to call.

- Were you surprised by what happened?

- Of course. How could I not have been—

- That wasn't your intention?

- My intention? No, how—there was no intention.

- You had no intention when you created the site?

- That's not how I work. That's not what we've been talking about.

- But visitors to your other pieces have had very strong reactions.

- Some have, yes.

- And wasn't that your intention?

- That these people would starve themselves? Supplicating in a concrete room for a week?

- It was a reaction to your work.

- I can't control someone's reaction.

- But you create the space.

Jess starts to speak but then stops herself. Her mouth tightens to a thin line.

Laura's voice returns, pressing.

- Someone died in that space.

Jess stands and walks deeper into the studio, creating distance, losing focus, shrinking in the frame against the blank white wall. She stops, her back to the camera, a hand on her hip, staring into the white.

The camera zooms in, pursuing Jess, pinning her against the wall. The only sound is the tiny clicking of film winding through the camera, then Laura's voice, which sounds closer now, as if she has also followed Jess across the room.

- What did that space mean to you?

Jess shakes her head, either unsure or refusing to answer. Laura speaks again.

- What did it mean to them? To the people who stayed inside?

FIRE SEASON

4

ISABELLA

YEAR OF THE RAT, TIGER, DRAGON, SNAKE, PIG

Nineteen seventy-two was the Year of the Rat. Miss Burton, Izzy's sixth-grade English teacher, told them all about the Chinese Zodiac. Izzy liked the idea that years could have animal characteristics, though the Year of the Rat made her nervous because she thought that from certain angles, in certain mirrors, she looked like a cartoon rat, with her stubby nose and jug ears. She kept her ears buried in her hair but there wasn't much she could do about her nose. Just cover it with her hand when she laughed, or when it seemed like someone was staring. Izzy was guilty of staring, too. She spent a of time looking at the other girls, wishing for their slender noses and delicate ears.

Those girls called her señorita because her father's family was from Mexico and Izzy had his coloring. A round, brownish face in every class photo, peeking out from within the slim white forest. Easy to overlook a darker patch amid all that light.

Except of course, when it wasn't, when they didn't, when the girls focused their attention on her and she didn't have enough hands to hide behind.

Once Izzy came home crying and told her mother about the nickname. Madeline reared up like a cobra, imperious and deadly, and said that Izzy's father made more money than most of her friends' fathers combined. Izzy knew immediately that telling her mother had been a mistake. For one thing, those girls weren't her friends. She didn't have many friends, except for Chloe. And the amount of money didn't matter. Her father owned parking lots. This made him, in the eyes of the girls at school, only a step up from a valet or a guy who worked at a car wash. Her father could strut around town with cash falling from his pockets and it wouldn't make a difference.

Her parents thought they were respected and admired. Chairman and chairwoman of the board. They were kidding themselves. Izzy saw it in the enraged, defensive flash in her mother's eyes when Madeline heard the nickname—it was all so fragile under the surface. Cold, deep water beneath thin ice.

She and Chloe had been friends since the year before. Chloe didn't get along with the other girls either. She thought most of them were spoiled fakes. Chloe was an actress, so she was away from school a lot, shooting parts in movies and TV shows. She was confident and opinionated, which Izzy admired but was a little afraid of, too. Underneath it all, Izzy worried about being a phony, and that someday Chloe would find out.

She had Chloe, and she had Vince. Vince's father had worked for her parents for years, keeping the grounds, fixing the cars—whatever needed to be done. On afternoons and weekends Vince came to the house to help. He was a year older than Izzy, tall for his age, thin and lanky. He dressed like a cowboy, but it never seemed fake like when girls at school tried on a new look. It was like he really believed he was a cowboy, so Izzy was willing to believe it, too.

Vince was kind of like a brother and kind of like a friend and, she figured, kind of like an employee. It was a weird combination. She never knew quite how to feel about him, one day to the next.

Izzy trailed around while he worked. He was a good listener. He didn't know anyone she knew, so she felt comfortable telling him things. She shared all her worries and fears and he listened, taking them with him at the end of the day, leaving her fewer of those things to carry around.

She was crossing the hall from Math to English, a late morning in late fall, getting toward the end of the year. Izzy was thinking about a dog, asking for a dog for Christmas. A golden retriever, she thought, a big blond bundle of exuberance. Their house and the surrounding grounds were large, they made Izzy feel small and out of place, and she thought that having a dog might shrink things down, help it all make sense.

And then, suddenly, she was floating in the middle of the hallway. Her feet had left the ground. For a moment she was scared, this was nuts, but then the fear left her, and that emptiness filled with something new. The light from the windows above the lockers rushed in. Her brain popped with what felt like fireworks traveling down the length of her body. Every nerve ignited, a million fuses lit all at once.

She wanted to cry out with joy.

She opened her eyes to whispers, snickers, murmuring. Izzy heard the clack of heels on the tile floor, saw Miss Burton coming into focus, her mouth open, eyes wide. Izzy's ears were ringing, and the ringing grew louder, splitting through her skull.

Someone said, What's happening? Why's she shaking like that?

Someone said, What's wrong with her?

Miss Burton knelt down beside her, calling out to someone down the hall. The ringing was all Izzy could hear, except for the gasps now, from the girls gathered around, staring, and then shocked and giddy laughter. She couldn't feel her fingers or hands or feet. All she could feel was the wetness and warmth spreading into her skirt, down her thighs, onto the floor.

Her doctor ran tests and gave her a prescription. The medication worked. She didn't have another seizure, but she had a new nickname: Señorita Shake. It followed her like that imagined dog. She heard it between lockers, under the pergola during lunch. They would never let her forget. Her father owned parking lots and she was the girl who fell to the floor and lost all control.

She didn't tell Vince about the seizure. It was the first thing she'd ever withheld from him. She was too afraid to put that picture into his head, of her thrashing in the hallway, wetting herself. No one could forget that, and she didn't want him to see her that way.

Whenever she thought of the seizure Izzy grew sick with shame, but she also felt a strange ache to return to the moment just before she blacked out, to recapture that sense of golden rising. When she was awake, she couldn't remember it exactly, but it came to her in dreams, and in dreams it wasn't cut off by the fall to earth, or by the sound of other girls laughing. In her dreams it continued growing, becoming so bright that the world around her disappeared, clearing the way for something beautiful and new.

She could stop taking her medication. That would do the trick, wouldn't it? But she didn't have the guts.

In the locker room she snuck glances at the other girls, sick with jealous desire for their displayed edges: cheekbones, hip bones, the smooth, hard ladder of ribs up a back. Statements of striking grace, beautiful in their strict simplicity.

In front of her bedroom mirror she pushed at the softness of her belly, her round cheeks. She pinched the inch of flesh at her waist in the same way her mother pinched whenever she walked by.

Nineteen seventy-four was the Year of the Tiger.

Once a week her mother visited the shops on Lake Avenue, dragging Izzy along. Like maybe if Izzy spent more time with clothes and jewelry she would start to care about those things. Izzy wandered around the racks while her mother stepped in and out of changing rooms, turning in toward the mirrors, appraising herself from different angles, absorbing compliments from the salesladies.

The salesladies asked Izzy if there was anything she wanted to try on. She smiled and shook her head. She had learned the smile to perfection but rarely used it, storing it away in her back pocket like a card trick, misdirection. These women were lulled by the smile, it was a language they understood, so when they turned away, trusting, Izzy moved something from one place in the store to another. A bracelet, a skirt, a blouse. The shivery clink of hangers along metal rods. Her mother and the salesladies chatted at the counter and Izzy snuck a cocktail dress across racks, feeling in the transgression a little burst, a tiny echo of that moment from before the seizure, her body gathering light.

She ate half as much as usual, then cut even that in half. The Appedrine pills she stole from her mother made her jittery, but at least they kept her awake when she started to crash. She ignored her hunger and felt powerful for conquering something. Hunger was a weakness. It made her angry, and she used that anger not to eat.

Now when she looked in the mirror she saw some of those edges— hollows under her eyes, the solid line of her pelvic bone. She still didn't think she looked like the other girls, but that no longer mattered. Something else was happening. When she stood too quickly or went a long time without eating she felt a moment of that explosive brightness, like during the seizure. She'd found another way to move toward that light.

She was obsessed with help-wanted ads in the newspaper. She liked to imagine herself in each of the jobs listed. Nanny, secretary, nurse. At the dining room table she watched other versions of herself for what seemed like hours until her mother broke those possibilities, Madeline's voice cracking through like a slapping hand, telling Izzy she was late for school.

One morning she found an ad for work at a movie theater out on Pasadena's eastern outskirts. Nineteen seventy-six was the Year of the Dragon. Izzy was fifteen. She ditched Chemistry and took a bus to the theater. She'd never been out that way before, where the city began to disintegrate into the desert. The streets were wider and emptier; the buildings longer and lower. Everything the color of sand. She walked along the sun-exposed sidewalk past little stucco houses, tired-looking strip malls, a savings and loan with a rotating sign in the parking lot showing the time and temperature.

The theater manager interviewed her while leaning against the lobby's concession counter. He was tall and timid and damp-seeming somehow, like a sponge that hadn't been squeezed dry. When he spoke he looked only at her chest until she folded her arms and then he looked over the top of her head.

She worked two or three nights a week. She told Chloe and Vince but made them promise not to visit. It was a place where no one knew her. She told her mother that she had joined a study group.

The theater was called the Bijou. Izzy liked to say the name under her breath as she vacuumed the lobby or helped someone find their seat. The sound of the word, the grin and release, like a sneeze, like something you might say to a baby to make her smile.

They showed mostly art and foreign films. Every week a new language filled the auditorium. When *Cleo from 5 to 7* opened, Izzy watched it from the back of the theater and then asked for extra shifts that week. She was drawn to Cleo, wandering through a Paris afternoon while she waited anxiously for test results from her doctor. Izzy understood this young woman who seemed so out of place, disappearing for a moment as she passed behind a mirror in a hat shop.

The film had been made by a woman. Izzy had never heard of a female filmmaker. When she asked the manager to name another, he stared at the wall for a moment and then shrugged. Izzy attended every showing she could, surrounded by this woman's fear and hope and anger glowing in the dark. The feeling was so strong that at times Izzy expected to find Agnès Varda sitting behind her, willing her vision up onto the screen. She was there but not there, like Cleo passing behind that mirror.

"You ever feel like you're not yourself?" Izzy said. "Or like the self you thought you were is wrong? That maybe there's another way to be you?"

Vince twisted himself around until his head appeared from underneath her father's Mercedes. Grease streaked his cheeks, a field of dark stubble shadowed his chin. He looked up at Izzy and squinted, considering maybe, or fighting the sun.

"That's a dumb question, isn't it," Izzy said.

Vince shrugged with his eyebrows. "I don't think it's dumb. I just don't know the answer."

The engine was running, he was looking for a leak of some kind, and as Izzy stood there she moved her hips into the car's dark blue flank. As Vince spoke she imagined him there instead of the car, the pressure and vibration, and then that felt wrong and weird so she backed away.

"Is that safe?" she asked, changing the subject. "Crawling under there when it's on?"

Vince smiled and scooted himself back underneath the car, his voice climbing up through the body.

"Probably not."

She stopped taking her medication, moving through the following days and weeks scared of what might happen and scared that nothing would. But the weeks turned to months and she didn't have another seizure. She was relieved and then furious at herself for her cowardice.

Sometimes she still went to the shops on Lake Avenue to move things from one place to another. Walking in on her own now, without her mother, and smiling at the women who asked if they could help. But she felt only a few fireworks popping here and there in her brain, nothing more. She needed to be bolder.

She smiled at the women in the stores and then stopped smiling. The smile made her appear harmless and then the lack of the smile made her invisible. In the dressing rooms she pulled blouses on under her blouse, skirts under her skirt, slipped bracelets into her underpants. Leaving the dressing rooms many-layered. Smiling again to ward off suspicion, then not smiling to disappear.

"You ever meet any guys at the movie theater?"

"Guys?"

"Yeah, you know," Chloe said. "Guys, men. Don't men go to the movies?"

"Of course."

"Do you talk to them? Flirt a little?"

"What do you think?"

"Maybe you find a handsome stranger, sit down beside him—"

"Come on."

"What, no necking in the dark? A hand job in the back row?"

"Gross."

"Missed opportunities."

They were walking across the La Loma bridge, just about dusk, heading over to Bullock's department store. On Saturday nights, everybody met up in the parking lot. Izzy didn't really like the ritual, she tended to wander at the margins sipping the same can of beer, but Chloe always wanted to go. Sunny and blond, with an actress's sexy smile, Chloe could make herself fit in anywhere.

On an impulse, Izzy climbed up onto the bridge's concrete balustrade. She felt dizzy looking down into the arroyo, seventy or eighty feet of open space dropping through the treetops to the thin concrete vein of the dry river. She lifted her head and started walking. The balustrade was less than shoulder-width wide, so she had to set one foot in front of the other, like on the balance beam in gym class. She always fell off the balance beam. That was no big deal, a foot or two to the mats on the gymnasium floor. Same up here on the balustrade, if she leaned to the left—a couple of feet back down to the bridge's sidewalk. But if she leaned to the right, she'd fall into that vast open space.

"What are you doing?" Chloe said. "Get down from there. You're going to fall off and splat. Arroyo pizza."

Izzy moved along the edge, unsteady, but alive now.

"Sounds like a restaurant," Chloe said. "We should drive off somewhere and open a nice little place. *Arroyo Pizza*. You wouldn't eat it, though. You're so skinny."

Izzy was closer to that feeling than she'd been since the seizure. A car whipped past from behind them and the momentum transferred. She swayed left and then right, her head exploding with those fireworks.

"We need to find you a boyfriend," Chloe said.

But Chloe's voice had faded to a drone, just part of the buzzing in Izzy's head as she walked, barely balancing, her body's weight evaporating.

Suddenly a burst of birds flew from under the bridge, blue backs straight, white wings stretched, gliding in a tight arrowhead. There were eight or ten of them, and Izzy felt like—no she was *sure* she could step off the balustrade and onto their backs. She could walk lightly from one to the next as the flock shuffled in front of her, rearranging, skating high above the treetops.

She took a step.

Chloe grabbed Izzy's shirt, pulling her away from the edge.

"For fuck's sake, Izzy," Chloe said.

Izzy stepped back onto the balustrade, the birds flying off, the feeling flying off, then that familiar deadened crash back into her body.

"Jesus Christ," Chloe said. "What's wrong with you?"

"Would you like some help in there?" The saleslady's voice was close, coming from the other side of the dressing room curtain.

"No," Izzy said. "I'm fine."

"Because we have a strict shoplifting policy."

Izzy stopped, the moment frozen, she could hear the ice cracking. One skirt halfway up her thighs, another bunched around her waist. Two blouses under her sweater. Purse crammed with bracelets.

The saleslady yanked the curtain open, her face buckled in anger and disgust. Izzy might as well have been naked. She felt naked. Up on one foot, balancing, the skirt in midpull. She didn't know whether to keep lifting the skirt or to lower it back down.

Her mother arrived and negotiated with the saleslady in low tones. Funds were exchanged. Driving home, her mother spoke in fragments, or fragments were all Izzy heard. *Mortified. Shopping there for years. None of those clothes even fit you.*

"How much?" Izzy asked, looking out the window, watching parking meters, storefronts, clean-limbed oaks roll by.

"Excuse me?"

"How much did you pay her?"

"*That's* what you want to know? *That's* your concern?"

"What does it cost?"

"What does *what* cost?"

"Making everything go away."

Her mother and Chloe had next to nothing in common, but they both had the same question. Izzy had it, too, for that matter.

"What's wrong with you?" her mother said.

The boy's name was Bradford, but everyone called him Ford or Fordy. He was a senior at Poly, a basketball player, a forward or guard, Izzy couldn't remember which. But the sport wasn't important. What was important was the way he looked at her, like she was someone worth looking at, his eyes curious and a little greedy. No one had ever looked at her that way before.

Ford and a couple of his friends had come to the theater to watch *Celine and Julie Go Boating.* They needed to see a movie for French class and chose that one without looking into the subject or running time. Two hours in, Ford walked back out into the lobby, bug-eyed with boredom. Izzy laughed, even though she had seen the movie twice so far, hypnotized by its detail and repetition, the magical world it spun. At the concession counter, she and Ford talked about school and movies. She was surprised how easy he was to talk to. She hadn't even realized another hour had passed until his friends stumbled out at the end of the film, blinking in the bright lobby light.

They ran into each other after school, and at the weekly gatherings in the Bullock's parking lot. They went to see another movie, a rerelease of *Vivre Sa Vie*. Ford held her hand and shifted in his seat while Izzy watched Anna Karina watch Joan of Arc in another theater far away.

Then there was the night his parents were in Lake Tahoe, and she and Ford unfolded on his living room couch in the dark, the glow from the TV making small rippling pools on his bare shoulders and arms. *You're so beautiful,* he said, his mouth pressed to her neck, his hands moving over her hip, along her ribs, and she chose to believe he meant it.

She turned the corner to find a small group of girls gathered by her locker in an excited buzz, sticking something to the door. Izzy saw that it was a sheet of notebook paper, ragged edged from where it had been pulled from its metal spiral. The girls turned at her approach, eager for Izzy's reaction. It was a handwritten list in blue and black and green ink, multiple colors from additions over time. She recognized Ford's handwriting, the cramped printing that looked like it took so much effort. It was a list of girls' names, or rather their nicknames. Not the girls gathered around the locker, but girls from the edges, like Izzy. The fat girls, the couple of brown girls, the girls with bad skin. The list was numbered one through ten, with a checkmark after each. Number ten was *Senoreta Shake*. He even spelled it wrong.

"It's his Pig List," a girl said. Andrea. She had been Ford's girlfriend the year before. "Gross, isn't it? I guess he wanted to see if he could do all ten."

The bell rang and the girls moved off down the hall. Izzy stared at the paper. She pressed her thumb against her shirt, the hard jut of a rib, pushing until the paper blurred into a white smudge, until she could feel the thin-skinned bruise forming, praying it would spread over her body, ruining it, finally, so it could fall away.

It was junior year, the Year of the Snake. But that was a lie. Izzy knew the truth.

Nineteen seventy-seven was the Year of the Pig.

5

JESS

SUMMER 1979

Jess opened her eyes, waking slowly. The room began to take shape. Her room, her bed, her apartment. She couldn't remember leaving the party or driving back to Venice. But she remembered Anton, and what he had told her about Isabella. The name free now, like the girl.

Anton had given his news and Jess had made her way through the party to Gabe and then worked through her bottle of iffy merlot. She couldn't remember anything else. No, wait—one quick flash: later, walking down Broadway toward her truck, someone stepped out of the alley and Jess screamed, expecting Isabella. But it was only a kid from the party, a boy with a beard and a woolly hat. He skirted around Jess, freaked out by her reaction.

So incredibly stupid. Walking alone through downtown in the middle of the night, then in no condition to drive home.

Her head pounded, her mouth was dry. She had left the curtains behind the bed open and the late-morning sun poured through unchallenged. The weather had turned. This was the time of year when, even at the beach, dark curtains should be drawn, blinds turned flat, when the heat pressed against the windows like an angry passenger on an overstuffed train.

In the kitchen, Jess cupped cool water from the faucet and drank from her hands. Through the windows she saw the Scout parked down on the street, one tire up on the curb. She could have killed someone. She thought of her parents' accident, the young man behind the wheel of the oncoming car. How much had he had to drink? A bottle of wine, the police had said. Home from college on summer break, driving from a friend's party.

"This is a message from Anton Stendahl. Hello, Jess. I'm in town for my show at the Hearst. Hopefully I'll see you there."

Jess stood with her back against the refrigerator, the machine's vibration soothing her achy joints. She held the phone to her ear and listened to Deidre recite messages from the day before. Deidre read the message the same way she read every message, with a flattened calm that Jess imagined was part of some kind of training, a tone designed to protect the answering service operators from the messy intricacies of their clients' lives. Jess had come to know the voice well, she expected and relied on it, all the news from the outside world delivered in Deidre's agreeable, artificial hue.

Jess had never met Deidre. She probably worked in the office in Thousand Oaks where Jess sent her monthly check. Or maybe she worked from home, standing in a kitchen not unlike this one, leaning against her own refrigerator, hungover, reading the message in this same morning glare.

"I don't know if you've heard about Isabella Serrano." The name now spoken by yet another voice, Deidre's, finishing Anton's message. "Call me at my hotel. I have some news."

After the gallery attack, Anton became obsessed with Isabella Serrano. Jess avoided the news but Anton called Jess about every article and TV story. Jess had never thought of Anton as a friend, but he seemed to believe they were bound together by the attack, and just as Jess ran from that moment and its aftermath, Anton embraced it, forcing himself into an ardent co-ownership.

She hired the answering service to intercept reporters' questions and Anton's unwanted dispatches, but of course the service fielded all of her messages, and Jess soon found that she preferred it that way. It was easier to ignore the concerned and well-meaning calls from friends attempting to draw her out, and then it was easier to ignore when those calls diminished and ceased altogether.

"That's it," Deidre said, her voice taking on a slightly more relaxed coloration after a message, an actress stepping offstage. "Have a nice day."

The front door buzzer sounded, a long, braying blast, and Jess fumbled the receiver to the floor. She fished it back and hung up the phone, then moved to the side of the windows to peer down to the street. There was a green sedan parked behind her truck. A small boy stood on the sidewalk beside the car. It was Alex—it was Alex as a boy. Her window had become the frame of one of Alex's old photos. She remembered looking at his childhood snapshots, imagining what it would have been like to know him at that age. Back then she had wanted all of him, his whole history and future.

The buzzer sounded again.

It wasn't Alex; that was crazy. It was Henry, Alex's son. He looked up, squinting in the sunlight, raising his chin with a familiar lift, that physical echo, and then he saw her in the window and raised his hand in a mirror image of his father's enthusiastic wave, which became a beckoning for Jess to come down and answer the door.

When she did, she found Christine standing on the other side.

"I'm here for the photos," Christine said, dropping her hand from the buzzer.

She was a beautiful woman. The first time Jess saw Christine, she understood Alex's attraction. Small and blond and fine-boned, but fervid and intense, a woman who organizes relief camps in a country her own government is trying to destroy. She wore a slim-fitting jogging suit, pale gray, almost the exact shade of her eyes. Her hair was pulled back. She seemed full to bursting with indignation, forced to return to the home of her dead husband's mistress.

"The photos," Jess said, intimidated into playing dumb, breaking her eyes from Christine's and looking back to the car where Henry watched, smiling now. She knew that smile.

"Alex left them here," Christine said. "You should have given them back."

"You were going to burn them."

"What?"

"You said you were going to burn everything he left behind."

"I was in shock. My husband was dead."

"Well, I burned them," Jess said. "I climbed up onto the bluffs in Malibu and scattered the ashes."

"Bullshit."

Jess lifted her hands, showing nothing.

"Do I have to get some kind of order?" Christine said. "A warrant?"

"A warrant?"

"Whatever it's called. Do I have to go that far?"

Christine's eyes held on Jess. There was contempt in that look, a little pity. How had Alex explained Jess to her? As an ex-girlfriend, a woman who had been in and out of his life since college. The last remnant of a delayed adolescence. A woman he would never bring home to his parents, never ask to marry.

The only other time Jess and Christine had spoken was a morning three years before, in this same spot. Christine had stood in the doorway, hugely pregnant. She told Jess to stay away from Alex. Jess, mistaking accuracy for truth, spat back that Christine had it all wrong, that it was Alex who wouldn't stay away. As soon as she said it, Jess realized she was having the wrong argument. She had missed the point. This was a married woman standing before her, carrying a child. Christine wasn't there to argue, she was there so that Jess could see, could get it through her thick skull. It was over. It had been over for a long time.

Here again with Christine on her doorstep, Jess felt the same way she had on that previous morning. Small, petty, ashamed. Here was the woman, the widow; here was the fatherless son. And here was Jess, the bad penny, turned up again.

Christine let out an exasperated breath. "I'm putting together a retrospective of Alex's work," she said. "There are a number of museums interested, galleries, publishers. They all have lawyers. Look around. Dig deep. See what you can find." She fixed Jess with a final warning look, then turned and walked to her car.

Jess looked away, down to the sidewalk, over to the flat brick wall of the pharmacy across the street, anywhere but at the woman with the righteous anger, the moral high ground, the paperwork. She looked to the shoddily parked Scout, to the green sedan behind, the boy standing beside his open door lifting his hand again in a goodbye wave, crushingly familiar.

The ringing phone pulled Jess back upstairs to her apartment, where she found Deidre's voice on the line again, apologizing. There was one other message from the night before.

"Miss Shepard, my name is Madeline Serrano. Isabella is my daughter. She was recently released from her incarceration, a year ahead of schedule. We were told that she displayed exemplary behavior. That she was a model citizen.

"We—my husband and I—hope that this is the beginning of a new chapter in Isabella's life. She has had her difficulties, but we do not want her defined by the mistakes of the past. Isn't that what we all want? For each other, for ourselves? To move on?

"I'd like to speak with you about that future. I believe that we have some common interests. I'll leave a phone number, and we can arrange a time to meet. It will be a private conversation, just the two of us. I look forward to hearing from you soon."

6

ISABELLA

SUMMER 1977

S itting in the dead VW Bug, windows down, four bare feet up on the dashboard. The car was half buried in the hill below Chloe's little house in Echo Park. Chloe had wiped a clean swath through the leaves and dust on the windshield so they could look across the hump-back row of neighboring hills into the smoggy dusk, the whole sky the same livid shade of red, as if the setting sun had burst.

"How much do we need?" Izzy said.

Chloe took a hit of her joint, then set it on the edge of the dashboard's ashtray.

"Depends where we're going."

"Anywhere. I just want to leave."

Shifting in her seat, Izzy heard the crinkle of the paper folded into her back jeans pocket. She kept the Pig List there, a reminder.

"Five hundred," Chloe said. "Maybe a thousand."

"Ugh."

"How much do you have?"

"Less than that."

"If we just get to Vegas," Chloe said, "I can make what we need. I'm a terrific gambler."

"They won't let us in."

"Of course they will. I paid good money for those IDs."

Chloe leaned forward and picked at a chip of light blue polish on the nail of her big toe. "I was in Vegas a few months ago and walked away with three hundred bucks."

"Three hundred won't get us far," Izzy said.

"That was one night at the tables. Half a night. If we're there for a week, we're talking something real."

The sun slipped below the dash. Izzy lifted her hands and held them out at arms' length, thumbs and index fingers in Ls or pistols turned to create a rectangle, a frame of film. One of her jobs at the theater was to hang up lobby cards, the cardboard promotional shots distributors sent along with their films. These were often production photos, directors visualizing a moment, men looking at women through a frame of fingers. Sometimes Izzy looked through her own this way, imagining that she could reframe the world before her into a new image.

"What are you doing with your hands?" Chloe said.

"Nothing." Izzy dropped them into her lap. "What if you lose? In Vegas."

"I won't."

"What if you do?"

"You need to trust."

"Trust who?"

"Me." Chloe sat back, grabbed Izzy's thigh, and squeezed. "The universe. The rightness of all things."

She needed to get out of the house, out of her head, so she asked Vince to drive up Mulholland so they could watch the day's end dropping slowly, like the curtain at the close of a play.

"Remember how you used to tell me about racing?" Izzy asked. "You wanted to buy a car and travel from track to track."

"You remember that?"

"Of course."

He looked at her for a moment, then turned back to the windshield, the road unfolding, one curve at a time in the lowering dusk.

"Do you still think about it?" she asked.

"I don't know. It's been a long time."

He sounded a little embarrassed at the old daydream.

"What if we did it?" she said.

"Did what?"

"Just kept driving, out there."

She gestured to the windshield, *out there*, whatever lay beyond the hilltop rising into view.

Vince pulled his Firebird into a gravel turnout and slowed to a stop. They were pointed toward the valley, the long, low expanse of lights coming on, street by street, in counterpoint to the night.

"I'm serious," Izzy said.

"Where would we go?"

Izzy turned to him, trying to read his face, to see if he was really considering the possibility. He looked like a man now, a leaner, more thoughtful version of his father.

"Anywhere," she said.

He took off his sunglasses and turned to her. She could see him struggling, not sure what to make of her sudden proposal. There were quick
moments of resolution, flickering in and out, where it seemed like he
would move into action, put the car back into gear and drive them down
through that long grid of lights. Izzy wanted to grab that look, that moment; she wanted to hold it and say, *Yes, let's.*

But she was too timid, then too late. Vince looked away, and his face
settled, back to earth.

"Your parents want what's best for you," he said. "And my dad, my
mom—we couldn't do that."

Izzy wished she could step back in time just for half a minute, long
enough to grab that moment, to meet him there and move them both
through. But it had passed, and in its wake all the anger and sadness that
had moved aside for that moment returned. She hadn't even realized it
was gone until it all came back.

"I don't know what I was thinking," she said.

"Izzy—"

"Forget it. It was a stupid thing to say."

"What time is it?" Chloe's voice on the other end of the line was thick
with interrupted sleep.

"Let's go. I have enough for a couple of bus tickets," Izzy said. "A hotel
room for a night or two."

"Comped."

"What?"

"They'll comp the room if we're gambling," Chloe said.

Izzy stood at her window, the arroyo a black slash below, the dark
hills above punctuated with tiny points of orange streetlight, porch light,
insomniac window light.

The phone at her ear was called a princess phone, the receiver white and smooth and curved like a swan's neck. Izzy had never really thought of the name of the phone until now. When the call is over she'll pull the cord from the wall and open the window and throw the fucking thing out into the night.

"Okay," Chloe said. "When?"

"Tomorrow."

"That's awfully soon."

"Not soon enough."

"Are you okay, Izzy? Because you sound—"

"Not soon enough."

7

JESS

SUMMER 1979

I don't think it's a good idea," Gabe said. "You don't owe this woman anything."

"That's not why I'd go," Jess said.

They were sitting on Gabe's courtyard patio behind his house in Culver City, teacups and Jess's wineglass on the broad wooden table. She had come over unannounced, hoping for reassurance that she was making the right decision. Gabe wasn't on board.

David poured her more wine, a dark, tannic red, its legs stretching down the sides of the glass. He was a movie stuntman, a big presence, but quiet and considerate. He hadn't weighed in yet.

It was late; the only light came from the living room window, a warm amber glow. Just above the rooftop, beside the TV antenna, Jess could see the outline of the old Helms Bakery sign a few streets away, the red-white-and-blue shield she remembered from the delivery trucks that stopped at Ruth's house every Wednesday.

"You want her to forgive you," Gabe said. "But you didn't do anything wrong."

Jess didn't know to whom she owed anything anymore. All the balance books were lost. She didn't know if she was looking for an apology or forgiveness. But there was a promise in Madeline Serrano's message. *Isn't that what we all want? To move on?* And Jess, hearing that question, had thought, Yes. Desperately, yes.

"Where's the daughter?" David asked.

"I don't know," Jess said. "Her mother only said that she wouldn't be there when we met."

Gabe ran his thumb along a crack in the tabletop, frowning. "What's she going to tell you that you haven't already heard?"

"Maybe nothing," David said. "Maybe Jess just needs to hear it from someone other than us."

Jess spent an hour working through her closet. Everything she put on looked wrong when reflected back in the mirror. What did one wear when meeting the mother of her attacker? Something that would protect her, like a suit of armor or a magic cloak. She pulled from the hangers, staring into the mirror, unconvinced. She had no idea what Madeline Serrano expected.

What Jess knew of the Serrano family had come from Anton's unsolicited dispatches. He had supplemented his amateur reporting with obsessive historical investigation, hours hunched in library carrels searching the Business and Society pages, pasting together a rough family history.

Bruce Serrano got his first job as a parking attendant when he was fourteen. By the time he was twenty, he owned the lot. He spent the 1940s buying every vacant lot in the city's northeast corner, just in time for the postwar car boom and the construction of the freeways. His business expanded with the city, out to the new suburbs where he built more parking lots and then reasons to park—shopping centers and office clusters and housing developments. Bruce and Madeline met at a Tournament of Roses fundraiser. By then he was a major donor; she was the daughter of a prominent Pasadena banker. A year later, they were married.

There wasn't much information on Madeline. She was the dutiful wife in most of the pictures, Anton reported. Charity galas and civic events, a beautiful gown, pale skin and a chilly smile. Stepford territory, he said. Or else she was the secret backbone of the operation, the one who opened doors, bridging the gap between a portfolio of parking lots and a director's seat on some of the city's major boards.

Anton had found only one mention of Isabella pre–*Zero Zone*, in a list of debutantes coming out at a Pasadena country club. Can you imagine, he had said one night on the phone—our Isabella, the belle of the ball?

Jess closed her closet, settling on a blue oxford, cream linen pants, beechnut-brown boots. The outfit felt solid, sober, safe. This was the kind of conversation she hoped for, the kind that Madeline's message promised. Two adults airing their concerns, negotiating a way forward.

A man with a low drawl had answered the number Madeline provided. He had given Jess a time and an address in the San Rafael Hills, a quiet, moneyed enclave nestled along the border between Pasadena and L.A.

Jess drove up the wide, leafy streets, climbing slowly. Above, the limbs of live oaks stretched into a sun-streaked canopy, making her windshield bright then dark then bright again. On either side, courtly homes sat above rich green lawns, marble fountains burbling, garden trellises heavy with boas of honeysuckle and grape. And then she reached the end of the road, the address in question, a high wall of river rock draped with English ivy.

She parked at the curb. A wrought-iron gate, at least twice Jess's height, blocked the Serranos' entrance. The points along the top looked like spear tips raised in defense of a hidden castle. Past the gate, a driveway of bleached stone stretched a few hundred feet before dissolving into a fog of morning mist and dusty sunlight.

A smaller, human-size gate stood beside the other, set into the stone. Jess took a shaky breath and pressed the call button. After a moment the gate unlatched.

She walked up the driveway, stones crunching beneath her boots. The air held an acrid tang from the stands of tall, peeling eucalyptus on either side of the driveway. In the distance, through the thinning mist, the Serranos' house spread out before her, a massive modernist ranch, all clean angles and glass, towering windows shining in the sun. A fountain splashed in the center of the driveway's roundabout. Jess knew the piece; she had gone to school with the sculptor. It was an arboreal monster of sharp steel triangles, like a Calder fever dream, spinning in every direction with the force of the water pouring down from its crown.

"She's waiting for you inside."

Jess recognized that drawl from her phone call. On the other side of the fountain, a young man leaned into the open engine of a royal-blue Mercedes. Jess circled the fountain toward the front door, catching glimpses of him at the edge of the car's raised hood. He was tall and lean, with a short dark beard and lank hair that hung past his chin. He wore a denim jacket one shade lighter than his jeans, and a white cowboy hat, the brim tied up to the sides with a thin leather cord. He scratched his beard while he worked, looking down into the engine as if trying to keep himself from staring at Jess.

She paused at the front door. Madeline had promised a private meeting, but how could Jess know that was the truth? She imagined the door opening, Isabella waiting on the other side.

The cowboy lifted his eyes over the top of the car's hood, watching.

Jess pressed the doorbell.

"Is it too bright in here?"

Jess looked away from the windows, the pool and tennis court below, the expansive view into the arroyo. Madeline Serrano had returned from the kitchen with a small tea service on a tray. She watched Jess from the other side of the living room.

"Your sunglasses," Madeline said.

Jess pulled them off, tucking them into the pocket of her oxford. She squinted in the brightness. "I'm sorry," she said. "I forgot I had them on."

Jess saw a slight hitch in Madeline's polished demeanor as she took in the scar. But she banished it quickly and set the tray on a glass-topped coffee table. She wore a pleated shirtdress, blue like the Mercedes outside, and a long strand of dime-size pearls. Jess studied her for hints of Isabella, trying to see one woman in the other, but came up short. Madeline carried herself with crisp elegance. There was no sign of what Jess remembered of Isabella, or what had metastasized over the years in her imagination: the slouchy, feral girl full of malice.

Sitting on the sofa, Jess turned to find a wall of photographs: Isabella as a smiling little girl on a tire swing, an uncomfortable teenager in a ballerina's tutu, a serious young woman in the passenger seat of the Mercedes. She seemed to grow thinner with each image, a girl disappearing. Looking at each photo, Jess felt a jolt. She had never imagined Isabella's life before the gallery attack. It was as if Isabella hadn't existed before that moment. Here was a history Jess had never considered.

Madeline passed a teacup and sat on the edge of a wingback chair.

"Thank you," she said, nodding to Jess's sunglasses. "I like to see some-one's eyes. Bruce says I'm old-fashioned that way."

Jess looked to a black-and-white wedding photo on the wall. There was Bruce Serrano, chest and chin raised, intense, defiant almost, hold-ing hands with a young Madeline, tall and thin in a long white gown. The hint of a smile played across her lips as she returned the camera's gaze. Ready to eat the world, these two.

"You and Bruce have met," Madeline said.

Jess turned back to Madeline. "We have?"

"Years ago. He was part of a group of investors renovating a shopping center. You were hired to create a piece there, a skylight. He stopped by the work site a few times. I remember how impressed he was with what you were making."

Madeline tried a smile. There were still echoes of the confident young woman from the photo, but her certainty now seemed forced.

Jess thought back to that early project at the mall in Panorama City, the skylight she and Gabe had built. Nothing else came.

"I'm sorry," she said. "I don't remember him."

There was that arch smile now; Madeline had found it again, amused that someone wouldn't remember her husband, or would have the arro-gance to pretend that they didn't.

"It was a long time ago," Madeline said, "and he was one of many men in suits, I'm sure. But Bruce has been interested in your work for quite some time. He even thought of commissioning something for this house."

Jess looked out into the room, its windows offering sweeping views in every direction: north to the mountains, east to the desert, then west to the sea, toward her studio and apartment in Venice. She felt watched. She imagined Bruce Serrano standing here, surveying his city. She imagined Isabella alone in the dark, looking out at the electric spread of lights, try-ing to pinpoint one in particular, a telltale beacon giving Jess away.

There was a noise from somewhere in the house, what might have been a footstep, the clack of sole on tile. The sound pulled Jess's breath tight, and she sat that way for a moment, coiled and waiting. When no one came, she let herself deflate a little.

"You said that you wanted to talk about your daughter."

Madeline sipped her tea, then replaced the cup onto its saucer with extraordinary care.

"I feel the need to apologize for Isabella's actions," Madeline said. "As I told you on the message, she has had her share of difficulties. And those, of course, become my difficulties. You're not a mother, Miss Shepard?"

Jess understood that this wasn't really a question. It was a statement, an assertion of authority. She thought of Christine in her doorway making the same point two different times, a baby in her belly, a little boy waiting beside her car.

"I'm not."

"But you are a daughter," Madeline said. "So you understand the ties between a mother and daughter, and the knots that sometimes form along those ties." Her face shifted into a close approximation of a frown; the gesture, at least, the intention. "Isabella has made a long string of poor decisions. But I love my daughter, Miss Shepard. I want what is best for her."

Jess was struck again by the thought of a trap. She listened for footsteps, the cry of a door's hinge.

"Where is she?" Jess asked.

Madeline lifted her cup again, holding it aloft for a shaky moment. A slosh of tea crested the lip, pooling in the saucer.

"We don't know."

Jess felt her body seize, fear like a giant hand, squeezing.

"I thought she had been released," Jess said.

"She was. But because she is now an adult, we were only informed after the fact. She left the facility on her own. We hoped—I hoped—that she would come home."

"Where else would she go?"

"It's possible that she's trying to find the others—those people from the room you built. Whenever I visited her, she spoke about them. Sometimes it sounded like she was just waiting until they were together again."

Jess turned away, looking back to the wall, and there it was, the photo Anton had described on the phone years ago: Isabella standing in a ballroom, centered in a row of debutantes. All the other girls were bright and blond, smiling with entitled radiance. Isabella stood shorter, even thinner, her eyes contemptuous, staring back through the pomp and bullshit. Jess had seen that look before.

"I didn't ask you here to assign blame," Madeline said. "There's more than enough to go around. But Isabella is a highly impressionable young woman. And it seems that your work, for some, holds an incredible power. My husband felt that power. Isabella felt it."

"It's not the same thing." Jess hated the sound of her denial: unconvincing and desperate. "Your daughter needs help."

"That's what I'm asking for. Your help."

It had been a trap all along. Jess should have trusted Gabe, trusted her own fear.

"If we can find her," Madeline said, "you could speak with her, reason with her—"

"She needs a doctor."

"She has seen many doctors over the years."

"Then you need to find another."

"Miss Shepard, it was your work—"

"*She* attacked *me*." Jess stood, knocking her cup with her knee. The tea spilled, puddling on the table, running off the edge in a long, thin stream.

"My daughter would not have been imprisoned without the room you built," Madeline said. "Imagine her, Miss Shepard, in that room. Your room."

"I *have* imagined her." Jess backed around the table, stepping in the tea, her boots pressing dark footprints into the snowy carpet. "I want to stop imagining her. I want this to stop."

"Then help us," Madeline pleaded, her voice betraying real emotion for the first time. It was all showing now. "You could explain how Isabella misunderstood your work."

Madeline took a step forward and Jess raised an arm to keep her back. She felt all her fear and rage move down to her fingertip, another wand pointed.

"Miss Shepard—"

"Keep her away from me."

Jess moved past Madeline and out the door, back into the overbright morning, toward the fountain, past the Mercedes where the cowboy watched from the open engine. She felt Madeline behind her in the doorway, heard Madeline calling out, *Miss Shepard, Miss Shepard*, an appeal, a demand, her voice following Jess down the driveway.

Back in the Scout, her body rattling, Jess remembered to breathe. The radio was blaring—somehow she had bumped it awake when she started the truck, a chugging rhythm like a cartoon train staggering down the tracks. Iggy Pop, "Some Weird Sin." When she switched it off and the flood of ringing sound finally drained away, she heard tapping on the passenger window. The cowboy was knocking on the glass.

He removed his hat and opened the door, leaning inside.

"Miss Shepard," he said. "Can I talk to you?"

She noticed the brightness then, the glaring light through the Scout's dusty windshield. Jess reached for her sunglasses but her shirt pocket was empty.

"She needs your help," he said.

"Mrs. Serrano has more than enough resources. She doesn't need my help." Jess reached behind her back, running her hands along the seat, feeling for her sunglasses.

"I'm talking about Isabella." His voice was soft and low. It sounded like he was trying to soothe a frightened animal.

"There's nothing I can do for her," Jess said.

"You don't really believe that."

Jess almost sputtered, irate, incredulous. "You don't know anything about me."

"That's true," he said. "I'm sorry. My name's Vincent. Vince. Nobody calls me Vincent except Mrs. Serrano."

His swerve into introduction knocked Jess even further off-balance. What was she supposed to say here, *Nice to meet you*? She bent forward, searching for her sunglasses on the floor of the cab.

"Isabella saw something you made," he said, "and it changed her."

"It's not that simple."

Vince raised an eyebrow, a gesture that seemed to Jess half consideration, half dismissal.

"Maybe not. But that doesn't negate the fact."

"What fact?"

"That none of this would have happened without you."

Jess looked back at Vince. His eyes were remarkable, soulful and sad, a pale denim blue, matching his outfit. All his energy was in those eyes. The rest of him—the lanky, unhurried quasi-cowboy—now seemed like a child's costume worn to protect that wounded sincerity.

He reached into his shirt pocket and produced Jess's sunglasses. A magic trick. *Voilà.*

He looked at Jess's cheek. "I'm sorry she did that," he said. "You didn't deserve it. But she didn't deserve this either."

Jess took her glasses and shifted the truck into gear.

"I've already told you," she said. "There's nothing I can do."

Zero Zone

(1977; in situ installation; 30 miles east
of Nara Vista, New Mexico)

Here is the ghost town, the abandoned military base crumbling into the flat, sunburned waste. Scrub brush, bare trees reaching. Here is the base's center, the single intersection: the PX, a gas station, a small office building. All vacant.

Here is the squat brick school, its skin tattooed with graffiti, its windows fringed with broken glass. The schoolyard's grass is dry and long and wild. A pair of bicycles lie on their sides as if they had flung themselves down, exhausted. A swing set, a rusted merry-go-round. Overhead the sky is wide and flat, marked with white cirrus brushstrokes.

Here is the tall, old man wearing a straw rancher's hat. He appears at the edge of many of the photographs, his back almost always turned, facing out in the same direction as the lens. In a few of the photos he points off past the buildings toward the smudge of horizon. In one image he sits on a tree stump, drinking a can of beer, looking past the camera, his bronzed, lean face lined from years of squinting into sun and wind.

Two decades before Alex took the photos, the military conducted a pair of A-bomb tests on the base's northern edge. Alex had found a film of the tests, and one night in his studio he projected it for Jess. What struck her first were the film's colors—the rich browns and greens of the desert and the uniforms, the brilliant blue sky. And then the soldiers—fresh-faced boys standing in trenches, joking, laughing, playing cards. For a few moments, the camera lingered on them, this loose waiting. Then a jarring cut, shots of dummies propped up in the no-man's-land above the trenches, stuffed uniforms topped by volleyball heads, hand-drawn faces with crude smirks. Another shot of the sky, a plane passing overhead, its bright contrail painting a straight line across the frame. Two more soldiers, looking somber now, a little tense. They bowed their heads and pulled their helmets low over their eyes. One of them yawned.

Then a flash, flooding the frame white. As the light decayed the soldiers stood, facing the horizon, shielding their eyes. The camera turned with them to find the rising mushroom stalk, the canopied cloud spreading against the sky. After a moment, the soldiers clambered over the walls of their trenches, running toward that dark bloom.

Alex found the place where the tests were conducted. The land was now owned by the man with the hat. His ranch stood far to the south, but he had purchased what remained of the military base as a buffer against other ranches moving in, oil leases, rumors of an interstate that would cut clear to California. Alex contacted the rancher and spent a few days walking the site, taking pictures. The rancher spent most of each day with Alex, asking questions about his cameras and drinking beer. Alex stayed in a spare bedroom at the back of the man's house. The rancher was lonely, Alex said. His wife had died of breast cancer a few years before. Alex didn't refer to the man by name, only as "the rancher." Jess could see that Alex liked the mystery the title conveyed. This man as solitary sentry, standing watch over fading history—his country's, his own.

When Alex returned from the base, they sat in Jess's kitchen and he told her about each image, describing the feeling of isolation or the quality of noontime light in the center of the exposed main street. Earlier that day, Christine had presented herself at the front door and in the hours since Jess had finally understood that the relationship was over. She and Alex were colleagues now, talking about work. They didn't touch, though she longed to brush the backs of her fingers across his stubbled cheek, to feel that sandpaper roughness, the field of soft skin beneath. Instead they sat across from each other and she looked at the images rather than at Alex, trying to place herself alongside him in the photographs, willing herself even just a few days into the past when she could have stood beside him, his hand on her arm, her lips at his ear.

There were other people in a few of the pictures, young men and women, travel-ragged, hikers and drifters. In one photo a young man with a patchy beard drank a can of the rancher's beer. The rancher stood in the frame's foreground. The young man was smiling at him, mouth full. In another, a young man and woman crossed in the distance, backpacks hiked high onto their shoulders, trudging like pilgrims through the dust.

Alex looked over Jess's shoulder at the photo. "There's a campsite about thirty miles east," he said, "and another one thirty miles west, and the travelers pass the base along the way. Some of them know the rancher. He's always got a cigarette and a beer, a well where they can refill their canteens."

Zero Zone, Jess had said when Alex asked her what he should call the photographs. She had no idea where the name came from; it just arrived in her head. But she liked the science-fiction sound of it, the buzzing double z's. It seemed to fit the emptied landscape, a place reduced to a null, waiting for something new to begin.

After Alex's crash, word came around that Christine, in anguished rage, was threatening to burn all his work. Jess hid the *Zero Zone* photos in a portfolio under her bed. She had named them; she felt that some part of them now belonged to her.

Those first few nights after the crash she turned and twisted on her mattress, desperate for the oblivion of sleep. She lay sweating in the dark, picturing the image from the newspaper, Alex's car sheared by the tree, and then the *Zero Zone* photos below her bed, heat spilling from the prints, spreading up across the sheets.

When she couldn't take any more, she carried the photos down to the Scout and drove through the day and the following night and morning, out into Arizona and New Mexico, finally parking her truck by the western campsite. She gathered the gear she had hastily packed and started along the trail. Two days' walk, Alex had told her. That was the word he had used, *walk* rather than *hike*, and it made sense to her immediately, traversing the flat, dusty ground. This was nothing like the hikes they had made over the years, into the Angeles Forest, up to Yosemite, climbing the hills around Palm Desert. Days of ascent and discovery, nights in the tent with the flaps tied back so they could watch the wheeling stars. This was different—quiet and severe. The flat ground, the vacant landscape, the dark line of mountains in the unreachable distance.

She walked alone, struggling to keep her head above her chaotic stew of grief and anger and guilt. After a while the walk began to seem like a pointless exercise, trudging to nowhere from nowhere. She fought the urge to turn around and drive back to L.A. But what was there for her now? She didn't know. So she continued walking, slowly falling into a rhythm of movement that began to lay a pattern for her breathing, the tide of her body swaying from side to side.

She passed other walkers, young and old, alone and in groups, but she couldn't speak, or even nod in passing. It just wasn't possible to engage in any way. That night she slept in Alex's old tent, shivering in the cold.

The following morning she arrived at the abandoned base. She walked the streets from Alex's photos, peered into the same broken windows.

She met the rancher, whose name was Lincoln. Jess thought of his wife, a woman in a bedroom mirror, her fingertips on her breast, feeling the curve of something new, a small hard lump.

She was able to talk to Lincoln. She recognized his grief, though it was older, more lived-with than her own. She wanted to ask him how he had gotten this far with it, how he managed to keep it from consuming him entirely.

She stayed at a motel about a ten-minute walk from the ranch. Lincoln offered his spare room, but Jess couldn't sleep in another bed where Alex once slept.

She spent two days walking the base and that stretch of trail, trying to understand why she had come. There was something she couldn't decipher in that final conversation with Alex as he showed her the photos. She hadn't understood his intentions that night. They were both in such unfamiliar territory, the kind of place he was drawn to photographing, the charged, quiet moments after a noisy end.

The second afternoon, standing on the trail, something sparked in the corner of her vision. Jess turned to see a wispy shimmer, an orange and yellow ripple of light that flapped once, like a flag, and then disappeared.

Coming up a few steps behind, Lincoln answered her unasked question.

"There's still radiation in the air," he said. "Not enough to cause any trouble, but you see things sometimes. I tried explaining it to your friend when he was here, but he couldn't see it." Lincoln took a sip of his beer. "He said that he didn't have those kinds of eyes, but he knew someone who did."

By the end of the week she had designed the structure: a concrete room, ten feet high, twenty-five feet long, thirty feet wide. She drew a narrow wooden door in the eastern wall, and long, slender rectangular openings in each of the other three, horizontal apertures five feet above the floor.

Gabe and a few of his students drove out, and they spent two weeks transforming Jess's drawings into a physical space. When it was finished, Jess found that it worked as she'd hoped. The room gave focus to those unique moments of light. In the early morning it captured the sunrise, the openings in the walls warmed orange and red. By midday, streaks of flat white light entered from various angles, crossing the space, converging slowly, intersecting and flaring before moving on and away. In the evening a velvety purple glow filled the space as the sun disappeared below the western window.

That final morning, just before leaving, Jess stood on the dusty path looking west, the way she had come. It seemed like months ago, years. The room stood just to the side of the path. A place to rest and reflect on what had been lost before striking out again.

Walking away, Jess looked toward the sunrise. Far in the distance she could see the tiny silhouettes of other travelers, new pilgrims approaching.

MARTHA

SUMMER 1977

S he brought the two girls drinks all night at the craps and blackjack tables, the roulette wheels, watching them lose and lose again. The taller of the pair was clearly in charge. She wore tight jeans and a fitted shirt tied up to show her tanned midriff. She was drunk and loud and demonstrative, a performer of some sort. Martha had worked in Vegas long enough to know the type, actors and actresses out from L.A., terrible gamblers who grew brasher with each loss, calling out for an audience when they started to twirl down the drain. If they had an audience the losses were bearable. It became less personal, a show. They paid for one with the other. Martha understood the impulse, though she had never been one to seek that kind of attention.

The girls were probably underage, but no one at the Tahitian scrutinized IDs too carefully. This wasn't the Sands or the Riviera, this was a little tiki-themed casino at the edge of the Strip where the waitresses wore grass miniskirts and plastic hibiscus in their hair and couldn't afford to turn paying customers away. At first, Martha thought the girls would lose a little money and then their nerve, would flee after a few hours in search of a more reliable good time. The performer, Chloe, told Martha that they were traveling cross-country and had stopped to make some money before moving on. Martha was always amazed by the confidence kids like this displayed. To be fair, sometimes it actually played out the way they intended, and after a run of good luck they cashed their chips and continued on their way. Other times their luck headed south and the kids got scared and got out before they bled dry. She had no reason to think these girls were any different, but every time she came back around they were still losing and they were still there.

The smaller girl was no performer. She hunched at the tables, her red-and-blue-plaid jacket buttoned up tight. She was stuck in the quicksand of the losses, sinking. Martha had seen her kind before, too. These were the girls who took it all to heart and ended up stumbling along a side road far from the Strip, or overdosing in a restroom stall, or perching on a hotel balcony with another audience gathered far below. Martha understood that impulse, too.

Chloe drank champagne, tossing back flutes as soon as Martha arrived with each new round. The other girl, Izzy, drank rum and Tab, sucking her umbrella straw with grim determination, watching the wheel spin and then each tower of chips pulled home by the dealer.

The girls' money wouldn't last much longer. The tips would dry up, and the performer would become belligerent and belittling. That was often the last part of this show, the ridicule of a dealer or waitress, an attempt to transfer the shame of losing. But something about Izzy brought Martha back, round after round. A nagging, sidelong familiarity, as if the girl had arrived from some half-remembered place, a blurred childhood memory or dream.

The girls continued to tank, pushed along in the casino's forced migration of loss, from the higher-stakes tables in the center of the floor to the lowball games at the margins, the last stops before the restrooms, the coat check, the plastic totem poles flanking the exits. At around three in the morning Martha found them wiped out at the far edge. Chloe had switched gears, chatting up a young man, a college kid on summer break, floppy-haired and blandly handsome. She turned up her charm, laughing loudly at whatever the boy said, leaving her hand on his arm. She had found another game to play.

Izzy sat alone in a booth, shell-shocked. Martha watched as Chloe attempted to draw Izzy into this new configuration. Izzy was unresponsive, and then she was angry. She had been lied to, again. She was sick of being lied to. Chloe responded with furious annoyance—condescending, cruel, overpowering. With every word that Chloe shouted Izzy shrank a little more, folding inward.

Martha set her tray on top of a jangling slot and walked between the girls.

"I think you should go," she said, looking at the college boy, then to Chloe. Martha was only about five years older than the boy but tried to project whatever authority she could muster. Chloe began to belittle, right on cue. The boy seemed worried that his chance with this pretty girl was slipping away. He talked Chloe down, throwing a few of his own insults Martha's way before pulling Chloe from the confrontation, back past the slots and across the floor.

Izzy was motionless in the booth. She looked nearly catatonic. Martha should have left her there. This was none of her business. How many girls did she see sitting in this same booth, busted and blank? They were fixtures of the landscape. But this girl wasn't the same. She was fading, disappearing, and Martha felt another wave of the anger and grief that had sloshed through her for the past year.

She sat in the booth beside the girl. Looking out across the casino floor, she expelled a long, tired breath, an exhalation she imagined blowing the whole place away, scattering the hollow totems and bamboo facades and thatched canopies out into the desert. She saw them all tumbling, gamblers and slots, dice like rolling pebbles, cards like dry leaves. It should have frightened her, a vision of that kind of destruction. Instead it came as a relief. And though she still had an hour left on her shift, she looked out over the wasteland, real and imagined, and said, "I'm done here." Then she turned to Izzy and asked if she was ready to leave.

It was a goose-bump night, the cool air pimpling Martha's bare legs. As they walked she hummed a tune that had been in her head all night, trying to place it as they passed from the flash of the Strip to the underlit employee parking lot.

Izzy still seemed numb. Sitting in Martha's car, she didn't ask where they were going. She just stared out the windshield as the view dimmed from the sparkle of the casino signs to the diners and pawnshops, the sleepy residential blocks, rows of dark houses, then under the freeway and into the apartment complexes on the city's east side.

Judee Sill's "Jesus Was a Cross Maker." Martha finally named the song stuck in her head. At first she thought it must have been on back at the casino, but then she remembered where she had last heard it. The song had played on the little radio in Misty's room at the hospital. The radio's antenna had somehow snapped in half, so whenever a song came on that her sister wanted to hear, Martha pinched the broken tip of the metal wand to encourage the signal. Body heat, maybe, clearing the static. She sat on the edge of the bed, holding the antenna while Misty sang along in a thinned, weakened version of her once powerful birdie warble.

Stopped at a red light, Martha looked past Izzy to the car pulling up alongside and saw Misty behind the wheel. Then the light turned and Misty was in the passenger seat of the van passing from the other direction. Martha saw her younger sister everywhere. Smoking outside a casino service entrance, pushing her grocery cart up the aisles of the Wonder World, walking in the front door of the Episcopal church on AA-meeting nights. Dreamlike visions, apparitions, memories like movie scenes. Misty holding a cigarette and laughing at a dirty joke, Misty buying Tampax and artichoke hearts, Misty walking into a church to join others who shared her disease.

Scrambled eggs, bacon, an English muffin browning in the toaster. Up in her apartment, Martha poured coffee and carried a mug to the kitchen table where Izzy sat cross-legged, her arms folded over her chest as if trying to tie herself into a knot. Martha cracked the window and lit a cigarette. She didn't offer one to Izzy; the girl didn't seem like a smoker. Martha liked to smoke while she cooked. The heat at her hands from burners and pans, the heat at her lips from the cigarette. Give her a dry, sunbaked day, a little burn on her neck and chest. Pressing her fingertips to her reddened thighs and watching the white patches form and disappear, little ghosts on her skin. Misty had always said that between the sun and cigarettes Martha was sure to die of cancer. Martha had answered that you have to die of something, glib and foolish, because neither of them yet knew just what that something could be.

An afternoon in June, two years back. They sat at a bar at the Riviera, where Misty was designing costumes for a show. She had just returned from a lunch-break doctor's appointment.

Misty laid out everything the doctor told her about the course of treatment and the odds. She sounded so matter-of-fact, as if staying calm would enable her to contain the illness, to keep it manageable. Martha was two years older, but Misty kept the cooler head. She'd spoken in that same sensible tone during her early days in AA, attempting to comprehend a monster from a clinical distance. But this time the facts bled through. Misty had waited too long to see a doctor. She had ignored and denied. She admitted this to Martha, there at the bar, as if owning up to her sins.

Martha listened, watching her sister but also distracted by the TV flickering for attention over Misty's shoulder, a muddy horse race on the East Coast. The leading horse's name was Dumb Luck, and Martha thought, That's all we need. Willing in that moment to accept the comfort of Misty's pragmatism, to rely on calm-headedness and modern medicine and, yes, a little dumb luck. She could see it, a difficult road, but one they would travel together, staying focused, following the rules to remission and health. Watching Dumb Luck take the race, Martha felt a sudden hope, a strength she believed would carry them through, until she turned back to Misty and saw the new glass glistening on the bar, Misty's hand shaking as she lifted it to her lips, her first drink in eighteen months.

Izzy wasn't going to talk, so Martha told a few stories about her home-town in Florida, a few casino tales.

"I came out here to sing. Can you believe that? I had visions of my own show in a dark, velvety lounge. I could see my gown—wine red and off the shoulders and long, trailing behind as I stepped offstage, carrying the song with me into the audience."

Leaning against the stove, she felt the pan's heat pulse across the small of her back.

"But I didn't have the voice," she said. "My sister had the voice. A strange voice, like a wounded bird. It wasn't pretty, but you had to listen.

There was something deeper there, urgent and sad and hopeful. I was the one who dreamed of singing, but she had the voice, so there you go."

She carried the pan to the table and slid the eggs onto a plate.

"I wonder if I always knew," Martha said. "I had to have known, right? That we would come out here, but I would never make it as a singer. But I think I needed the force of that belief to move me. To move both of us, to get us out of that place."

Back at the sink, she set the pan under a stream of cold water. An angry hiss rose from the metal, insistent and unsatisfied, finally finding form in a cloud of gray steam.

"You want me to help you get home?" Martha asked.

After a moment, Izzy looked up from her untouched eggs. Martha saw her face set. The girl was sure of something for the first time all night.

"I'm never going back," she said.

9

TANNER

SUMMER 1976

H e rode the crowded bus over the hill and into downtown, holding the hanging strap, his back to the other passengers so as not to create a disturbance. The bus swayed like a ship at sea, what he imagined a ship at sea felt like. Unmoored. Looking up to the wide rear-view mirror to find the driver's eyes before the man quickly looked away.

The other adults on the bus also looked away, down to books or newspapers, a suddenly interesting splotch of gum on the floor. Children, though, stared. They were bold, curious, unashamed. They pointed and called out and asked what he was. The adults yanked them back, scolding them for their rudeness but also pulling them closer, protecting.

On the twenty-seventh floor he pushed the mail cart up and down the rows of desks. The secretaries and paralegals acknowledged him with a nod, but their eyes stayed lowered to their typewriters or phones or fingernails. A few lifted their heads to say, *Thank you*, while looking at a spot a few inches past the borders of his face.

He existed just to the side of the world around him.

It was as if when he was born he had somehow shifted out of phase. That shift had damaged him. His body was covered with hard, bulging growths, some the size of pinheads, others the size of grapes. As a boy his appearance made him invisible, and this invisibility made him desperate. He wanted to move into the lines of sight, no matter how cruel that sight could be. Twenty years later he still carried that need, but increasingly he felt it tinged with something new—a desire to leave this place and return to where he belonged. He knew it was out there; it had to be. And if he was out of phase, if this current state was a cruel mistake, then a correction was possible. There must be a way to move back through.

The new secretary's name was Georgia. She had a kind, round face, a dimple pressed into her left cheek. She heard his cart and looked up, just to the side of where he stood.

His mother had called them bumps. *Our bumps.* She didn't have them, her skin was smooth and clear, but by naming them this way she tried to share his affliction.

Tanner at seven or eight years old, just out of the bathtub, sitting on the closed toilet, listening to his mother's gentle singsong. *Don't cry, don't cry.* Her calloused fingertips spreading the cool cream on his face and neck and chest, covering the hard bumps.

The doctor had a long and complicated name for his condition. To Tanner it sounded like the name of a spaceship, a hardened exoskeleton that might take him to another planet, if only he knew where to find the controls.

His mother called them bumps but the children at school said he was made of rocks, throwing some, shouting: *Here's some more.*

He loved his mother fiercely but she wasn't like him, not really. As he grew older he began to resent her attempts to insert herself into his struggle. It wasn't something they could share. And then there was the other fact, lying between them like a broken bridge neither could cross.

I'm not really your mother. She yelled this once during an argument. Tanner was thirteen, at least a foot taller than her. He didn't trust his size, what he might do standing so close, so he walked away, deeper into the apartment, but her words brought him up short, like a dog at the end of his chain.

I am and I'm not, she said, quieter now. Ashamed, maybe, of voicing that harsh truth.

You know that, she said.

Did he? Did he remember someone else, another mother, another apartment in another part of the city? An enormous man with a heavy beard taking him from that place? The man was an official of some kind; he wore a name tag with the city seal. Standing in the doorway to Tanner's bedroom, he told Tanner to empty all the toys from his kindergarten backpack and fill it with clothes. When Tanner was finished, the man looked at the scattering of broken plastic army figures dumped on the floor and said that Tanner might as well take some of those with him, too. All the while the woman shouted from the other room, threatening the man but not moving from where she stood, smoking and trembling with rage.

Riding in the back seat of the man's car, Tanner looked through the window at streets and buildings and neighborhoods he had never seen, neon signs in incomprehensible languages glowing in the night.

Then here, with the woman he would always think of as his mother.

Sleeping that first night in a bedroom she made for him, that he would later realize had been hers. She hadn't always slept on the couch. The room decorated hastily for a boy she didn't yet know. Pictures cut out of a TV magazine taped to the walls: Howdy Doody and Davy Crockett and the Mouseketeers. She set a book out for him, *The Little Engine That Could*. That night she sat beside him and as she read he ran his finger over the bump of the library sticker at the base of the book's spine.

That first day at the new school the kids stared at him like he was something that fell from outer space. The teacher steered him to the front of the classroom and said, *This is Tanner. I want everyone to welcome him and say, Hello, Tanner.*

Tanner stared out and the kids stared back and no one said a word.

The after-work crowd in Pershing Square, the simmering onset of a summer evening, cigarettes and bus exhaust, smoke in the air from fires off in the hills. Businessmen and homeless men and mothers with strollers, joggers weaving through, fruit carts, ice cream carts, jangling bells, voices in Spanish, English, Japanese. Conversation and argument and salesmanship, connection, each person, one to the other. Friends, strangers, lovers, families.

Realize that while standing in the center of this crowd you could shout and no one would look at you. You could sing, you could scream. You could explode.

Every morning Tanner bought two mini-bottles of rum at the liquor store by the bus stop. Usually he drank them in the men's room before his first round of mail delivery, but today he saved them until after lunch, just before heading up to the twenty-seventh floor. The rum gave him the anger and courage to continue holding Georgia's mail while she nodded and looked off to the side, staring uncomfortably at nothing, her smile quavering like water in a puddle.

Finally she took a breath and moved her eyes to his. He handed her the mail. She smiled again, apologetic, and said, "I'm sorry. Of course. Thank you, Tanner."

And then he was the one who couldn't breathe.

A few days later he screwed up enough courage to ask her out for coffee. He didn't drink coffee, but he was aware that this was what people did when they were getting to know one another. He saw it all over the city—nervous pairs at café tables trying to find common ground. Every time he passed a scene like this he was filled with envy, a desire to hold one end of the uncertain, electric thread that could form between two people. He walked by and they stared and then looked back at each other, and he imagined that for some of them he became that thread, an uncomfortable moment they now shared.

He and Georgia arranged to meet at a coffee shop on their building's ground floor. Tanner arrived first. He sat at a small table on the sidewalk and looked through the books in his backpack. He always read three or four at a time, carrying them wherever he went. He had learned from an early age that he could step into a book in the same way he could step out of a room. He read a lot of science fiction, and books about religion. There were interesting intersections between the two. A yearning for something else, a refusal to accept the world as it stood. He had begun to form his own theory: that this world was simply a mask hiding another, more beautiful place. The books were fuel to the fire of his ideas. He read Philip K. Dick, Stanisław Lem, Ursula K. Le Guin. He read about John the Baptist and Joan of Arc and Shahid al Thani. The science fiction stories went in many directions but the stories about the prophets all ended the same way.

He heard Georgia's voice and looked up from his book. She met his eyes and smiled.

They sat outside the coffee shop for hours. She wanted to know all about his reading. He told her about his ideas, and then felt self-conscious and silly but she asked him to continue.

This is fascinating, she said. And you have the most wonderful voice.

He didn't want to ruin things, but he had to know. Why had she said yes to having coffee with him?

Her face flushed a little, embarrassed.

You just stood there and waited for me to *see* you, she said. I wish I had that confidence.

Tanner was astonished. He'd never thought of what he had as confidence. He'd thought it was anger. But maybe Georgia was right. Or they were both right, and maybe he could turn what he had into what she wanted to see.

They continued to meet after work for coffee or dinner. She left little notes on his desk in the mail room, index cards folded into complexities that opened to reveal something he had said the night before that she remembered and felt was important enough to show back to him, like a mirror with the horror of sight removed.

Sometimes when they were out together a co-worker passed and made a stunned double take. Normally this would have filled Tanner with embarrassment and rage, but now he stepped forward into those moments. He offered his hand and his name, and they looked at him for the first time.

For years he had checked out books on sex from the library and he had a small collection of pornographic magazines. Twice he had paid prostitutes at a motel by City Hall. These encounters briefly extinguished his physical need but only served to widen another, stronger desire. With the second girl he offered to pay extra if she would lie beside him and run her hands over his body. She accepted, and when he was naked she moved her hands quickly along his chest and shoulders and then stood from the bed and gathered her things and her money and left.

In the dark, on their first night together, Georgia guided him gently, expertly. Another kind of confidence, he thought, following her lead, forgetting the books and magazines and the two women before, feeling like he was floating above his body, as if every touch set more of him free.

He began talking to people at the bus stop, in the mail room, in the offices. Now they listened when he spoke. He told stories from his books. Sometimes the stories were from the accounts of the prophets and sometimes they were science fiction but more often he blended them into something new, and these were the stories people responded to most. When they stood beside him on the bus or by the coffeepot in the break room, leaning in, their eyes on his, Tanner felt what he thought Georgia must feel when she touched him, that power, the ability to lift someone from the falsity of their body. To bring them along into that phase between worlds.

10

JESS

SUMMER 1979

An alarm system, a dog, a gun. These were the options before her. Insufficient or terrifying or absurd. Picturing herself with a weapon made Jess want to laugh or scream. Once, she would have thought it impossible to imagine that fractured version of herself, but now it came with sickening ease. Eaten alive by fear with a gun in her hand. Isabella arriving through a door, a window. And then what? Jess hated every ending that choice demanded.

She called Zack. She needed to hear her brother's voice, though she couldn't even be sure she had the right number. He changed or disconnected it every few weeks, certain his phone was being bugged by the

FBI or the Motion Picture Association or both. Whenever Jess expressed frustration over how difficult he was to contact, Zack responded with stories of fellow film dealers woken by midnight knocks, handcuffs, interrogations in bare-bulbed rooms.

Since those early film-collecting days in his room above Ruth's garage, Zack had become a major player in the underground market, moving prints of lost classics and Hollywood hits. The vast majority of the prints were illegal, duped or stolen from the studios. But to Zack, this wasn't a crime. Film was an art, and he was saving it from the greedy, shortsighted executives who saw nothing but profit and loss up on the screen.

The real trouble came from other stolen films moving through the network, private movies of the rich and famous. Intimate, secret, compromising moments. Zack didn't talk much about these films. When he did, it was in terms of rumor and innuendo, reels of celluloid or videotapes that might or might not exist. If they existed, they were a means to an end, a source of income to fund his preservation crusade.

Jess had always thought Zack's paranoia was unwarranted or exaggerated. It didn't seem so crazy now. He of all people might understand her panic. But after a few more rings a recorded operator's voice came on the line: *We're sorry. This number is no longer in service.* He must have changed it again.

An alarm system, a dog, a gun, a hotel. Jess threw some clothes into a bag, unsure how much she would need. Two days' worth, three, a week? She thought of those timid guest stars on TV cop shows, stashed away in a motel by the interstate, told to lay low, dye their hair, change their name. Witness protection. They were always found, though, weren't they? At some point in the episode the long-feared hand comes knocking.

She checked in to a hotel by the airport, a bland, gray-toned high-rise catering to business travelers, less a destination than a pause on the line between two points. Everyone in motion in the hallways, the lobby, in and out of conference rooms, the restaurant and bar. Waiting for the elevator, men in suits and women in skirts and blazers moved briskly around her, no eye contact, no touch. Maybe this was safety, she thought. Invisibility.

At the windows in her room, past the rising floaters, the city smeared before her in a smoggy haze: the clutch of towers in Century City, continuing along Wilshire and into downtown, the web of streets and freeways like veins in a body, movement in every passage. Far to the north and west she saw a small gray tuft hovering over the hills, the first dark breath of smoke. She had heard warnings on the radio driving down. It was the beginning of fire season.

She needed a drink. She needed to decide what to do next, where to go where she would be safe, if such a place still existed.

From her bag she pulled out a dark skirt and blouse, sheer hose, black flats, the pair of small emerald studs Gabe bought her to celebrate that shopping mall commission years ago. This was the kind of outfit she once wore to meet with potential clients and funders. The blouse hung off her shoulders now, the skirt was loose at the waist. She had lost weight in the last two years. But this way, at least, she would look the part. She could imagine she was here scouting a future project rather than hiding from the repercussions of the past.

She had a drink down in the bar, her attention pulled to a TV showing a baseball stadium in Chicago, what looked like a riot in progress. Hundreds of people ran from the stands toward a bonfire in the outfield. Some held signs and banners, *Disco Sucks*, throwing records like Frisbees. The police tried to push them back but the people kept coming, dropping over the outfield walls, scaling down the foul poles, undeterred by the smoke filling the stadium. Other fires flared along the basepaths and people danced around the flames, what looked like thousands now, shaking their arms at the sky, overtaken by joy or anger, a shared mania to burn.

Jess retreated from the violence filling the screen, across the hall to the restaurant, a quiet, dark steakhouse. She set a cocktail napkin on her table and held a pen in her hand because this was what she once did in places like this, when she was able to see them as possibilities. Tonight the napkin stayed blank. She was only playing a part.

She noticed him sitting a few tables away. He was sturdy and blond, fair-featured. He wore a crisp blue suit. He looked, in some canted way, like a movie version of Alex: larger, clearer, sanded smooth of all the rough edges. Her first impulse was to tell Alex—*I saw this guy who looked like the actor who would play you in a movie*—because Alex would love the idea of a doppelgänger out in the world. But that wasn't possible, so instead she snuck glances at this stranger, feeling a misplaced physical longing. She was truly disappearing now, chasing ghosts.

The man sat alone, squinting at a brochure in the candlelight, a pen in his hand, making notes or corrections. He saw her looking and smiled, then nodded toward the empty chair on the other side of his table. Joining him would be out of character, but what character was she now? If another version of Alex was here, then it stood to reason that she could also become someone else.

When she arrived with her drink he stood and introduced himself as Carl Cook, from Guelph, Ontario. He was the western U.S. sales representative for a Canadian textile manufacturer. He held up the brochure, a little awkwardly, as proof. He was on his way to Phoenix but there were mechanical problems with his plane so they had diverted to L.A. for the night.

They sat and ordered more drinks. Jess told him that she was an artist commissioned to design an installation for the hotel. He asked what kind of installation and she said that she didn't know yet. This was the beginning of the process—staying in a place for a couple of days to get a feel for it, to understand its rhythms, its spaces and movements. He smiled, looking perplexed and impressed. Then he reminded her that she hadn't told him her name. She introduced herself as Anne Del Mar, what

sounded like a soap opera name, but there it was, spoken with prepos-
terous ease. Anne with an *e,* she told him, doubling down. She thought
he would laugh, seeing through the ridiculous fabrication, but instead he
said, "It's very nice to meet you, Anne."

Carl asked about her work, and Jess found herself describing projects
she had never made, stillborn sites that existed only in her sketchbooks
and head. Anne Del Mar's projects, maybe. She gave them names and lo-
cations, construction anecdotes, falling deeper into the disguise. She was
beginning to feel safe here, the further down she went. Carl was a good
listener. He asked questions and for the first time in she couldn't remember how long she had answers.

She noticed that what she had first thought were small checks on his
tie were actually birds, a repeating pattern of birds in flight, so she risked
one small truth among the lies, telling him about *Vol,* the installation she
had created in an old barn in the Loire Valley. She had spent a few days
there, just as she was doing here, getting the feel of the place, looking for
clues.

"Clues to what?" Carl asked.

"That's the question," Jess said. "Clues to something that I can't quite
feel or see. Until I do."

The clues she found at the farm in France were the large flocks of
birds that flew over the barn at the same time every day. Due to what
seemed like a peculiarity of the air currents, the flocks passed the barn
and then turned, again and again, before they finally found the direction
they sought and wheeled away to the south. She brought in Gabe and a
crew and they cut openings in the roof, creating a giant camera obscura
that projected the shadows of the birds down into the empty barn, where
the shadows then flew along the floor and walls, soaring, turning, passing
through and away.

"That was where I got this," Jess said, touching her scar. "I fell from
the scaffolding."

The farmhouse across from the barn was a bed-and-breakfast, and Clarice, the woman who owned both, wrote to Jess a few months after the site was completed. She said that the barn had become something of a destination. Guests told her they felt as if they were flying within the flock. Adults and children stood in the center of the barn with their arms out like wings, turning in place. Others said that it felt as if something was passing through them—not the birds, really, but something *of* the birds, an essence that moved in their bodies before the birds took flight again.

About a year later, during a week of gallery visits and meetings in Paris, Jess returned to spend a couple of nights at the bed-and-breakfast. It was the off-season, and the only other people around were a young Irish couple. Clarice said that they had spent every day that week inside the barn. They'd lost their child recently, due to circumstances they didn't offer. Jess sat at the window of her room in the farmhouse and looked out at the gyroscopic flocks of birds and then down to the barn, which now seemed so full of loss that she could imagine the walls and roof blowing apart.

On her final morning there she encountered the couple in the courtyard. Clarice had told them that she was the artist responsible for the site. That was the word she used, *responsible*, as if directing blame for whatever the couple felt inside the barn. But they greeted Jess with a bruised and shaken warmth. They wanted to thank her. They couldn't quite explain why they spent so much time here, they said, during a trip where every hour was planned with destinations and activities designed to exhaust them into forgetting. They didn't know exactly what they felt when they were inside, the young man said. The father. He couldn't describe it. Looking back to the barn, the space above where the birds returned every morning, the mother said, *Maybe it's peace, or something like it.*

Jess never told anyone this story—not Gabe, not Alex. She didn't think it was hers to tell. But sitting across from Carl she felt a sudden juvenile desire for him to believe all those stories of transformative experience spun around her pieces. A man dreaming again for the first time after a stroke; a young couple finding some measure of peace within their grief.

Carl wanted to know more about *Vol*, the details of its construction, how a camera obscura worked. It occurred to Jess that she was giving something away, that if Carl really wanted to investigate he could discover, fairly easily, that Jess Shepard was the artist behind *Vol*. But here in the dark restaurant it didn't feel like a possibility. It didn't seem like anything would ever leave this place.

They ordered more drinks. Carl had a warmth that Jess perceived, or decided to perceive, as genuine. She knew he could be lying as well. The things he told her about himself were tangential to any facts of real meaning. Stories about travel and growing up in the country. He had strong, expressive hands, and he gestured as he spoke, a skilled salesman drawing his listener close. He might not even be Carl Cook of Guelph, western U.S. sales representative. Or he might be, and the sin was in the omission, the wife and children back home. But she chose to take him at his word, as he seemed to have taken Jess at hers. An unstated agreement.

She could see a path here. A new name, new persona. Leaving the hotel and boarding a plane. Landing in Phoenix, Sydney, Seoul. Maybe she could create again, live again, as someone else.

They went up to his room rather than to hers. Riding in the elevator, Jess said she'd like to see it for research purposes. Neither of them laughed at the joke, the weight of the coming moment beginning to press.

Maybe it's peace, or something like it. Had the young mother really said that? It sounded too perfect, too rehearsed. The neatened end of a story, tucked in like the corners of a bedsheet. Or had she, instead, told Jess about their son, and then their days in the barn, the shadows moving across their arms and faces, and then gone silent, staring at Jess until Jess looked away?

In his room Carl kissed her and she felt nothing. She hadn't been with anyone since Alex's death. Another retreat. She tried to move back into her body. He began to unbutton her blouse but she didn't want him to touch her, not yet. She lifted his hands away and led him back to the bed. She pulled off his tie and unbuttoned his shirt, then stepped away and watched him undress in the dark, glimpses of pink skin in the dim room. She unzipped her skirt and slid it down over her hips. Folding her arms behind her back, she unhooked her bra and stood naked, a cold draft swirling around her ankles. Stay here. Stay inside yourself. She was whispering and hoped he didn't hear. He pulled back the bedspread. There was a formality now that Jess thought she could handle, expected movements and gestures. She placed her palms in the curly hair on his chest and eased him back and then lifted herself over his hips and reached down for him, guiding, lowering her weight.

Sex with Alex had been intensely physical, muscular, bruising. Afterward she would lie awake, sweat cooling between her breasts, behind her knees, her fingertips touching scratches on his skin and sore spots on her own. It was as if they were grappling with some presence that existed only when they were together. Physically he was so much stronger, but he wouldn't let her win, so Jess used every tool at her disposal: teeth, nails, unexpected submissions and offerings so he would lower his guard, a blind animal smelling blood, and then she would turn the tables again.

Jess imagined that the sex between Alex and Christine was gentle, comforting, a balancing counterweight to their own ongoing conflict. But where was her balance? Both with and without him she was lopsided, incomplete.

Carl moved slowly, gently, following her lead. She tried to feel his body beneath and within, his hands on her arms, his eyes on her breasts and then up to her eyes and then closed. When he said a name, she didn't know to whom he was speaking, and then she remembered. She was Anne. She had been Jess and now she was Anne and then who would she become?

Afterward, Carl asked more about *Vol*. He wanted to know what species flew over the barn at what times of year. When he was a boy he had had a junior ornithologist's guide, and for a while made notes and drawings of birds he had seen. Jess asked where it was now, and he shook his head. He said he hadn't drawn a bird in twenty years.

"The northern lapwing," she said. "The golden plover."

Carl smiled, his eyelids heavy. He repeated the names, looking up at the ceiling, the arcs of paint there like flight paths, turning and then away.

"Anne," he said, "those sound like beauties."

When Carl began to snore she dressed quietly and left his room. Back in her own, she sat on the carpet by the windows and waited for morning. In the dark, Isabella appeared again, holding her metal canister above her head. Jess had always seen rage in Isabella's face, murder in her eyes. But now, staying for once in that remembered moment, she wasn't so sure. The gallery's security guard was still so far away; Isabella had plenty of time to strike again. Maybe it wasn't rage. Maybe it was fear or confusion, the face of a girl wondering what she had done.

Outside, the smoke above the hills was spreading, lit by the sun's first red paring to the east. The edges of the city dissolved in the bloody light. If she sat here that light would pass over her, too. She would disappear. This was what Alex had felt, in those final moments speeding down Beverly Boulevard. Finally, she knew. She watched that terrible choice open before her, barreling unmoored toward that tree.

She showered and dressed back in her own clothes, leaving Anne's folded on the bathroom floor with the towels. At the checkout desk she saw Carl heading into the restaurant. He smiled, a little sadly, and nodded, and Jess tried to accept this kindness, to absorb it as strength in the face of what might come.

From a courtesy phone she called the Serranos' number and waited for the cowboy to answer.

THIS
WORLD
AND THE
NEXT

11

MARTHA

SUMMER 1977

Rotting fruit—that was the image that curdled Martha's thoughts. Misty's body shriveling, her skin bruised, her breath sour when she spoke. Within a couple of months of the diagnosis Martha was sleeping on her sister's couch, helping Misty to shower and dress, driving her to the clinic. During Martha's shifts at the Tahitian she called Misty every hour, and when there was no answer she rushed back to the apartment, blowing through traffic lights and stop signs, fumbling with her keys at the door, steeling herself for the worst and then almost sinking to her knees in relief when she heard a cough from the bedroom or water running in the kitchen sink.

Every time she raced in or out of the building she passed a fig tree, its rotting fruit strewn across the sidewalk, their leathered skins burst and their insides spilled out, wet and red, covered in ants.

Martha moved a cold washcloth along Misty's forehead, held Misty's hand as she fell into a brittle, troubled sleep. Her strong, beautiful sister was falling away, sliding down a hole inside herself, leaving this burning husk behind.

At night, Martha left the TV on while she tried to sleep. She had never cared much for TV, but the glowing screen was a comforting presence, the only light in the dark room while she drifted on the couch.

Sometimes she woke in the night and didn't know where she was until the flickering image reminded her. Heart pounding, she watched whatever was on-screen until the program ran out and the national anthem began to play, the flag rising up the pole, flapping in the prerecorded wind. And then nothing, just static, and those were the worst hours, the world gone quiet except for her heart and head. After those nights Martha had never felt so grateful to see the first bright curl of sun in the purpling windows. She wasn't religious, she couldn't remember ever saying a prayer, but Oh thank God was what she thought when those nights finally turned over into morning.

She didn't tell Izzy these stories. That first night in her kitchen Martha told happier stories, summer mornings back in Florida, she and Misty jumping off the bridge into the river by their house, holding hands as they fell. Or Vegas stories, those early days of parties and shows, seeing Misty's costumes onstage for the first time—gowns with plumage that spread like peacock feathers, starbursts of sequins and rhinestones, dazzling in the spotlights.

"My sister never performed, but she looked like a showgirl. All legs and gorgeous skin. Turning every head."

Martha couldn't bring herself to say Misty's name. Instead, in every story she said, *my sister*. She hadn't said Misty's name since her death.

She thought that if she did she might break apart, or sink completely into herself, or maybe even become infected, as if somehow Misty's name also carried her disease.

The shame of this thought blocked her breath. She imagined one of those rotting figs lodged in her chest.

"What's wrong?" Izzy asked.

Looking across the kitchen table, Martha saw Izzy's concern. It was the first time the girl had moved outside of herself. Martha imagined finally opening up, sharing everything she was holding in. But she was still too afraid and ashamed, so she managed a smile and said she just had too many stories and memories.

She looked out the window and saw Misty standing under a streetlight looking back.

"I've got to get away from this place," Martha said.

"The trail cuts across the northeastern corner of New Mexico. It doesn't have a name," Misty said, "or it has a lot of names, but nothing official. People think of it as a pilgrimage. Some go west to east and some east to west. There's no right or wrong direction, but you start at one end and by the time you reach the other you've changed. Here. Look."

For as long as Martha could remember Misty kept journals full of articles cut from newspapers and magazines, photocopied pages from library books. Around these pieces she wrote her own notes and thoughts and little poems. The journals were different colors and sizes, but they all grew equally fat over time, swollen with the clippings taped to their pages.

Misty slid the journal across the table. They were eating breakfast, oatmeal and sausage links. Or rather Martha was eating and Misty, with no appetite, worked her way down the row of vitamin bottles lined up beside her plate, shaking tablets into her palm, swallowing each with a sip of ginger ale.

The article was from one of Misty's New Age newsletters. Two or three of these arrived in the mail every week. She had abandoned the clinic's treatment plan, becoming increasingly obsessed with the idea of a cure outside the realm of what she now called *Western medicine's very limited imagination*. This was the reason for their most intense arguments—that Misty was spending the last of her money on newsletters and vitamins instead of real medicine and doctors, throwing away her chance for survival on a bunch of voodoo bullshit. Martha couldn't stand to see Misty looking for some miracle in the mimeographed pages, or rambling about how time was nothing but a phony construct and a real cure would require transcending the idea of time, returning to a past moment of health and carrying that moment into the future.

"The pills make me sick," Misty would shout during their fights, shaking one of her prescription bottles in Martha's face. "Why should I take something that makes me sick?"

Martha looked over the article on the pilgrims' trail. A black-and-white photo sat at the top, the view from the middle of a wide dirt road. A mountain range stood in the far distance. Just visible, eclipsed by the tallest peak, was a bright white sliver of either the rising or setting sun. The land on either side of the road was nothing but sand and scrub. To Martha it seemed a lonely, desolate place, until something in the photo caught her eye: a pair of tiny figures far down the trail, backlit into silhouette.

"See?" Misty said. "That's us. We can go back to whatever time we want. We can go forward."

Misty sounded so hopeful that Martha didn't have the heart to argue. She smiled, covering Misty's hand with her own.

"We're not stuck here," Misty said, "if there's no reason to stay."

They poured Misty's ashes into an urn and handed Martha the plain copper container. Holding it felt obscene. Her sister wasn't there. This was another lie, comfort as home decor.

Driving back from the crematorium, Martha pulled over to the side of a highway overpass and threw the urn as far as she could, off into a large construction site, a flattened plot of land crawling with backhoes and bulldozers. She watched the ashes fly, catching for a moment in the wind before falling back to earth.

When they were kids, Misty had claimed she was a twin, but that her other sister had never been born. They had been together in their mother's belly but Misty was the only baby who made it out. She repeated the story when she was angry with Martha, and Martha understood that it was intended to wound her, to imply that there was some spirit or ghost with whom Misty felt a deeper connection. Martha was too afraid of the possible answer to ask their mother if the story was true. So it hung over her childhood, a presence that was most likely a lie but that at times felt real enough, a nameless girl following at a slight distance.

One evening before the diagnosis, driving back from an AA meeting, Martha brought up the missing-twin story. Misty swore she couldn't remember ever saying such a thing. "That would have been so awful of me," she said. "I'm sorry if I did that."

After dropping Misty off at her apartment, Martha sat in her car and tried to feel if that presence was gone now, finally banished. But no—it was still there, *she* was still there, the other sister. Indistinct but nearby.

Martha stood in the stale, hot dark of her bedroom and looked down at the sleeping girl curled into a comma on top of the sheets. Was that what she had felt earlier in the casino, when she first saw Izzy losing at a blackjack table? That the unnamed ghost who had been with her for so long had finally stepped through? And if that was true, then what else was possible? Could she step through the other way, as Misty had claimed throughout those final months?

No borders, Misty had written in her journal, on the page behind the photo of the pilgrims' path.

no lines on the map,
no walls,
no time or space that cannot be
joined together,
world without end—

Martha lay on the bed, mirroring the curve of Izzy's body, leaving a small gap along that line between them. She smelled her own smoke and Izzy's sweat and the cheap fruity shampoo found in nearly every hotel bathroom on the Strip.

World without end. Wasn't that a line from a prayer? Had Martha heard it on one of those nights waiting in her car for Misty's AA meeting to finish? Had it come from inside the church, the deep vaulted room glowing in the night?

Over the last year she had seen Misty everywhere, but now she finally felt her, far off but present, waiting.

For the first time since the crematorium, she whispered her sister's name.

12

JESS

SUMMER 1979

Vince suggested they meet at a Mexican restaurant at the bottom of the Serranos' hill, just past the freeway on-ramp. It was late morning, between breakfast and lunch. The dining room was empty and mostly dark, lit only by the dim umber glow of the electric-candle sconces along the walls. Two waitresses in colorful dresses cleaned, the older woman wiping tables while the younger woman pushed a carpet sweeper.

From his stool at the bar Vince looked over his shoulder, watching the waitresses.

"My mom worked here when I was a kid," he said. "She had a closet full of those dresses. Five or six different colors, one for each day. One time I asked her which was her favorite and she said, *mandarina*. I had never thought of a color having a flavor, or a scent."

He gave a sheepish smile, disclosing a jumbled row of white teeth, then tucked his hair behind his ears. His cowboy hat sat on the empty stool on his other side. He had removed it when they entered the restaurant.

The older waitress came around behind the bar, opened a bottle of Coke, and set it in front of Vince. Jess ordered a coffee. The waitress poured a mug and set it on the bar and as she turned to leave Jess asked her to add a shot of tequila. The waitress added the shot and said something to Vince in Spanish, her voice low and disapproving. Vince smiled again. "Todo está bien," he said. The waitress didn't seem convinced, fixing Jess with a skeptical look as she left the bar.

Jess said, "She thinks I'm trying to corrupt you?"

"Something like that."

Jess sipped her coffee, feeling the tequila move through, her body unwinding, coming in for a soft landing. Vince looked away to a foil Cinco de Mayo banner still hanging behind the bar, giving Jess the space she needed to quiet her nerves. Intuitive, this one. Observant.

"Did Madeline ask you to chase after me the other day?"

Vince shook his head. "I'm on my own."

"Where's Mr. Serrano?"

"He's been living in a hotel in Beverly Hills the past few months. Mr. and Mrs. Serrano have had a hard time with all of this."

"How long have you worked for them?"

"Since I was a kid. My dad kept the grounds, maintained the cars. Whenever I was around, Mrs. Serrano gave me things to do. When my dad couldn't work anymore, I took over."

"You're about Isabella's age."

"A year older."

"And you were friends?"

Vince looked at his hands for a moment, considering. His fingers were long, with rusty stains of oil or grease in the gutters around the nails. He seemed self-conscious that Jess noticed and began working at the nails of one hand with the fingertips of the other.

"She didn't fit there," he said. "In that house. Ballet lessons, which fork to use with whatever. She was out of place. The first time we met I was probably seven or eight. She was hiding in the hedges that used to line the driveway, tearing the sleeves off her blouse. She told me that if I didn't say anything, I could keep the sleeves. I felt like the luckiest kid in the world. The sleeves were red silk and I thought I could tie them together to use as a bandana when I played cowboy. So I never said anything."

Jess smiled at the image, a smaller Vince with a smaller cowboy hat, red silk over his face, firing at imaginary foes.

"We played games," he said. "Hide-and-seek. We talked a lot. Some nights when we were older, she'd argue with her parents and ask me to drive her somewhere. She didn't like to drive. She never even got her license."

"Why not?"

"She said she didn't trust herself. She was worried she'd hurt somebody."

Vince took a sip of his Coke, looking into the mouth of the bottle, remembering.

"We'd go up along Mulholland," he said. "We both liked that tunnel through the trees, how you take some of the curves real slow, and the lights of the city appear, just for a few seconds, down below. Then another turn and they're gone."

Jess had taken that drive with Alex many times for the same reason. She wondered about cars they had passed on the lonely curves, faceless silhouettes in the front seat. Vince and Isabella, maybe, sharing a slow turn.

"She talked about leaving," Vince said, "She wanted to go somewhere no one knew her, where she could be somebody else. She asked me to go with her. And for a minute, I could see the whole thing. Starting over somewhere new. But I was too scared, or loyal, maybe. I thought of my father and the Serranos. I told her I couldn't do that. Right then I knew I had broken something."

"When was the last time you saw her?"

"The night she left. I drove them to the bus station."

"Them?"

"Her and Chloe, Izzy's best friend."

"Where were they going?"

"To Vegas. She told me it was just for a couple of nights, for Chloe's birthday. But then she kept going."

The questions came like cars on a dark road, emerging one after another in the headlights. Mulholland curves. Each time one appeared, Jess asked. It seemed insane to her now that she had never asked before. She had tried to contain Isabella in the dark, where her image, her memory, festered and grew. But with each of Vince's answers that image took another step forward, loosening from the shadows.

"That's not true," Vince said. "That wasn't the last time I saw her. One time I drove Mrs. Serrano up to that detention center. I was waiting outside the visiting room and looked through the window in the door and saw Izzy. I almost didn't recognize her. She looked like somebody had stripped away parts of her. All I could see was this core, like an apple core, dark and spiky. This secret inside part was all that was left."

The dining room was empty now. The waitresses had disappeared. Jess looked into the mirror behind the bar. Past the streaks and floaters, she saw Vince staring into the mouth of his Coke bottle, his somber, gentle face, his anxious fingers scratching at the glass. But the woman sitting beside him was not who Jess had expected to see. It was the face of a scarred, haunted stranger. All the courage that had gotten her this far—in her life, in her work—had been stripped away.

She didn't know why this surprised her. Of course this was who people saw; of course she hadn't hidden it well. This was who she had become. Just this secret inside part was all that was left.

Jess took the last sip of her coffee, and when Vince turned to her she said, "Where do we start?"

13

TANNER

SUMMER 1976

I 've felt that way, too, sometimes. Like how you described. Between things, almost. Here but not here. Isn't that what you said?

They found him at the mail-sorting tables, or riding up in the elevator, or in the halls outside the partners' offices. Clerks, bookkeepers, paralegals, even some of the lawyers. The new secretary who sat a few desks from Georgia asked if there was somewhere else they could talk. Standing close in the break room, the heat from the coffeepot and the heat from her hand on his arm.

He thought of Georgia out there at her desk. But then he thought of all the time he had wasted, all those years before he understood what he was capable of.

After work the new secretary drove him back to his apartment. They smoked a joint and Tanner spoke about what he knew, what he believed. She listened in the darkening room, her face rapt in the glow from the security lights hanging outside the building. When he finished, she took off her clothes and stood before him, pale and smooth and perfect. Then she began to undress him. Tanner didn't feel what he once would have, that familiar shame and embarrassment. Those things were gone now, rats that had jumped ship. Instead he felt such power as she knelt before him, moving her hands over his body.

So beautiful, she said, lifting her mouth to his.

Her name was Juliet. Sometimes she came to Tanner's apartment with flowers tied into her hair, daisies and posies, multicolored faces looking out through the thick brown waves. Sometimes she brought baggies of weed and tiny pink tabs of acid. They smoked the weed and dropped the acid and Tanner talked and saw his words open windows all around. A revelation. There was another place. He had been right all along. But those windows were still just out of reach. No matter what they did in that room, he couldn't pass through.

I don't like what's happening to you, Georgia said.

I told you it was just one time.

I'm not talking about the girl. I'm talking about how you're acting.

How am I acting?

Like this. Scary. Shouting at me. Cornering me. I want to leave.

We're in the middle of a conversation.

This isn't a conversation. Let go.

I'm not finished talking.

Let go, she said. I want to go.

He was nearly blind with fury and fear. If Georgia left his room he knew she would never come back.

He pushed her down in the corner of the bedroom and walked out, shutting the door, wedging a chair under the knob. Georgia pounded on the door and shouted from the other side. He left the apartment. He needed to clear his head, to find some way to talk to Georgia, to make her understand.

He started up the hill toward the freeway. Evening was settling in; lights blinked on in apartment windows as he passed. The rain that had been gathering all day began falling in soft *plaps* on the asphalt. When he was a kid he loved lifting his face to the rain; the cool drops on his skin felt like reminders of a better place. He lifted his face and tried to remember that feeling. Cars honked and swerved around like circling dogs, engines snarling. He closed his eyes, willing himself through. There it was—still so far away but visible, like the first glimmer of sunrise on the horizon. He could show her. He could convince Georgia to follow him home.

Back at his apartment, the police were waiting. Neighbors had heard Georgia screaming and pounding on the walls. As the officer pressed his head to lower him into the back of the squad car, Tanner saw her one last time, shivering inside the building's front door, her hair wet with rain and sweat, a blanket over her shoulders.

Six months in the county jail was nothing. This surprised him. Tanner expected the terror-filled chaos of prison movies: sadistic guards and shower assaults. Instead, the men were afraid of him. It was hard not to laugh. He had a benign skin condition and these men, many twice his size, gave him a wide berth. He realized that he needed to keep his mouth shut for a while so that when he started talking it would carry greater significance. He was right. The men began to gather around him in the gym and the yard. When the guards tried to break it up, he started talking to them, too.

His mother came once. She cried and reached for his hand. Tanner told her that she shouldn't come back. Her son loved her, he said, but her son was no longer here.

One morning in the gym a new inmate jumped him, pulling him down to the floor and pressing his wide thumbs into Tanner's windpipe, gritting his teeth and slathering like an animal. Tanner was surprised by how calmly he moved through the moment, his body relaxed and light, before the other men rushed in and pulled the new inmate off and beat him ragged while the guards kept their backs to the room.

Afterward, a muscle-bound, baby-faced Latino kid asked if he could touch the thumbprint at Tanner's neck. Tanner nodded and the kid placed his fingertip on the sore red circle. Tanner watched the kid's face, the flawless skin that once would have burned him alive with envy, and saw, instead, that same ache in this kid's eyes as they moved across the bumps on Tanner's throat. The kid wishing, Tanner knew, that the craggy shell was contagious, that he would give up his own perfection for something more.

Out of jail, he took a room at the Y downtown. There was a bookstore on the other side of Flower Street called the Rising Lotus that catered to New Age space cadets. The owner was an angular, middle-aged hippie named Lynch, who had a long neck and a vulture-beak nose. The front of the store was filled with books and pamphlets on meditation and natural healing and Eastern religions, but the real action was in the back room where Lynch sold a variety of illicit substances. After a week or so of Tanner hanging around, Lynch asked if he wanted a job keeping an eye on the front of the store, like a security guard or bouncer. If the cops showed up, Lynch said, Tanner could either hand over some cash or raise his voice to warn everyone in the back, depending on the cop in question. If a junkie or rival dealer barged in, Tanner should kick them out of the store. Tanner said that he wasn't much of a fighter and Lynch looked him up and down and laughed and said, You don't really need to be.

Most of the time, though, the store was quiet, so Tanner spoke to customers about the truths he had uncovered. Certain nights some of the women who hung around the store brought him home with them. Lynch marveled at this. You're like some kind of fertility god, he said. I should rub the top of your head for luck.

No, Tanner said, but you could let me speak in the store. Every night for an hour or so. People would come to listen.

They sat in a half circle of folding chairs, two and then three and four rows deep. Tanner spoke about this world and the other, the phase between the two. He spoke about his childhood, his new mother and that first day of first grade. He talked about growing up in this skin, about his job at the law firm and Georgia and jail. The more honest he was, the more rows of chairs surrounded him at the back of the store.

One night he saw a familiar face in the crowd. Tanner worked his way through the parting bodies to the baby-faced kid from the county jail. They embraced. The kid was strong and held on for a long time. His name was Danny. He had gotten out a couple of weeks before and had come by on an errand for the guys who ran his block. Old habits, he said with a shy smile. But what else can you do?

How many bodies did you step over to get here tonight? How many people sleeping on the sidewalk? How many times did you gag from the smog choking the air? What violence and cruelty did you see in the news that made you feel helpless or afraid? High school kids rioting in Florida. Someone stabbing a famous actor in an alley just a couple of miles from here.

I don't care what you believe in—whoever or whatever you think made this world. This can't have been their intention. There's been a mistake. We're all afraid to say this, but we know that it's true.

He looked out into the surrounding crowd, the seated rows and then those standing between the bookshelves. He needed to make eye contact with every single one, creating the connections that fueled him as he spoke. He felt the phase opening. With enough of this energy he could push all the way through.

Have you ever gone somewhere—you're waiting for a meeting or an appointment—and realized you're in the wrong place? Or as a kid you walked into a classroom and everyone looked at you like you had two heads and you were shaken by the understanding that you were supposed to be somewhere else. That's what's happened here. We're in the wrong place. You know this. And you're waiting for someone to show up and tell you where you're supposed to be.

Face to face to face, each pair of eyes, holding until he felt all of them at once.

You can stop waiting. I've seen it—the world where we belong.

Mei Sheng was a grad student working toward a master's in journalism when she was diagnosed with lymphoma. She came by the bookshop on the days she went to Good Samaritan for radiation. Looking for hope, she said. Usually, I don't believe in all this stuff, but I don't know what else to do.

At first, she told Tanner, she had been afraid of him. Not because of his appearance. It was your intensity, she said, the first night she brought him back to her apartment after one of his talks. Your confidence scared me, but I think I need to be around it now.

Tanner was drawn to her, too. Another pure soul trying to leave her shell.

She had lost most of her hair and covered her head with a series of pastel bandanas. That first night at her apartment, Tanner told her to stop wearing them. She untied the pale green cloth and let it fall away, revealing the short, rough patches of hair that sprang from her scalp like weeds in an otherwise vacant lot. She looked at him and raised her eyebrows as if she had made an irrefutable point. She started to retie the bandana and Tanner said, What do I see?

Mei Sheng lowered her hands.

A body, Tanner said, trying to fall away. Nothing more. What are you fighting?

The group that gathered for his talks grew. They nodded and clapped and called out when he spoke, coming alive as he came alive, repeating some of his phrases for emphasis. Many of them used the word *sermon* to describe what they had come to hear.

Lynch began accepting donations at the door. He offered Tanner half of what he collected and Tanner laughed and said, How about I give you twenty-five percent? Lynch told him to go fuck himself and Tanner said that if he did go fuck himself it would be in somebody else's store. From then on, Danny collected the donations while Lynch stood behind the counter, shooting hostile looks.

Back in college, Mei Sheng had gone on a road trip with a boyfriend. He was studying philosophy, she told Tanner, and liked to take these long soul-searching hikes. He had heard about this trail that cut across northern New Mexico, right through an old army base where they once tested an atomic bomb. At least, that was the story. A few of his professors walked this trail every year. He wanted to go and asked her to come along.

Spring break, she said, managing a weak smile. Pretty sexy stuff, walking for days through the dust.

She'd had a radiation session that morning and now sat on the floor beside the toilet in her bathroom, resting her head on the plastic seat. The afternoon was sullen and overcast, but all the shades were drawn. After a session, almost any light bothered her eyes.

Tanner stood in the bathroom doorway, listening.

I haven't thought about that hike in a long time, she said. But this morning when I was lying on the table and they started the machine I pictured a bomb blast. The flash, the mushroom cloud. Then I thought of the story of the test site.

And you're wondering, Tanner said, if one thing follows the other.

Mei Sheng shook her head, rolling it a little on the seat.

I don't think anyone has ever become sick from that hike, she said. My old boyfriend is fine. The thought wasn't so much cause and effect as a kind of echo, maybe. A reverberation across time. I thought I could almost hear it, like a gong, sounding years ago at an explosion in the desert and then again this morning when they turned on the machine.

She smiled, the slightest upturn at the corners of her mouth.

I sound like you now, she said.

Tanner had tried to convince her to stop the radiation, but she was stubborn and scared. Her parents met her at the hospital for every treatment but despite their appeals, she refused to move back home. She was caught in the middle. Tanner understood. He had spent his entire life that way. She didn't yet realize that fighting against the body was useless, that the body was useless. The only way to be free was to leave it behind.

He absorbed so much energy from the crowds at the bookstore, but he couldn't quite find a way to move through the phase. Mei Sheng was the key. The gift of disease had brought her halfway there. He imagined her letting go, allowing the cancer to take her body completely. He would be with her in that final moment, that first moment, holding on to her essence as it fled its shell, pulling him through the phase like a string in his hand.

Mei Sheng turned her head and heaved, her thin frame convulsing with the reflex. Nothing came up and so she spit feebly into the bowl.

She lifted her head and ran her palm across her scalp, now completely barren.

I haven't worn anything on my head in weeks, she said. People don't look at me anymore. Not even my parents. They look to the side.

He waited for her to turn her head again, for her eyes to reach up to his.

I look at you, he said. I see you. You're almost there.

In the back office, Lynch began harping again about his cut of the donations. He needed at least half, he said. The sermons or whatever the hell they were brought a lot of people in, but those people didn't buy much and were in fact cutting down on the other product he was trying to move. His other customers didn't like coming into a place that was so busy. So we can either agree on fifty percent, he said, or you can indeed go fuck yourself in someone else's store.

Tanner was only half listening. He looked around the room. Lynch's desk was a riot of cassettes and 8-tracks and receipts, as well as a couple of tell-tale clues from his other business—a small spread of rolling papers and a bare razor blade, grains of white powder still clinging to its edge. Metal shelves of pamphlets and books lined the walls. The title of an oversize paperback caught his eye: *Modern Pilgrimages*. The cover photo showed a wide trail leading back across a flat, arid landscape.

I know you think you're hot shit, Lynch said, with your groupies and your meathead flunky. But we both know better. You don't believe that garbage you're spouting. So let's deal with this like businessmen.

Tanner took the copy of *Modern Pilgrimages* from the shelf and walked past Lynch, their shoulders brushing in the tight space. He lifted the razor from the desk and saw the quick fear in Lynch's eyes. Tanner walked out into the store and as he heard Lynch's relieved sigh Tanner drew the razor down the side of his own neck, pushing hard into the bumps, through the skin, ear to trapezius. By the time he reached Danny, the razor was away in his pocket. With his wet, red hand he pointed toward the back room where Lynch stood openmouthed in the doorway, as Danny, huge with wrath, followed that silent order, crashing back through the store.

He convinced Mei Sheng to cancel the day's treatment, and instead they drove to Venice and walked along the canals, stopping every few yards so she could catch her breath. She spoke again about that walk across the edge of the desert a couple of years before. She thought about it all the time now, she said, dreamed about it, as if she hadn't understood the significance of the experience while it was happening. Or maybe the experience worked in a delayed fashion, like some kind of seed finally sprouting, watered with time and distance and illness.

Her dreams about that walk were so vivid, she said. She could see each stone and footprint on the path, could taste the dust and sweat, feel the heat of the naked sun. Then she woke in her apartment and looked around the familiar room that now seemed foreign and false. Even here, she said, walking with you doesn't seem real.

They stopped on a narrow wooden footbridge spanning one of the canals. She turned to Tanner and touched the long cut running down the side of his neck. She asked him what had happened. He smiled and told her he didn't know, that he woke up that morning and it was there, tender to the touch, red and livid in the bathroom mirror.

He showed her the book from the store. She looked at the pages on the New Mexico trail and shook her head, disappointed. This is nothing, she said. Pictures, descriptions. Dead on the page. I can't tell you how alive it is in my dreams. I wish I could pull you in with me.

As she spoke, she held him by the arm and he could see her distress, the desperation in her eyes.

This sounds crazy, she said, but if it wasn't for the cancer and the radiation, I wouldn't have remembered. I wouldn't have these dreams. I wouldn't have met you.

She pressed the book back into his hands, then squeezed his arms, her strength surprising, fingertips pushing bumps into bone.

You need to take that walk, she said. I think if you started, you would finish in a very different place.

He woke to hands grabbing his arms, his hair, dragging him up from the floor. He slept on the floor because Mei Sheng could no longer tolerate another body in the bed. Any touch was like a blow. These were blows now, kicks to his stomach and ribs, folding him back down. One of the men attacking him was Mei Sheng's brother. Tanner recognized him from a picture on her desk. The men pulled him into a corner while Mei Sheng's parents and two paramedics rushed into the room. Mei Sheng was too weak to scream, so Tanner screamed for her. The men held him while the paramedics lifted Mei Sheng onto the stretcher. Her mother was crying and speaking in rapid Chinese, what sounded like a prayer. Her father stood in front of Tanner, his face wrenched with disgust. He looked like he wanted to spit. Then he did, onto Tanner's bare feet. As the stretcher passed, Mei Sheng turned her head and looked at Tanner and he could see that she was leaving, this would be the day. He struggled to reach her, to hold on to what remained of the presence dimming in her eyes, but her brother and his friends were there, pinning Tanner's arms, covering his mouth, stomping, punching, kicking.

The room was not in any of Mei Sheng's recollections of the path. It was not in the guidebook. He and Danny walked for two days and then this astonishment simply appeared, revealed after the rise of a low hill. Stark, preternatural, a small concrete building in the middle of the trail. It robbed Tanner of breath, pulled at the mercury in his blood.

Oh, Tanner said. A sigh of recognition. He had no knowledge of how it had come to be, of what was inside, but he knew that this was the room, this was all rooms. He was inside, dumping toys from his backpack. He was inside, pushing Georgia into the corner. He was inside, holding on to Mei Sheng as she led him through the phase.

Here it was, finally. He walked toward the open door.

From *Light + Space*

(1977; 16mm film, sound; 82 minutes;
Laura Lehrer, dir.; unreleased)

Jess turns and walks back toward the camera, stopping behind the chair. She places her hands on its back. A shield between her body and Laura's questions.

- Has something like what happened at *Zero Zone* ever happened before? That kind of extreme reaction to your work?

Jess looks down at her hands. Her knuckles are pale from gripping the chair. She opens them slowly, prying each joint.

The camera's focus breathes a little, blurred and then clear. Laura speaks again.

- There are essays and reviews, accounts of engagement with your work. Life-changing experiences. They're always positive, at least those that I've read.

Jess nods, still watching her hands, curiously, as if they belong to someone else.

- But another possibility is always there, isn't it? A different kind of experience?

The Way Out

(1962; makeshift studio installation;
Claremont, California)

They pulled girls from campus sidewalks, cafeteria tables, their dorm room beds. Husky boys with hands like grizzlies' paws clamped the girls' forearms, under armpits, escorting, lifting, dragging if necessary. Outside the student union in the early-autumn heat they marched the girls one at a time onto a locker room scale. They wrapped lassos of measuring tape around hips, waist, bust. They moved the metal weight across the top of the scale, forward and back. They called out numbers. Students gathered around. The boys cheered or jeered as if the measurements were football scores. The girls watched with forced smiles or pained smiles or smiles that looked like bright red cuts across their faces.

The weigh-in was a first-year rite of passage, they said. All in good fun.

Jess was eating lunch with a couple of girls from orientation when they heard the mob arrive. The girl beside Jess tensed up; Jess felt her own body stiffen in reply. The girl across the table started to giggle nervously, covering her mouth as she chewed her egg salad. The boys burst into the cafeteria singing some kind of fight song. They went table to table, pulling the girls up from their chairs and ushering them outside while other boys laughed or clapped or looked away.

Jess stood on the scale and they called out her weight, wrapping the measuring tape around her breasts, their hands everywhere, one even on her throat for a moment, a thumb pressed into her windpipe, turning her into position. She just wanted it to be over. The noise around her was an unbroken roar. Then a boy slapped her on the ass and she stepped off the scale and into the cheering crowd. She turned and watched the next girl, the one who sat beside Jess in the union. The girl stood on the scale, her body rigid as a plank of wood but her chin jumping, her mouth dropping open as she moaned, a low sound running beneath the noise. Jess felt the moan enter her body, swirling in her chest and throat to find her own moan trapped there, a wail of disgust and fear and shame.

The next year Jess stood in the crowd and watched every time a girl was weighed and measured. She tried to catch their eyes when she could, to be there on the other side of the noise, and if that wasn't possible then she would bear witness. Afterward she walked off campus to the little storefront Alex rented as a studio and stalked the space, wanting to cry or shout or break something. At one point Alex handed her a cup of coffee and Jess threw the mug across the room, thrilled by the satisfying burst when it exploded against the far wall.

Gabe brought curtains from the theater department and they cordoned off a corner of the studio into its own room. Then they made a corridor of curtains leading from the front doors, what Jess saw as a soft approach, a velveteen tunnel of deep reds and purples guiding you in. They shopped a weekend's worth of yard sales and filled a rack of shelves in the curtained room with plates, mugs, glasses, vases. She spread the word in the dining hall, the union, the classrooms. When the first girl arrived, Jess was waiting at the beginning of the curtained corridor with safety glasses and a pair of rubber dish-washing gloves. Five minutes later the girl reemerged into the bright afternoon, flushed and sweating, a small cut on her cheek, another on her calf. She handed Jess the gloves and glasses and then stayed to help clean, to ready the space for the next arrival.

They stayed open for hours after every weigh-in. Sometimes no one came; sometimes three or four girls were waiting by the door when Jess arrived. Some of the girls broke everything they could get their hands on, screaming or shouting so loud their muffled voices could be heard through the cinder-block walls. Some were silent, and when Jess went back into the space to clean she found that nothing was broken, only moved a little, or simply left alone.

Some took off as soon as they finished, but others fell into folding chairs outside the storefront, talking and smoking, then going quiet when someone new arrived, giving them that gift of silence as Jess handed over the glasses and gloves.

Alex asked her what it was called.

"What's what called?" Jess said.

"This piece. You should give it a name."

She hadn't thought of this as art. What she was still trying and failing to do with paint was art, or an attempt at art. This revelation, finally discovering what she had been searching for, was exhilarating. She remembered Aunt Ruth on the night they finished building their breezeway, standing with her eyes closed, her arms out, whole for a moment.

One afternoon a group of football players showed up at the studio, beery and loud, demanding to be let inside. Jess blocked the door, her legs like jellyfish, and told them she was going to call the police. One of the players stepped up and put his hand in her hair as if to kiss her or break her neck. She kept her eyes on his, her voice as steady as she could make it, and told him to leave. He squeezed her hair in his fist, a warning, a reminder, then released her. The boys walked away laughing, weaving down the sidewalk.

The next day, Gabe came by so Jess wouldn't be alone. They only had one visitor, who had been inside so long Jess had forgotten her until Gabe suggested one of them go in and check.

Jess walked down the curtained corridor, listening for shouts or screams or cries, glass breaking, singing even, which was how some of the girls told her they had spent their time. Jess didn't know the girl's name, so she called out *Hello?* and waited for a response. Her voice died in the tunnel of fabric. She stepped through the last curtain.

Everything was broken—the glassware, the crockery, the shelves. The girl lay on her side in the bull's-eye of the wreckage, knees to elbows, motionless. Her eyes were open but lightless. Deep cuts crosshatched her cheeks and arms. She hadn't worn the glasses or gloves. Jess knelt beside her and placed a hand on her shoulder. The girl's muscles were tensed, her body hard as a rock. She was taking short, shallow breaths, little gasps. Jess stood and called out to Gabe. Her voice broke and then fell to her feet, more shards. She called again, louder, hearing her own wild panic, then she ran back through the corridor toward the doors that Gabe had just come through.

They drove the girl to the infirmary, where a doctor asked them what the hell happened. Jess tried to explain and the man watched her with increasing indignation. When Jess asked if they could stay, the doctor looked at her like she was out of her mind. "Haven't you done enough already?" he said.

The girl's name was Bonnie. She was small and blond and fair; Jess had seen the pale blue veins in her neck and wrists when she'd found her on the studio floor. None of the other girls knew her. She was quiet and shy, or at least she seemed that way in those early weeks of the semester, her first time away from home. Within a couple of days she was back in classes. Jess saw her in the library and walking between buildings. But every time Jess thought to approach she held back. She couldn't explain why she avoided the girl, as if Bonnie had done something wrong. Jess hated herself for her cowardice, her lack of courage to engage, to do more than create something and then step back and watch.

A secretary from the dean's office came by Alex's studio and told them to close down the site. Some of the girls continued to meet outside, discussing other actions they could take, a letter-writing campaign or a petition to the dean. Bonnie disappeared from campus; someone told Jess that she had transferred to a school closer to home.

She brought it up with Alex the night they took the curtains down. He listened as Jess let it all out, what felt like a confession, her frustration and sadness over what had happened. When she was finished, he paused for a moment up on his ladder.

"It's a risk," he said. "And I don't think the risk is just to the artist."

Almost a decade later Jess heard that the college, under pressure from students and alumni, had finally banned the weigh-in. That night, celebrating the news at the Brig with old friends, a gap opened in the noise, and for a moment Jess saw Bonnie there, just the way she remembered. As toasts were made and glasses clinked, Jess looked at the girl curled on the floor of the bar, the floor of the curtained room, drained and pale and broken like the plates.

14

MARTHA

SUMMER 1977

She spent most of her paycheck and tips at a sporting goods store not far from the crematorium. The checkout girl keyed in the prices of the tent and kerosene lantern, the sleeping bags, two pairs of hiking boots. It would cost nearly all she had, leaving only a couple hundred dollars to take with them on the trip. Martha watched the receipt lurch up from the register, line by line, her body charged with a swirl of fear and hope, what she imagined gamblers must feel when they finally resolved to bet it all.

"When I was younger, I was scared of directions," Izzy said. "They made the world seem flat, like a map."

They headed south on an empty county road, the mountains at their back, the desert ahead. In the passenger seat, Isabella looked up from the map in her lap and stared out the windshield across the long red view.

"Thinking of north as climbing up and south as sliding down," she said. "I was scared of the word. *South*. I wouldn't say it. It felt like you could take a step in that direction and fall forever."

They stopped for dinner at a truck stop about an hour from the pilgrims' path. A few men sitting at the counter eyed them all through their meal and when Martha walked to the restroom, one of the men followed. She came back out to find him leaning against the wall, the payphone receiver to his ear, but she could hear the dial tone's drone as she passed back to their booth. She decided they would spend the night in the car. Martha felt safer knowing they could drive away if they needed to.

In an empty post office parking lot they put the seats back and cracked the windows for some fresh air. Izzy slept soundly, but Martha left the key in the ignition, trying to stay vigilant.

In the middle of the night she woke to a single point of orange light in the dark distance, what seemed like a baleful, roving eye, but which she soon realized was a cigarette lighter, along with the shadowed form of a man standing by the front doors of the post office. Martha's heart sped up, her pulse thudding in her ears. The man lifted his arm, slowly, and Martha felt her breath rise with the movement. Then the lighter went out and the figure moved away, off down the street, visible only in the short gaps between buildings, a darker shape against the dark night.

•

The next morning, as Martha and Izzy organized their gear in the parking lot, a young man approached and asked if they were heading to the trail. He was squat and muscular and spoke softly, with an accent. Martha was wary, so even though this young man seemed gentle she turned down his offer. He looked slightly hurt by her rejection, but then he smiled again. He said his name was Danny and he hoped to see them out along the trail.

The ground was hard and rocky and she was out of shape. Her knees and thighs ached, and the calluses that had formed on the balls of her feet from working the casino floor began to tear and bleed, her body's last remaining armor peeled away.

They hadn't brought enough water. After only half a day they had already run out, and Martha wondered if they would need to turn back, aborting the journey before it had even begun. But then they began to find milk jugs full of water at the side of the path, left by pilgrims with experience and compassion.

When the wind blew they covered their faces with bandanas against the swirling dust and Martha couldn't help but see it as crematory ash. She tried to push the vision to the side of her mind but it was insistent: this was a trail of the granulated dead, lifted by the wind to cover her boots and clothes, her hands and hair, inhaled through the bandana's thin fabric. Bodies within her body. The idea terrified her for most of the first day's walking and that night's restless sleep in the tent, but when she woke at the second dawn she thought of it in a different way. What if these were the souls of all those who had dreamed of making this walk but had been unable to reach this place? What if she could carry those souls with her along the path?

The thought was no longer fearful; it was a responsibility, an honor. When they began to walk again Martha left her bandana rolled in her backpack and when the wind blew she breathed freely. Izzy asked why she no longer covered her face and Martha explained her realization. For a moment, spoken aloud, it sounded crazy again, but then Izzy nodded and untied her bandana and walked uncovered for the rest of the day, too.

At times, Martha saw two figures walking side by side up ahead on the trail. Usually, after a few moments they disappeared in a shift of light, but every so often she saw that the figure on the left was Danny. The other was a tall, thin man who spoke continuously while they walked, his long hair swaying from beneath the bandana tied over the crown of his head.

Every once in a while, the man lifted his hand to make a point and Martha saw what she thought was the same movement that had raised the lighter outside the post office, that languid intensity, confident and controlled, a conductor gathering the moment to a single point of focus.

She knew that she should be afraid, or at least wary, but so much had changed within her since that last night at the casino, so many useless alarms had finally fallen silent, that she found herself staring after the man whenever she saw him far ahead, and waiting for that movement, hoping for it, almost—the pull in the air he created just by lifting his hand.

For the last hour, Martha had watched the lone figure approaching from the opposite direction. It wasn't Danny, or the taller man. Eventually Martha saw that it was a woman. When she was maybe fifty yards away, the woman raised her hand in greeting and quickened her pace.

The woman was out of breath but smiling, happy for the company. She was older, in her sixties, maybe, a weathered and energetic presence, with bright white grooves in her sunburned face and her gray hair pulled back in a loose ponytail.

"Are you on your way to the room?" she asked, drinking from a canteen on a strap slung crossways over her body, her eyes open and alight while she swallowed.

"What room?" Izzy said.

The woman told them that an artist had built a structure at the midpoint of the trail, just north of the old army base. "I'm calling it a room," she said, "because it seems like part of something larger, as if it isn't really complete in and of itself. And God was it hot in there. I was only able to stay for an hour or so before I worried I would start to cook. But I loved that someone had made it—this surprise rising up in the middle of what I thought I knew."

They moved into the patchy shade of a short, bristly yucca, and the woman, whose name was Helen, lifted a pear from her backpack and sliced it with a pocketknife, sharing its wedges with Martha and Izzy.

The fruit had ripened perfectly in the heat. Each slice was soft and sweet and heavy with juice. Martha couldn't help licking her fingers, the taste of the pear sharpened by sweat and dust.

"Did you pass a big guy going that way?" Martha asked. "Hispanic?"

Helen nodded. "He and another young man came into the room just as I left. You could be there by nightfall. Do you know them?"

Martha shook her head. She wasn't sure why she had asked. It had less to do with Danny than with the man traveling with him.

"You meet all sorts of interesting people along the path," Helen said. "Everyone comes for their own reasons, and everyone finds their own way." She finished her last slice of pear and readjusted her pack, ready to walk again. "Stay open to those surprises that rise up in the middle of what you thought you knew."

It wasn't there, the trail ahead was empty except for the ever-present mountains in the far distance, and then it appeared, maybe a quarter mile away, a short gray rectangle that looked as if it had been cut out of the sky at the horizon, slowly gaining texture and depth as they approached.

"The room," Izzy said, and Martha knew, from the way the entire world seemed to funnel into that space, that the man was inside.

She stopped and Izzy turned and asked what was wrong. Martha wanted to run; her body screamed for flight. But there was another feeling behind the fear—a sense that events were falling into place. Stones surfacing in a stream, waiting for her to cross. She thought of Misty's journal, the photo of two pilgrims on the path.

Izzy reached out to her. Martha took her hand and they walked toward the room.

He was only handsome from a distance. A tall, commanding silhouette in the doorway, his hair falling over his shoulders. Then Martha was close enough to see his face, the hard, round pustules or tumors that bubbled from his skin, forehead to neck. He lifted his hand in greeting and she shook again at the familiar gesture and saw more pustules ringing his wrist, in the gaps between his fingers. He wore long sleeves and hiking pants but even without seeing the rest of him Martha knew that his body was covered. When they were a few yards from the doorway he smiled. Even his lips were crowded with those hard growths, and Martha wondered if they hurt.

He looked at them with an intensity that was impossible to turn from, his blue eyes like magnets. Martha felt herself pulled, her body bending toward him, into the doorway beyond.

When he spoke, his voice was a surprise, warm and smooth, the sound of the sun rising, finally, after an interminable night.

"Welcome," he said. "You're finally here."

15

ISABELLA

SUMMER 1977

The room was a bare cinder-block box. There were horizontal openings in three of the walls and a door in the other. It was late afternoon, so the room was mostly dark, shadowy in the corners, the openings glowing weakly in the spillover light. Somehow, this place made sense. Izzy understood its brutal simplicity, like a body pared to essentials, waiting for something more to arrive.

The man with the lizard's skin was behind them in the doorway. That was a terrible way to think of anyone, she knew how it felt to be judged, but that's what he looked like, a craggy creature of the desert. Danny was there, sitting on a bench in the middle of the room. A young couple sat in a far corner, a guy with glasses and a thick blond beard and a girl with an open satchel between her legs. From the satchel she lifted a camera lens toward the light and peered through the glass, dissatisfied. Izzy felt like she and Martha were disturbing a private moment, but then Danny smiled and motioned for them to come farther in.

The young man with the glasses offered them water from a plastic jug. Izzy drank greedily, her body wobbly with thirst, her stomach growling with hunger. They hadn't eaten since that morning. The young man said his name was Ernst. The woman didn't offer her name. Danny stood by the man at the door and they spoke quietly.

The woman in the corner worked on a small movie camera. She seemed frustrated by the machine or her inability to make it do what she wanted. Finally, something snapped into place and she let out a loud sigh of relief.

Izzy wanted to ask her about the camera, how it worked. She wanted to ask if she could look through its viewfinder, to see if what she saw there was the same as what she saw in the frames she made with her hands. But the woman seemed closed off and annoyed, so instead Izzy moved to an opening in the wall and lifted her hand to feel that outside breath on her skin.

She turned from the window to see the lizard man watching her. She was shaken by the force of his gaze. Everyone else in the room fell away, sliding south off the map.

She stepped toward him and suddenly the air in front of her tore, a rip opened in the space. Izzy flinched from the brightness and heat, the burning white disc that unfolded from the rupture, growing, reddening, filling the center of the room.

Izzy gasped, staggering back, but then the light was gone. The room returned, stuffy and dim. They were all watching her, Ernst and the woman with the camera, Danny on the bench. Martha crossed the room, concerned. The man in the doorway hadn't moved. He studied Izzy with even more interest, if that was possible. Izzy shook Martha off and leaned back against the wall, her hips and legs weak, her stomach somersaulting.

After a moment, the man in the doorway asked, "What did you see?"

She wanted to say that she had seen the feeling she had chased for so long, that burning light, but nearer now, almost close enough to touch.

Instead she said, "Nothing. I'm just tired from the walk."

The sun dropped away, leaving the room glowing gray in the weak afterlight. The outside world disappeared. They floated in the abyss. She slid down the wall and sat on the floor. Martha joined her, taking Izzy's hand. "You're freezing," she said, and Izzy realized that she was shaking, her teeth were chattering. She imagined the room wheeling through space, an infinite field of stars surrounding them. She could see those stars through the roof, could even see them through the man's dark form standing in the open doorway. His voice seemed to come from out there, beyond his body. Izzy remembered sitting in the planetarium at the Griffith Observatory, a sixth-grade field trip, holding Chloe's hand in the dark, watching the pinpoint stars revolve in the vastness above, stories of old gods and the constellations they placed in the heavens, a narrator's voice that came from unseen speakers: *This is the secret history of the world.*

"My name is Tanner," the man said. His voice sounded close but hidden, as if coming from those same unseen speakers.

"And I believe," he said, "that we're all here for a reason that is making itself clear."

Tanner spoke through the night. He told of his childhood, growing up monstrous and apart. He talked about sadness and sex and violence and prison with an honesty that Izzy found incredible, laying himself open without shame.

Everyone listened in silence. After a while Tanner was silent, too, and

Izzy felt afraid, abandoned. Without his voice there was only the night. She reached for Martha in the dark but found nothing. She was floating away, through nothing. She was about to call out when his voice returned, pulling her back.

"What did you see?" Tanner asked again, and this time Izzy spoke the truth, because he had shown her how such honesty was possible.

"A sun," she said, her voice a bright white slash cutting through the darkness. "Another sun coming."

He spoke about this world and another, a phase between the two. How he had seen glimpses throughout his life but had never been able to move through. This was the place, though. He knew it the first moment he saw the room. "Did you know it, too?" he asked, and Izzy wasn't sure if he was speaking to her. Then a voice from the darkness said, "Yes." Martha's voice. Then Danny answered, his accent rolling the word like a smooth stone.

"You recognized it, didn't you?" Tanner asked. He was speaking to Izzy now. She could almost see his pebbled face in the dark, his eyes on hers.

"Yes," she said.

"What you saw," Tanner said, "is the sun that will burn this world clean."

"And then what?" Martha's voice.

"And then," Tanner said, "we'll be free."

The first milky light of morning. A bird called from far off, a single repeated, questioning cry. Looking up through the openings in the walls, Izzy saw the high branches of a few trees, a small ring of circling gnats. The world had reappeared. Everything that happened—the new sun,

Tanner speaking through the night—faded in the light. Izzy wanted to curl up, shutting everything out.

Then Martha unspooled beside her, wrapping her arms around Izzy, pulling her close, the cool tips of their noses touching.

"No, no," Martha whispered. "You're here. It really happened."

Izzy looked into Martha's eyes, the warmth there, the belief.

Martha kissed her forehead, her cheek.

"You saw it," Martha said, her lips wet with Izzy's tears. "You can take us through."

In a blink, the heat returned. Izzy was covered in sweat, couldn't drink enough water. She looked around the room at the plastic jugs and wondered what would happen once they were empty.

Ernst and his girlfriend huddled in the corner. He was upset, raising his voice. He wanted to leave. His girlfriend tried to calm him in indecipherable whispers. The woman had an accent; Izzy hadn't noticed before.

After a long while it seemed like the woman won the argument. She returned to her camera, but with a renewed sense of purpose, attaching a film magazine like a soldier in a movie assembling his rifle. She started shooting from the corner. The whirring film was the only sound in the room. Izzy turned away, self-conscious.

The afternoon burned on. The sun hung at the low end of its arc, staining the room bronze and gold. Danny sat on the bench, eating from a jar of apple sauce. He held the jar out to Izzy, offering. She shook her head, she wouldn't allow herself to give in to hunger, not here. She stood to get some air at the window and her legs went woozy, weaker than she thought. Then the room dimmed and dropped away and the air in front of her ripped open, flaring brightest white.

Izzy fell to her knees.

It was immense, gorgeous, terrible. Swelling white then yellow then bloodred. The heat was almost unbearable. Her skin felt like it would burn from her skull. She covered her face, reflexively, then lowered her hands. There was fear, but also longing. Let the longing have more power. Bring it through. This was Tanner's voice, from beside her.

"Can you see it?"

"No," he said. "You're the only one."

She was soaked with sweat. She reached out, an embrace, knowing if she could touch the sun it would pass through, but then the air wavered and the room snapped back into place.

Izzy fell forward on her hands, the sound of her breath hard in her ears. Martha rushed over, her arm around Izzy's shoulder. "You're burning up," she said. Danny brought a jug of water. Ernst watched from the corner, stunned. Even his girlfriend lowered her camera. Martha helped Izzy to her feet, pressed her lips to Izzy's hands, the bruises forming there from the concrete floor.

Izzy looked up to Tanner, standing where the sun had been, his eyes closed, his face clenched as if he, too, felt its loss.

16

JESS

SUMMER 1979

They rode in Vince's emerald-green Firebird, taking side streets down into Echo Park, hooking into the afternoon's traffic once they turned onto Sunset. They would start with Isabella's friend Chloe. She had been a child actor, Vince said, playing in a number of kids' movies a decade or so back. Never the star, but the tomboyish best friend, the girl with more than a little troublemaker in her. That had proved good casting, or Chloe had carried the persona offscreen, because by her early teens she had problems with drinking and drugs. For a while, she hadn't been allowed in the Serranos' house. Mrs. Serrano worried that she was a bad influence on Isabella. But they found ways to get together, Vince said.

He helped them sometimes, when Isabella asked, telling Mrs. Serrano that Isabella had gone one place when really she and Chloe were together in another.

"She's been in a few other movies since," Vince said. "Cheapo horror pictures and comedies. Boobs and blood. I don't know why she keeps making them. Maybe she needs the money. Or she just likes to be on-screen. She always had to be the center of attention."

Jess remembered the debutante photo, Isabella's discomfort in the frame. Isabella and Chloe might have seemed mismatched, but Jess understood that kind of relationship, where one partner's confidence provided cover for the other's reservations.

"What did the Serranos do when they realized Isabella was gone?"

"They called the police," Vince said. "They thought she'd been kidnapped. Some kind of ransom thing, like that oil family kid."

"Getty."

"So I told them the truth. They weren't too happy, but they were relieved. The fact that she had run off was better than the alternative. Then Chloe showed up a couple of days later, looking for Izzy. They had gotten separated somewhere. Mrs. Serrano called the police again, but they didn't give her much hope. They told her it was a big country."

"Chloe didn't know where she'd gone?"

The light ahead turned and Vince eased to a stop.

"If she did, she didn't tell me. Chloe always thought of me as the help."

They waited for a moment, until it seemed Vince had run out of patience. He looked up and down the cross street, then stepped on the gas, pushing through what remained of the red light.

"Somehow Izzy ended up in the desert with those people," Vince said. "In that room you made. We didn't know she was in there until it was all over. Mrs. Serrano flew out to Santa Fe, but Izzy was gone again."

They passed liquor stores and carnicerias, their walls branded with graffiti. Echo Park was gang territory, a cluster of scruffy hills warrened with a maze of narrow streets, perfect for getaways. Vince steered off Sunset and started up a steep side street. Between the garage doors pressed close on either side, Jess caught glimpses of the small cottages on the slopes above, half-hidden by palms and magnolia. Dogs behind chain-link barked as they climbed, the Firebird's engine waking them into action.

After a few switchback turns, Vince pulled to the curb. He lowered his head and looked through the windshield to a garage fifty feet farther along. A stone staircase beside the garage led up a hill covered with orange poppies.

"I'm assuming this is still Chloe's place," Vince said. "She bought it when she was in high school. She sued her parents to become an adult or—there's some other word for it. To control her own money from the movies." He pointed toward the staircase. "Izzy used to shout up from the street," Vince said, "but if I remember, that gate doesn't lock, so you can just go right up to the house and knock."

"You're not coming?"

"Chloe won't say anything if I'm around. She'll think Mrs. Serrano sent me."

"How do we know she'll talk to me?"

"I guess we don't."

Jess had imagined herself playing second to Vince's affable investigator. Going in alone wasn't a possibility she had considered.

She got out of the car and crossed the street, setting the dogs off again, a wave of barking that rippled back down the hill. For a moment she stood at the gate, which was not only unlocked but had no latch, simply sitting on its hinges, slightly ajar. She looked back toward the car for reassurance, hoping for a nod or—she didn't know, a thumbs-up, even—but the sun's glare had washed Vince's windshield white.

She started up the stairs. Halfway up the hill, in the shade of a flowering magnolia, an ancient VW Bug sat half buried under a cover of dead leaves.

The windows were open or broken away. Jess smelled pot and stale cigarettes from inside. She turned and looked out across the smoggy spread of rooftops and telephone poles, the never-ending cat's cradle of wire, the bright windows of the houses nestled into the neighboring hills. She imagined sitting here with a friend, a high school summer night, smoking, watching the city darken and then come alive again with firefly points of streetlight.

She could be here now, of course, inside the house above. When Jess knocked, Isabella might be the one who answered the door.

Jess looked back down to the street, but the side of the neighboring garage obscured Vince's car. All she could see was the front bumper shining in the sun. She turned and continued up the steps, brought back for a moment to the opening night of *Spectrum*, watching the initial visitors step through her studio door into that first dark room. One woman, Jess remembered, looked at her with a nervous smile, and then, as she crossed the threshold, held her breath.

"I know who you are," Chloe said. "I watched the news."

She leaned in the doorway, tall and long-limbed, filling the frame at a diagonal. Her jean shorts were cut ragged and high; her sleeveless T-shirt bared pale arms like birch branches. She was a few inches taller than Jess, and probably ten pounds lighter. *Willowy* was how a movie agent might have once described her, Jess imagined, a gilded description of a girl whose addictions didn't run to food. But those days were over. The addictions had won. Chloe looked hungry and raw, her lips and nostrils chapped, her hair hanging in greasy tangles.

"I was hoping I could ask you some questions," Jess said. "About Isabella."

"There's nothing to say." Chloe straightened up to her full height, an attempt to intimidate, maybe. "I haven't seen her in years."

"Could you tell me what happened in Vegas?"

Chloe expelled a single derisive snort. "You're a little late, don't you think?" She stepped back inside and started closing the door.

"She's missing again," Jess said.

Chloe paused. "I thought she was in jail."

"No one knows where she is."

Chloe stared at Jess for a moment, searching for the lie. She looked over her shoulder, back into the house, listening, considering. Finally she opened the door again and turned away, walking barefoot across the living room. It was an actress's stock gesture, an ambivalent invitation. Jess had seen it many times in Zack's favorite noir films. Which made Jess the reeled-in heavy. It was her job to show some interest and follow.

The house was a Spanish-style cottage with a terra-cotta floor and low, arched doorways. A charmer at one point, but now a murky, slummy cave, with dark bedsheets over the windows and paint scabbing from the walls. In the living room, a half stick of incense burned on the fireplace mantel. The only decorative touch was a movie poster hanging above the saggy couch: *Sorority Psycho*. Chloe's name was there in the credits below the painted image of a buxom, screaming co-ed in a torn nightie.

Chloe dropped onto the couch and nodded to a wooden dining chair by the front window. A big cereal bowl sat on the wicker coffee table, *Sesame Street* characters parading around its sides. Big Bird and that hairy elephant-looking creature, the imaginary friend. Jess couldn't remember its name. The bowl was filled with a rainbow assortment of pills, which Chloe began sorting by color into little baggies.

Jess took off her sunglasses and sat in the dining chair. Chloe looked up from her bowl. Her eyes widened at Jess's scar.

"Shit," she said. "Izzy did that to you?"

Chloe lifted a thin joint from an ashtray. She lit it with a kitchen match and took a hit, watching Jess through the smoke.

"You two have been friends for a long time," Jess said.

"You've obviously talked to Vince."

"He's worried."

"And you're worried, too? After what she did to you? That's a serious guilt trip you're on." Chloe waved some of the smoke from her face, looked back down at her work.

"Why didn't you go any farther than Vegas?"

"We ran out of money."

"But Isabella went on," Jess said. "Alone."

"Not alone. She made a friend."

"Who?"

"A waitress at one of the casinos. She brought us drinks and we tipped her until we didn't have anything left. The drinks kept coming, though. I thought maybe she was into me, like it was some sort of come-on. But then Izzy had her breakdown and it was obvious who the waitress was interested in."

Jess heard noises from another room—buzzing, muffled voices, a TV or radio. Chloe followed Jess's gaze, looking down a hallway that disappeared back into the house.

"My roommate," Chloe said.

Jess thought of Vince, down in the car. She wondered how loudly she would have to yell for him to hear.

"We lost all our money," Chloe said, "and it really hit her, that this was as far as we were going to get—five hours from L.A. We weren't going to make the break we'd always talked about. And maybe she realized that I probably never wanted to make the break in the first place. It was just a game to me, I guess. A fantasy. But Izzy fell apart. It was like all the glass inside her broke. That was when the waitress stepped in."

"Do you remember her name?"

"Are you kidding? They're all the same—the casinos, the waitresses."

Chloe reached to the ashtray, stubbing out her joint. Something caught her eye. She blew the ashtray clear and held it up for Jess to see. *The Tahitian Hotel & Casino* was imprinted in the tin.

"This was the place," Chloe said. "I took this on my way out."

Jess saw movement at the edges of her vision, what she thought was another empty shadow, but when she turned she found a man standing in the hallway. He was tall and bony, bare-chested. His eyes swept the room, then Jess, edgy and suspicious.

"Everything cool?" he said.

Chloe smiled and nodded to Jess. "An old acting friend," she said. "She played my mom in an *Afterschool Special*."

The man scratched his neck, looking at Chloe, then Jess. Dark purple marks covered his chest, radiating out from his heart, a starburst of broken capillaries.

"Toss me one of those," he said. Chloe picked up a baggie of blues and underhanded it across the room. The man caught the baggie, gave Jess another bald appraisal, then turned back down the hall.

Chloe looked at the ashtray and lowered her voice. "I left the casino with a guy I met. I didn't want to deal with Izzy. She was so upset, making it seem like it was my fault."

"And this waitress stayed with her?"

Chloe began picking pills from the bowl again, little octagons, butter yellow.

"I went back to the casino the next day, but Izzy wasn't there. Neither was the waitress. I waited, but they didn't show." Chloe frowned. "I shouldn't have left her. But that's easy to say now, right?"

Jess watched Chloe's face, the first admission of regret complicating her features. She nodded to Jess, her scar.

"She would never have done something like that before whatever happened in the desert."

"Chloe." The man's voice called out from the other room.

Chloe looked to the hallway, then back to Jess.

"You should go," she said.

17

MARTHA AND ISABELLA

SUMMER 1977

The room seemed to expand and contract, maybe due to the day's heat or the relative coolness of the evening. Like a body breathing, Martha thought. The light and absence of light made rooms within the room. At times the others disappeared within those shadowy folds, only to reemerge hours later in a new window of light.

She was terrified of Tanner but unsure whether her fear was of him or the things he said, his voice like the answer to the question at the center of her body. Whenever she imagined grabbing Izzy and running from the room, Tanner spoke again, and Martha realized they needed to stay.

Misty was right. Martha could exist in two places at the same time. Here in this stifling room, and in the space that opened when Izzy saw the new sun. Watching Izzy staggering, arms raised toward her vision, Martha felt Misty in that opening, waiting on the other side.

"Someone's coming."

Danny stood in the doorway, looking down the path in the last of the sunset, the fading orange outside world. Tanner joined him, the two men shoulder to shoulder.

Izzy watched, sitting with her back against the far wall. Two figures approached on the path. From their size and the heavy swagger of their walk she could tell they were men. As they got closer she saw that they were about her age, college boys, maybe, handsome in a soap-commercial way. A little scuffed now from the walk, their faces streaked with dirt and sweat, their hair matted from the heat. Both were humped with large backpacks like turtle shells. One wore an Oklahoma State T-shirt, the other a grimy white tank top.

Tank Top smiled at Danny and Tanner, raising his hand in a weary greeting. His arms and chest were sunburned lobster red. Izzy hadn't considered that others might arrive at the room. It felt like an intrusion. Anyone else entering might pierce the skin of what was happening, popping it like a bubble.

"So this is the place," Tank Top called out. "We heard there was something new on the trail."

Oklahoma State shrugged off his backpack. Tank Top guzzled from a canteen. Tanner and Danny stayed in the doorway. The woman in the corner lifted her camera but Ernst told her to put it away. She ignored him. Film began to whir.

"Holy shit," Tank Top said, seeing Tanner up close for the first time. Then: "Sorry, man. You must get that a lot, right?" He stepped toward the door, still smiling.

"You have to go around," Tanner said. "Or back the way you came."

"What? Why?"

"This place isn't open to you."

"What are you talking about?" Tank Top looked into the room. "What's going on in there?"

"You heard him." Danny's voice was hard with threat. "Go around or turn around."

Oklahoma State unzipped his backpack and reached in. Danny said, "Stop," and he stopped, one hand deep in the bag.

Tank Top was still looking into the room: at the woman filming, then Ernst, then Martha and Izzy sitting against the wall.

"Are you okay in there?"

He was speaking to Izzy. She wanted to scream at him. She wanted to tear at his big idiot face, his accusing eyes.

He stepped forward and Danny shoved him back. Tank Top stumbled and fell on his backside in the dirt. Oklahoma State pulled a pocketknife from his backpack, holding it out awkwardly. Danny grabbed his wrist, twisted, clubbed him in the side of the head with a grapefruit-size fist. Oklahoma State let out a groan and fell. Danny moved toward Tank Top, who scrambled in the dirt. *Get away from me get the fuck away from me.* Danny kicked his chest and back, his head. Oklahoma State rolled on the ground, ears between his elbows, moaning.

"Stop," Ernst said. "Make him stop."

Tanner turned to face the room.

Izzy felt overrun with rage. She wanted to be out there with Danny, kicking, driving the men away.

"Do you want him to stop?" Tanner asked her.

Izzy shook her head.

"Not until they're gone," she said.

"We're leaving," Ernst said.

"Please keep your voice—"

"We're not staying here. This is crazy."

Ernst grabbed his girlfriend's rucksack, shoving her gear inside. She pulled it back, holding the bag and her camera to her chest. A small box of film fell to the floor.

"You want to stay?" he asked, incredulous. "They just beat the shit out of a guy."

"It got out of hand," she said. "They were protecting—"

"What are they protecting?" Ernst turned to Izzy, his face wrenched with fear and disgust. "This has gone way too far."

The two college boys were gone. Tank Top had finally got to his feet and dragged Oklahoma State up and they ran back the way they came. An awkward, embarrassing flight. Izzy hated them but she also knew that feeling, trying to run from shame. They would run forever. She imagined them still running years from now in the scorched landscape the new sun would leave behind. Like figures from a parable, a pair of bad examples.

Danny stalked the outside perimeter, kicking at the low mounds of dirt, slowly defusing, as if he wouldn't come back inside until all his anger was spent.

Martha sat beside Izzy. When the boys first ran off she said, maybe to herself, *Why did I think that?* Izzy asked her what she was thinking, and Martha said, *That I wished Danny had killed them.* Her voice was pained and thin.

"Just a little while longer," the girlfriend said.

"No." Ernst grabbed the bag from her again, then the camera, then one of the last plastic jugs from beside the bench.

"We're taking some water," he said to Tanner, who watched from the doorway.

"Take it all," Tanner said.

Izzy wanted to call out, joining in. *Yes, take it all. We don't need it anymore.*

"Let's go," Ernst said.

His girlfriend looked around the room, unable to decide what to do. Izzy wanted to spit in her face. Those two never should have been inside in the first place. Impurities. Doubters. They kept the sun from moving through.

"*Go!*" Izzy shouted. Beside her, Martha's body shuddered from the violence of the sound.

The woman followed Ernst to the door. Tanner stepped aside to let them pass. Ernst looked at him and shook his head.

"You're all fucking crazy," he said.

Tanner smiled, boyishly pleased, like he had just won a game.

Through the openings in the walls, Izzy saw Danny passing back and forth in the gray twilight, still stalking the edge of the path. Martha said, "I'm thinking it again." It sounded like she was going to cry. "Please don't hurt them," she said, her voice too small for Danny to hear. They were just words to counteract the words in her head. Izzy understood. She took Martha's hand. Ernst and his girlfriend started off down the path.

Martha knew now that she had made a mistake. She had been wrong about Tanner; or she had been right and hadn't trusted her instincts. They were trapped now with these two men. She wanted to yell for help, but there was no one to hear. Those two college boys had been driven off; the young couple was gone. She should have left with them, dragging Isabella along like Ernst had dragged his girlfriend. But every time that thought entered her head, Tanner turned on her, his eyes bolting her to the wall.

She whispered her sister's name in the dark, as she once had when they were girls, two beds in the same room. She waited for an answer, a lifeline, Misty's hushed voice in the night.

"Everything all right in there?"

An old man's voice, gray and twangy, called up the next morning from the southern approach, the direction of that abandoned army base.

"Some boys came by," the old man said, his voice closer now. "Told me there was trouble up here."

Danny moved to the door, grabbing the handle. When the old man pulled, Danny pulled back. Just the thinnest sliver of light in the doorway and then it shut tight again.

"All right now, open up."

Dull thuds of a fist on the door.

"This is my property."

Bootsteps in the dirt, the dry crunch of pebbles outside the room. Izzy and Martha sat under the western opening, Tanner under the southern. The old man appeared in the opening just above Tanner, peering. Under a battered rancher's hat his face was furrowed, a farmer's field in a lifetime of drought. Bushy white eyebrows, pinprick pupils. Izzy wondered what he saw. Just the darkness of the room, maybe Danny's broad back at the door.

"Hey," the rancher said, the kind of call into nothingness that sounded as if it should echo. He couldn't see a thing.

"I can get my rifle," he said.

"I'm sure you already have your rifle." Tanner's voice came from just below the rancher's face. The man stepped back, spooked.

Tanner said, "You don't want to see what we have."

The rancher's face receded, small and brown in the morning sun. "The woman who built this thing called the sheriff," he called back. "You should move on before he gets here."

Tanner stood, looking out the southern opening, watching the man shrink into the distance. Then he turned to Danny and said, "Bar the door."

The police arrived at nightfall. *Sheriff's deputies*, a voice called out. Flashlight beams played through the openings, garish yellow streaks in the dark room.

"Stay back," Tanner called.

"We're back," the deputy said. "Why don't you come out so we can talk?"

This was the voice Martha was waiting for. She crawled close to Izzy and whispered, "Let's go, let's tell them we need help."

Izzy set a finger on Martha's lips, keeping her silent.

"It's okay," Izzy said. "We're almost there."

How many days had it been? How many nights? Izzy passed in and out of a shallow sleep and woke in a panic that the police had broken in. But Tanner and Danny were always there, keeping watch.

Danny tore the bench from the concrete and used it to force the door closed. The food was gone, the water almost gone. There was a bucket in the corner that they were using for a bathroom but even that stopped hours ago. Another inessential stripped away.

She was no longer hungry, but she was thirsty in a way that exposed the obscene insufficiency of the word. It felt like her body was made of sand. When she slept she dreamed of water on her face, in her mouth.

Each afternoon the new sun appeared and moved closer but she couldn't quite pull it through.

Izzy heard little squawks from the police radios back at the base, car doors opening and closing, a helicopter circling overhead. They're trying to break us, she thought.

A man spoke through a megaphone and Tanner told them to ignore it. "They're trying to break us," Tanner said, and Izzy heard the repetition of her own thought and knew it to be true. She felt such hatred for the man and his megaphone. She wanted to crawl out through an opening and walk down to the line of police cars and bash the man like Danny had bashed Oklahoma State, using the megaphone like a giant fist.

"If you let the women go," the man with the megaphone called, "we can all take a breath."

"Leave us alone!" Izzy yelled back, standing and shaking, strong again, her rage like an earthquake.

The air around them pumped in and out suddenly, as if in concussive response, the deafening chop of the helicopter's blades right overhead, filling the room's openings with dust, roaring past before returning to its original height.

They gagged and wretched and coughed, and when Izzy could breathe she screamed at them again, dust in her eyes and mouth, the copter's throb still racking her chest.

The air shuddered, folding back. It had heard her. It was here, finally. The room filled with light. Izzy raised her arms, ready to finally burn free.

Martha heard the loud metallic *clank* of something slamming against the outside wall. There was a loud hiss and the air twisted with an acidic burn. It felt like she'd taken a face full of pepper. She clawed at her eyes, shouted for the police: *Help us!*

Another shot clanked against the outside wall. More gas filled the room. Someone outside yelled and the room flooded white. Martha was blind: she could only hear Danny shouting, Izzy shouting, the men outside shouting, *Move move move.*

The door burst in. Izzy felt Danny rush by, as if sucked into the vacuum of that opening. A man shouted, *Get down, get down,* and then there were gunshots. Izzy had never heard real gunshots before, the fast chain of tight explosions. With each blast a part of Danny's chest burst open, spurting blood. Her hearing dropped away. In the silence, she reached for Danny, but then he collapsed, hitting the ground beside her, and in the moment of impact the sun flared out, leaving the room strangled with smoke, men shouting, Martha screaming, Danny lying motionless in the doorway, Tanner with his hands raised to the police saying, *Thank God you're here.*

The man on the megaphone barked, *Kneel kneel kneel.* It all rushed back now, everything she thought she'd let go: shame, fear, rage. Two men grabbed her. She kicked and bit and thrashed. Martha reached for her but was pulled through the door. Izzy screamed again, the muscles in her throat tearing, her voice giving out, dragging her fingertips across the wall, leaving skin as she was wrenched away from the room.

From *Light + Space*

(1977; 16mm film, sound; 82 minutes;
Laura Lehrer, dir.; unreleased)

What did you think when you saw the news? The standoff, the
police siege—
- I didn't.

Jess is still standing behind her chair, her right hand up at her left
shoulder, kneading a muscle. She looks uncomfortable in her body, out
of alignment.

- You didn't have a reaction?
- I didn't watch the news.
- You didn't—
- I couldn't. I tried, but—
- You just ignored what was happening?
- My brother watched.
- Your brother?
- We talked on the phone those nights. He watched it all.

- So you didn't have to?
- You don't understand.
- Then explain.

18

JESS

SUMMER 1979

She drove up through the Cahuenga Pass and into North Hollywood, along the broad boulevards lined with burger joints and gas stations, billboards at every intersection, *Abogados de Accidentes* and *Solarcaine*; *Cheap Trick Coming to the Fabulous Forum*. The afternoon was hot and tinder-dry. On the valley's far side, plumes of gray smoke rose from the mountain peaks as if from a row of chimneys. The radio news said the fires were getting worse.

Zack's phone number was still out of service. They'd fought about this the last time they spoke—his tendency to disappear for weeks at a time, to a convention or on a film-searching expedition, or off the map entirely, when he disconnected his phone and refused to answer his apartment buzzer. She told him to call when he was going away so she wouldn't think he was being held in a dark basement by the FBI, and sometimes he did, humoring her, but more often he didn't. Then it was Jess's turn to go silent, fed up with her one-way effort in the relationship. But before too long he'd do something thoughtful, appearing on her birthday with a supermarket cake or inviting her to a screening in town. She'd cave and they'd restart the cycle. It frustrated her to no end but she couldn't break loose. She was still his little sister.

He was twitchy and nervous even before their parents' accident, but his work had made it worse. She was always surprised when she went to one of those screenings—a lost classic at the Egyptian Theatre or a private showing at a client's house in the hills—and saw him interacting with other people. In the right mood he could be charming, and all those hours watching movies had made him a good storyteller.

Sometimes he came to one of her pieces, but they never talked about the work. They talked about mechanics: materials she used, the building process. They skated along the edges. She had no idea how he felt about any of it. She was afraid to ask, worried that his judgment would shut her down. It shouldn't have mattered, but it did, stirring up guilt she had never exorcized. Zack stopped drawing after their parents' death, but for Jess it was an opening. He had been the artist, then she took his place.

The gallery attack seemed to confirm his worst fears—a late-night assault from out of the blue. He grew even more secluded. Jess wanted to think Zack was internalizing his concern for her because he didn't know how to show it, but she didn't know if that was true. Maybe he was being selfish, neglecting her pain in favor of his own paranoia. Either way, it suited her. He didn't ask when she was going to get over her fear and rejoin the world. He already knew the answer—part of her never would. Once or twice a week they talked on the phone deep into the night. Usually, they watched movies this way. One of them called when they found something on channel 2 or 11, and they watched and commented, Zack giving movie history context and Jess marveling at or deriding the use of light and space. Those nights, sitting in front of her TV with the phone cord stretched out from the kitchen, her brother's voice in her ear, Jess felt, at least for a little while, safe.

His building was a long stucco two-story that butted up against the back end of a second-run theater. The apartment was cheap, owing to the dicey neighborhood. Jess was sure he could afford better—some of the films he sold went for high prices—but the seediness of the location suited Zack's vision of himself as a hunted man, a character from his beloved crime pictures.

She couldn't remember if the intercom worked. Pressing the button, she squinted up to Zack's window. Nothing but a bright white rectangle, reflecting the day. Then the speaker cleared its throat and she heard Zack, slightly distorted, a movie robot's tin-can voice.

"Yeah?"

"It's me."

"What?"

"It's your sister, Zack, open the door."

A pause, then a loud buzz and the *clank* of the dead bolt falling away. Jess pushed the door open and started up the staircase. She carried Ruth's Beethoven sonatas under her arm, a peace offering after their last argument.

When she was halfway up Zack appeared on his landing, looking even more disheveled than usual. He wore a striped bowling shirt and clashing shorts, scratching the top of one socked foot with the toes of the other. He had put on weight. His face was fuller and his belly pushed against the seams of the fabric. He pulled at his goatee, a nervous habit indulged ever since he had been able to sprout facial hair. Jess always imagined that Zack thought the goatee made him look like a South American revolutionary or a French intellectual. He considered himself an amalgam of the two, minus the politics. His only ideology was cinema, but his faith was as deep and defiant as that of any true believer.

She was about to call up to him when the movie soundtrack boomed next door, filling the stairwell, a low throb Jess felt deep in her chest.

"Did you call?" He sounded put out that she had arrived unannounced.

"The number's dead," Jess said, reaching the step below the landing, catching her breath. Too many cigarettes, not enough exercise. "How are you?"

"Busy. In the middle of a few things."

"Can I come in?"

His face tensed. She was disrupting his routine. Jess thought of how good it once felt when he had included her in his plans and projects. Those Somerville summers on their front porch, drawing mazes for her to work through or asking her to hold a handful of pipe cleaners as he twisted them into a complex armature, branching like a spiderweb.

Zack was the artist, she had told Laura Lehrer years ago, and the filmmaker had asked, What were you?

She had been his apprentice, his shadow, and that had been enough for her, until it wasn't.

Jess took off her sunglasses. He looked at her scar and then quickly away. The physical proof of the attack usually made him even more uncomfortable around her.

His apartment was dark, shade-drawn, and smelled of sweat and dust and the vinegary tang of old celluloid. Metal film canisters sat in tight rows on shelves and stood in high stacks against the walls. The front room was large—actually the living room and a bedroom combined. Right after he moved in, Zack had knocked out a wall between the two, creating a space long enough to throw an image. A screen hung down at the far end, a dim white apparition in the dark.

Zack sat on a stool at a large butcher-block table covered with tools and metal parts. A half-dismantled projector stood open amid the disorder, lit by a single desk lamp. Holding a pair of needle-nose pliers, he leaned in to the body of the machine, carefully threading a wire behind gears.

Jess held up the records. "I was listening to these the other day and thought you might like them."

"I don't have a record player."

She turned to take in the surrounding hoard of machinery. "You're kidding. Then I'll take them back."

"No, it's fine. Leave them."

She set the records on a shelf full of cardboard Betamax boxes. Over the last few years, videotape had become an increasing part of Zack's business. He'd resisted at first—he'd told Jess many times that tape was a shitty substitute for film—but the ability to record TV programs won him over. Unsurprisingly, he'd become obsessive about it, taping late-night movies and cop shows along with hours of TV news.

The apartment rumbled a bit with the sound of the movie playing in the theater next door. Zack didn't seem to notice. Jess imagined that it was background to him now, a comforting wash of sound and vibration, the feel of movies all around him even when he wasn't watching.

"What are they showing?"

His eyes stayed on his work. "*The China Syndrome*. Have you seen it?"

"I haven't gone to the movies in a while."

"It's about a nuclear accident. Kind of like Three Mile Island. Lots of screaming and sirens."

"I was downtown the other night," she said. "They were showing *Border Incident*."

"The Million Dollar Theatre. That wasn't my print. They asked for it, but I told them they were crazy. Their projector's a fucking lawn mower."

She thought of his old room above Aunt Ruth's garage, the small gaggle of the professor's friends who came to watch movies. She wondered who Zack saw these days, if anyone came up here or if he was always alone.

She had rooms like this now. She held off for years but had finally suc-
cumbed. Instead of pulling him out, as Ruth had asked, Jess had followed
his path into isolation.

"I was hoping you could show me something," she said.

"I don't really have time for a movie."

"Not a movie. News footage."

"Of what?"

"*Zero Zone.*"

He leaned back from the projector but kept his eyes on the gears.

"I thought you didn't want to see that."

"I changed my mind."

"Why?"

"It's something I made," she said. "And people were hurt there. Someone was killed."

"That's not your fault."

"But I shouldn't have looked away."

Zack set his pliers on the table and looked up at her, finally. She wondered who he saw. Probably the same scared, haunted woman she had
seen in the mirror at the Mexican restaurant with Vince. The same terrified girl standing at the top of the staircase on the night of their parents'
accident.

"Do you still have it?" she said.

He made a face, a comically sheepish twist of his mouth. It was a ridiculous question. What had he ever thrown away?

The apartment's second bedroom was filled with more videotapes heaped
on shelves and stacked in unstable towers on the floor that looked like
stalagmites or pillars from some ancient ruin. Zack maneuvered his bulk
around them expertly. Each box was labeled in black marker with the jag-
ged, impatient handwriting that hadn't changed since he was a kid. *NYC*

Blackout, Unabomber, Death of Elvis. Jess sat on a small love seat while Zack scanned a shelf.

"Local or national?" he asked.

"Your choice."

Two TVs sat side by side on a dresser, each with a videocassette machine on top. Zack pulled a tape from the shelf and fed it into one of the machines, then switched on the TV below. The picture rolled in a liquid waver, fuzzy-edged and discolored, then settled into a local newscast. An anchorman with a perfect helmet of hair spoke to the camera. Over his left shoulder, a small rectangle showed another image, a still photo of *Zero Zone*. Jess's spare concrete room was a dark silhouette against a brilliant sunset.

The anchor said that a small group of hikers were inside this art installation, refusing to leave. Temperatures were expected to reach triple digits over the next few days, and the woman responsible for the room, Los Angeles artist Jess Shepard, had told the owner of the property to call the authorities.

Jess felt her chest joggle when the anchor said her name. For two years she'd believed that ignoring and denying kept her hidden, like a child who thinks she disappears when she covers her eyes. But of course she'd been a central fact of the story all along.

The rancher, Lincoln, appeared on-screen, a cigarette in his tight mouth, a microphone pushed toward his face. He was angry and concerned. He believed there were four people inside the room, though he couldn't be sure. Hippies or dropouts of some kind. The sheriff had had no luck talking with them and threatened to knock down the door. That was when one of the hippies, a man, said that they had a weapon inside, to be used if any violence was enacted upon them. That was how this man put it, Lincoln said. Those kinds of words, like out of the Bible.

A different newscaster was on-screen now, a high-haired blond woman speaking in grave tones. A negotiator had arrived from Santa Fe.

This was another night, another station. Zack had edited the footage together. There were no commercials, no other stories. Jess wondered how long he had worked on this tape, how many times he'd seen this footage. She remembered the nights of the standoff, alone in her dark apartment, on the phone with him while he watched his TVs. She hadn't wanted him to describe what was happening, but she'd needed him there, absorbing the awful news, just as he'd answered the phone on the night of their parents' accident, a bulwark against the full force of the disaster.

He never said much those nights. Jess just heard his breathing and the muffled voices of the newscasters, a few mechanical clicks in the background. Zack pressing buttons. Even then she knew he was recording.

There was a wide still shot of *Zero Zone* in a golden dusk, what Jess thought might be a photograph until there was the slightest movement, a bird crossing the top of the screen. The image held for a long time. Jess tried to imagine what was happening in the room, what Isabella saw or felt. She wondered if it was anything like what she had seen, that initial waver of light that seemed to speak to her grief for Alex, the inexplicable loss made physical. A vision that had led her to the impulsive and illogical act of building a room in the desert.

And then the footage jumped, the camera shaking. The cameraman was running. Police officers passed and charged ahead. There was a loud pop, a weapon fired, a cloud of gas rising just outside the room. Another pop, another cloud. Police shouting, *Move move move.* Spotlight beams appeared, finding the edges of the room, the dark openings in the walls. The cameraman stopped, but the police continued on, guns drawn, sprinting toward the distant room. Night was falling fast. Jess squinted at the screen. The police reached the door, shouting, weapons raised, and then they fired, quick loud shots, bright muzzle flashes leaving white stains on the video, smearing as the cameraman adjusted his angle. The police disappeared into the room. More shouting. The spotlights found them again, reemerging. Two police officers led a long-haired man out, his hands pulled behind his back. Then two more officers helping a woman. They all stepped over something as they came through the doorway. A body. The camera zoomed in, blurry, then back out. Another couple of officers now, struggling to get through the door, pulling someone, Isabella, screaming and kicking, thrashing to get free of their grip, her body twisted back toward the doorway.

Another cut. A succession of photographs on-screen. An older mug shot of a stocky young man, Danny Aguado, described as the leader of the group, killed by police during the raid. A second mug shot, the long-haired man, his face pebbled with growths or tumors. Tanner Helm, the newscaster said, an accomplice at first, then held hostage by Aguado, with the others. A photograph from a casino floor, a young woman with pretty, tired eyes: Martha Reed, a Las Vegas cocktail waitress. There was another hostage, the newscaster said, who they would not identify because of her age. A runaway who had come to the room with Miss Reed.

The screen went black. Zack reached down and switched off the TV.

"I need a minute," Jess said.

"Okay."

"Jesus Christ."

"Yeah."

She wanted a drink. She wanted a cigarette but knew she couldn't smoke in Zack's apartment. Celluloid was highly flammable. She often worried about him in here, a stray spark from one of his machines setting the rooms ablaze.

Jess said, "Isabella Serrano is missing."

"I thought she was in jail."

"She wasn't in jail, Zack. She was sixteen when this happened."

"Whatever they call it. Juvenile detention."

"Her mother thinks she's trying to reconnect with these people."

"What are you going to do?"

Just a few days ago, Jess had called Zack hoping for an answer to this question. Expert advice on how to disappear. Now, she took a deep breath and said, "I'm trying to find her."

"What? Why?"

"Because she needs help."

"Let her parents help. Or the police. She tried to kill you."

"No, she didn't."

"Then what the fuck was she doing?"

Jess looked back at the blank screen, feeling the ghost of the last images, the police tearing Isabella from the room.

"I don't know. I don't think she knew. But I can't leave her out there again."

From *Light + Space*

(1977; 16mm film, sound; 82 minutes;
Laura Lehrer, dir.; unreleased)

Jess stands behind the chair. She appears wounded, retreating inward, her face set against further harm.

- I don't have anything more to say.

Laura's voice grows steadily, rising up each step of accusation.

- You created that room. You left it open for interpretation. Those people locked themselves inside. Did you ever think about what they were going through? A man was killed in there—

Jess turns away. She looks off-frame, her chest rising and falling with great effort. She can't get enough air.

- All that pain in a place you made, and you couldn't watch?

- We need to stop here.

- We're not finished.

Jess looks back toward the camera, ignoring the lens, her eyes fixed on Laura.

- Turn it off.

- Ms. Shepard, I want you to—
- *Turn it off.*
Her shout fills the studio, a sudden blast in the white room.
The frame goes dark.

19

ISABELLA

SUMMER 1977

The hospital was noisy and bright, smelled of metal and bleach. They pumped Izzy full of fluids and calories and antibiotics; a doctor conducted a physical. Izzy stood naked in front of the man but really she was back in the room, that glorious moment, leaving her body, moving toward the new sun.

When the doctor left, the police came in, a sheriff's deputy in uniform and a detective in a brown suit, a self-assured man with a neatly trimmed mustache. Izzy sat on the edge of the bed. She didn't want to get under the covers like a patient. She wouldn't allow them to make her feel there was something wrong with her.

She refused to talk to the police. This didn't seem to bother them. The detective said that Tanner had already told the whole story—how Danny convinced them all to stay in the room with the promise of everlasting life. Tanner said he had gone along with it for a while but changed his mind after Danny attacked the college boys. Then Danny refused to let any of them leave.

She didn't have to be afraid of Tanner anymore, the detective said. Even though he regretted his part in all of this, he'd still spend a couple of years in prison.

The desert room was some kind of art installation. The artist, a woman named Jess Shepard, was the one who called the sheriff in the first place. If it wasn't for her, the deputy said, who knows what would have happened to you.

Both cops called her Miss Serrano. Martha had given them Izzy's name. Breaking her silence, Izzy asked if she could see Martha. The detective told her that wasn't possible. Martha had been taken to a different hospital. They were overwhelmed with the press attention. You're like movie stars, he said.

Finally the police left, joining the noise outside her room, doctors and nurses walking up and down the hallway, their footfalls heavy and urgent. With each thump Izzy saw Danny collapse in the room. She saw Tanner fall to his knees, welcoming the police. His lies filled Izzy with guilt and gratitude. He and Danny had sacrificed themselves to protect her.

Izzy's nurse was young and slight, with soft eyes and long hair twisted into a bun. She seemed uncomfortable, moving constantly, checking the IV bag, adjusting the bed, talking nonstop, as if worried to leave any opening for Izzy to speak.

They were in Dalhart, Texas, the nurse said, less than an hour from where Izzy was rescued. That was the word she used, *rescued*. There were reporters all over town, but Izzy shouldn't worry. She was a minor, so the police hadn't released her identity. Nobody knew who she was.

"But your parents are on their way," the nurse said. "When they get here, I'll send them right in."

The nurse heard her name summoned by the PA in the hall and let herself out with obvious relief.

A neatly folded pile of clothes sat on the chair in the corner. Hand-me-downs from the hospital thrift shop, the nurse had said, but clean and probably close in size. Izzy pulled the IV from her arm, took off her paper gown, and got dressed. A pair of Lee jeans soft at the knees, a baggy yellow blouse with a beaded spiral on the front. Her wallet was there, too, with what was left of Martha's cash. Back in Vegas Martha had asked Izzy to carry the money, joking that even on an empty desert trail she'd find a way to spend it.

Izzy opened the door and slipped out into the hall. From a speaker in the ceiling, the PA voice called for a Dr. Michaels to report to Radiology. Another nurse came out of a room a few doors down and approached, walking briskly. Izzy remembered that smile she had perfected years ago, shopping with her mother. She stretched her face into that smile, feeling herself disappear as the nurse's eyes ran over her quickly, sliding past. The nurse continued on down the hall.

Izzy walked toward the elevators. She pressed the button, pressed it again, impatient, sure that at any moment someone would shout her name. Two women huddled together by the window at the other end of the hall. One was making loud, quick wheezing noises, her body jerking with the wild reflex. Izzy couldn't tell if she was laughing or crying. The elevator dinged and the doors opened. Two men were already inside. They looked like businessmen. One man's suit was light, the other charcoal gray. The man in the light suit held a cowboy hat down by his belt buckle; his wide forehead was marked with a red band where the hat had pressed into his skin. Izzy thought of Vince for a moment, a million miles away. The thought felt out of place in her head, like it belonged to someone else. She walked into the elevator and stood between the two men, turning to face the closing doors. The man on her right cleared his throat, as if he needed to make some kind of noise to break or claim the silence. Izzy looked at their reflections in the metal doors, wavy abstractions, a tall tan blob and a tall gray blob and a small yellow blob between them. The seam where the doors met split her right down the middle.

Out on the first floor, she walked past the thrift store, the gift shop, toward the front doors, where two cops stood outside, smoking. She didn't hesitate, only turned her head away when she pushed through, back into the welcoming noontime heat after the hours in this air-conditioned icebox. One of the cops said, "Hey," and Izzy picked up her pace, ready to run, but then the other cop whistled, a catcall directed at her backside, so she continued through the parking lot, across the road into town.

The canister was a strange machine, strange thought, strange hope. Izzy saw it through a pawnshop window, half hidden behind the guns and guitars—a metal canister like the ones in the hospital alongside the old people in wheelchairs, a big smooth silver bullet. The strange hope was that she could bring the canister back to the room and open its top and let the machine breathe in the air of that place. Then maybe that air could be moved somewhere else, the way blouses and skirts could be moved in and out of the stores back home.

The man working in the shop showed her how it worked. There was a wand with a trigger that sprayed whatever was inside. "They're used for pest control," he said, "though I know some folks use them to kill weeds in their lawn."

A row of old mirrored beer signs hung on the wall behind the counter. Izzy watched a news van's reflection roll by from one to the next, through *Stroh's Spoken Here* to *Old Style* to *Miller Genuine Draft*. She felt the van moving on the street behind her, searching. *Eyewitness 5*, and then another right behind the first: *Newswatch 13*. She reminded herself that they didn't know her name or what she looked like. Not yet. But as soon as the police found her empty hospital room they would be after her again, and her parents were coming soon, if they weren't here already.

"So what do you have?" the man asked, tapping the canister with a fingernail. "Pests or weeds?"

Outside, a pickup truck with mismatched green-and-blue doors was turning around in the pawnshop's parking lot. Crossing the lot with the canister, Izzy stuck out her thumb and the truck pulled over. The driver was an old man with a white beard and curlicued eyebrows and for a second Izzy worried it was the rancher who had said he owned the room. But this man's voice was different, whispery, as if it had been damaged or worn down. The man asked where she was headed. Izzy said that her father had been in the army and she was looking for the base where he had been stationed. The man said there had just been a shitload of trouble out there. Izzy said she didn't know about any trouble. She wasn't from around here.

They drove through the late afternoon, the sky rusting atop the mountains. As they approached the base, Izzy worried they would encounter the rancher, the police, reporters snapping pictures. But the base was empty, just some husks of old buildings kneeling on dusty streets. It looked like a movie set, more the idea of a place than a place itself. She got out of the pickup, lugging the canister. With every step she expected to see the room appear on the horizon, but there was nothing, only flat ground stretching to the mountain line. Panicked, she stopped and turned, looking out everywhere. Then she saw the trail, its long dark line cutting the monotony of the landscape.

Izzy ran along the trail, the dirt rutted with tire- and bootprints. She could still taste the acidic breath of tear gas in the air. She heard the police shooting, saw Danny falling, the new sun folding back in on itself. They had been so close. Another few seconds and, she was sure, they would have passed through.

The fence was at least fifteen feet high. Large plastic signs hung on the chain-link: *No Trespassing* and *Violators Will Be Shot.* Izzy looked to the room beyond, surrounded by the fence, a prisoner in a cage. She tried to climb but couldn't while carrying the canister. She scraped her fingers into the dirt, digging like a dog, but the ground wouldn't give. She wanted to cry. She wanted to bash her head in with the canister. She could lie down and die here, fading, dust to dust.

Then, quickly, a flash in the air. That familiar glint. Could have been a trick, or her imagination. But no—it was there, she'd seen it. She stood and unscrewed the top of the canister, holding it over her head, willing that light back into her arms.

Back outside the base Izzy hitched again, this time with a lady trucker who chain-smoked Winston Longs and talked nonstop about Jesus. Speeding west along the interstate, she asked if Izzy had found her own personal savior. Izzy said yes.

At a motel near the Arizona border she paid for a room with a little of Martha's cash and locked herself inside. The TV showed spotlit film of the siege, police storming the room in the tear-gas haze, then a mug shot of Tanner, old pictures of Martha and Danny. A black silhouette of a girl's head appeared next, a flat, featureless shadow. The third hostage, the newscaster said, a minor from the Los Angeles area. Then a picture of Jess Shepard working in her studio in L.A., standing over a large table covered with papers and what looked like plaster models of rooms. The newscaster said the artist wasn't speaking to the press.

Izzy unplugged the TV and turned its face to the wall. She sprayed a puff of air from the canister and knelt on the floor, eyes open, waiting.

Nothing came.

She slept and woke, drifting in and out, unsure from one moment to the next which side of the phase she was on. She dreamed of the desert and the hot red room, of Tanner's voice and Danny falling, of Jess Shepard in her studio. She tried other motel rooms, hitchhiking to other towns, asking only women for rides; she didn't trust the men. Using the rest of Martha's money, six dollars a night, eight dollars a night, she sprayed, she knelt, she waited, but the air was dead. She was stuck here, in this body. The realization wrapped around her, hands smothering.

In a motel in Needles she rose from her knees and turned the TV back to face the room. The date the newscaster gave didn't make any sense. A month since the attack: *Looking back at the events that shaped the summer.* Time was meaningless now, like everything else. They showed the police firing into the doorway, Tanner's mug shot, Danny's body covered by a sheet. Then the picture of Jess Shepard standing over her plaster models, so smug and confident, looking down on her creation.

A warm, muggy night in Santa Monica. Izzy could feel the ocean a few blocks away, out there in the darkness. A heavy presence, like a hand on the small of her back, pushing her forward.

She crossed the street toward the glow of the gallery windows. She forced herself through the crowd, past the photographers and young leather-jacketed leeches and rich old ghouls with their death smiles and mine-shaft eyes. Moving toward the two figures standing together, their backs against the wall.

Jess Shepard looked like her photo, confident and proud, a big smile in the bright lights. Izzy stared at that smile and felt nothing but rage. She stepped forward, meeting the artist's eyes. Jess Shepard looked at Izzy like Izzy didn't make any sense, like she didn't belong in that place, and then her smile dropped away. A flicker of understanding. Izzy pointed the wand.

She told the artist why she was here. She intended her voice to be a shout heard by everyone in the gallery but instead the sound only wheezed out, an airless rasp.

You took this from us. I'm giving it back.

She pulled the trigger. A woman in the crowd screamed. Jess Shepard stumbled from the force of the dead desert air. All of Izzy's rage pushed down to the sharp tip of the wand. She swung it at the face holding that big false smile. The artist fell to the ground. Izzy lifted the canister over her head. She wanted to bash Jess Shepard like poor Danny bashed that college boy, like she should have bashed her own head outside the fenced room.

Jess Shepard looked up, a terrible slash marking her cheek, blood and torn skin. Izzy hesitated; she couldn't believe what she'd done. This woman's face. Her anger faltered, falling from her hands. She dropped the canister.

More shouts and screams from the other side of the gallery. Someone knocked her to the ground, a security guard, his body falling onto hers as she hit the floor. Izzy's face was just a foot from Jess Shepard's face. Jess's confidence was gone. It was a mask; Izzy saw this now. Underneath, Jess Shepard was cracking, coming apart. Izzy knew that look. She understood where it came from. A secret shame revealed.

The security guard pulled her hands behind her back, then twisted Izzy's head the other way to face the blank white wall.

LIGHT AND SPACE

20

JESS

SUMMER 1979

In her kitchen, Jess called Information in Las Vegas and asked the operator if she had an address for Martha Reed, but there was no listing by that name. She called the Tahitian, but the woman who answered told Jess the casino never gave out information on its employees. "We get a lot of creeps asking after the girls," she said.

Jess hung up the phone. She was aware of her hypocrisy, searching for a woman who might not want to be found. Jess paid the answering service six dollars a month to avoid calls just like the ones she was making. But Martha was the only real lead.

She and Vince would have to go to Vegas. If they did find Martha, they would need to be careful. Jess knew their sudden arrival might feel like an ambush.

She called Deidre to get her messages: Gabe checking in about Jess's meeting with Madeline Serrano, Anton Stendahl suggesting they consider starting a project together. Then Deidre said she had a message from Zack Shepard. His name sounded so strange in Deidre's voice. Zack had never left a message with the service. He didn't like anyone writing down what he said.

"He was very curt," Deidre said. She sounded a little put off. "No hello, no goodbye. Just, *Tell my sister I found something.*"

"After we watched the news here, I asked around a little," Zack said. "I thought somebody might have more footage."

Jess stood with her back to the wall Zack's apartment shared with the movie theater. She felt the low shiver of the soundtrack's deeper registers, what sounded like city traffic, heavy vehicles crossing uneven pavement.

"I told someone your story," Zack said. "A guy who collects art film, avant-garde, experimental stuff. He knew who you were, he'd heard about *Zero Zone.* He said there was another guy I should talk to."

Zack sat on the stool by his worktable. He held a small screwdriver and turned it in his hands as he spoke.

"This other guy," he said, hesitating, "is someone I've only dealt with a couple of times. And only on the phone, never in person. He's pretty specific in his tastes. Old stag shorts, pornography. Some darker stuff. He told me he'd seen a film."

"A film."

"A film that was shot inside *Zero Zone.*"

The words clanged in Jess's ears, meaningless for a second.

"How is that possible?"

"I don't know if it is," Zack said. "He could be full of shit. Some of these guys just like to talk."

"But you think he's telling the truth."

"I don't know."

"That's not what you said in the message. You said you found something."

Zack turned the screwdriver. He didn't want to continue. Jess didn't know if he was embarrassed about giving her this glimpse into the shadier corners of his world or of he was trying to protect her. Maybe both. But she couldn't let him back away.

"Zack, tell me."

"He said he saw this film once, after-hours at a gallery downtown, but a few minutes in, the director stopped the screening. Just switched off the projector and turned on the lights. This client thought it was some kind of performance, or maybe a way to increase demand for the print. He made an offer, a couple of offers, but it wasn't for sale."

A siren rushed by in the movie behind her. Jess felt it roll across her lower back.

"He couldn't really describe it," Zack said. "He told me he'd seen a lot over the years, but this was something else."

A large, dark form moved into the edge of Jess's vision. She knew better but still turned, chasing shadows, the form breaking into a flurry of dark spots, a snowstorm in photonegative.

She said, "You think he's telling the truth."

"I don't know. But he gave me a name."

"Whose name?"

"The director." Zack set his screwdriver back on the table. "The woman who made the film."

21

MARTHA

SUMMER 1979

J ust outside of Twentynine Palms, she rented a single-wide at the end of a long gravel road. The woman who owned the trailer offered to cut the rent in half if Martha fixed the place up. The rooms were stale and empty, the siding faded colorless from years of constant sun. But Martha saw a blank canvas there, a chance to start fresh.

She had spent the last year and a half back in Vegas, desperate to re-create her life before the room. Denying what had happened out in the desert seemed like the only way to survive it. She returned to her apartment, even begged for her old job, enduring breathless questions from the other waitresses and the floor manager's Patty Hearst jokes. When she read the news that Izzy had attacked the artist who created the room, Martha pushed it to a far corner of her mind, trying to ignore the guilt and fear she felt in equal measure. She needed to return to her old life, haunted but safe, following Misty's ghost around town.

Except Misty was no longer there. Martha had trailed her sister's memory into *Zero Zone*, but she came out alone. She no longer saw Misty at traffic lights, outside the church, in the grocery store. She didn't know if she felt abandoned or free. Maybe somewhere in between. But nothing was keeping her in Vegas, so she sold just about everything she owned and played a game she and Misty loved as girls: close your eyes and point to a spot on the map, letting chance and fate decide where you'll start a new life. When Martha opened her eyes, her finger pointed to Twentynine Palms.

It was a drowsy desert town, with a short main drag of shops and diners and bars, then a loose orbit of houses and trailers scattered a few miles in every direction. A mountain range stood in the distance, the low peaks leaning like crooked bicuspids. The country around Martha's trailer was flat and rugged, strewn with scrub brush and broken boulders. The closest neighbor was a quarter mile down the road. There were very few signs of other life, just the sharp cries of hawks circling high overhead, the plaintive howls of coyotes in the night. It seemed like an Old Testament landscape: stark, ancient, indifferent. She felt suitably small here, hidden.

She cut her hair to her chin, dyed it from brown to black. She got a job waitressing at a honky-tonk on the main road, a dark, wood-paneled bar with local acts on weekends and Waylon Jennings on the jukebox. At the thrift store in town she bought a bed, a wicker love seat for the living room, a Formica-topped table for the kitchen. She opened all the trailer's windows to air the rooms, scrubbed the linoleum with Spic and

Span, bleached the bathroom. With her Polaroid she took pictures of the sage growing along the edge of the trailer's dirt driveway and asked the man at the hardware store to mix paint to match, with the same breath of purple in the flat, soft gray. She bought rollers and brushes and a ladder, and spent the next week painting: slowly, gently, coaxing this home back to life.

She still had bad days, where she woke from a nightmare of the room, or of Izzy in a prison cell. They had both gone crazy. The room made them crazy or Tanner made them crazy. They carried their grief and need into the room and then those things came alive, ravenous animals, jaws snapping. On the worst of the bad days Martha felt her body covered with those bites. She stopped herself from checking for marks on her skin. That would be crazy.

In the gun shop across the road from the bar she bought a little .38 special, not much bigger than her hand. The man working the counter took her to a back-room shooting range and showed her how to load and aim and fire at a paper target. She put the gun in the drawer of her bed-side table. The man at the shop told her to keep all five chambers full. An unloaded gun is a paperweight, he said.

A straggly manzanita grew outside her kitchen window, and in the mornings while Martha drank her coffee a fat, happy hummingbird arrived to dip its beak into the little bell-shaped flowers. With some of her leftover paint, she brushed a small portrait of her new friend on the corner of the kitchen table. She wasn't much of an artist, the bird was only vaguely bird-shaped, but she got the color and movement right, the slash of pale purple across its throat, the blur of its wings working hard to stay in flight.

In the afternoons she left her car at the trailer and walked to work, though it reminded her of that other desert walk, the sun and heat and crunch of her shoes in the dirt. But she felt she needed to endure it, as a form of penance for what she had led Izzy into, and as a path forward, a way to move through the memory and return to this world.

The letter arrived with a small bundle of mail forwarded from Vegas. The corner of the envelope was blotched with an over-inked stamp of the return address, a youth correctional facility near Fresno. Martha's name and her old address were written below.

She didn't know what to do with it. Throwing the letter away felt like a violent act but opening the envelope seemed akin to some kind of self-harm.

She pictured Izzy in handcuffs, in a cell, manhandled by guards. Izzy in a gallery in Los Angeles, murder in her heart.

Martha didn't open the letter, or the letters that arrived every few weeks after. She kept them—she needed to keep some part of Izzy close—but she wouldn't allow herself to be pulled back.

One night she let one of the regulars drive her home from the bar. Sam was a phone company lineman, quite a bit older than Martha, a little rough around the edges, sad in a way she recognized. Missing someone beyond reach. He had a good sense of humor. He made wry jokes out of the corner of his mouth when she passed or leaned over him with a fresh Jack Daniel's. He kept his jokes clean and his hands to himself, even in her bed in the dark. She lifted his hands and placed them on her hips, her breasts. He tasted like whiskey and woodsmoke. She hadn't been with anyone in a long time. It was part of her life that slipped away with Misty's illness. But here he was, this sad, gentle, funny man, his hands cold on her skin, shaking a little. They were both new to this again.

Later, she woke to a noise from the kitchen. In the lunar light from the range hood she saw Sam sitting at the table in his undershorts, his belly hanging over the elastic in a single firm roll, a steaming coffee mug in his hands.

"Sorry," he said, nodding at the kettle. "I tried to grab it before it howled."

She sat and he poured her a cup. He said he had trouble sleeping. Too much to think about, work and old shit from way back that ran through his brain, repeating like a song he couldn't switch off. "You know what it's like," he said. It wasn't a question; it was an acknowledgment. Kindred spirits. His voice was even lower in the night, a smooth rumble Martha wanted to wrap around her shoulders to keep warm.

He set her mug down on the table, just below her hummingbird. When she first painted it, Martha saw the relentless beating of the bird's wings as inspiration to keep moving, staying ahead of a past that seemed intent on eating her alive. But maybe running was the problem. Running from Misty's death, from what had happened in the room. Running from Izzy, who wasn't to blame for any of it.

"I want to tell you something," she said to Sam. "And I'll understand if you want to run for the hills. But I've got to tell someone, and right now you're here and half-naked so it seems you have to listen."

Sam smiled. He leaned back and turned the burner beneath the kettle on, then nodded to Martha and looked at her, really looked at her.

She took a deep breath and began to tell her story.

Two weeks later she drove north and west, following one of Sam's maps, highways to small-town streets to back roads, then through the front gates, signing in at the guard shack, steering her hatchback into the vast, nearly empty parking lot. A solid-looking brick building stood at the far end, the same color as the parched farmland on the other side of the fence. Martha pulled into a spot and lit a cigarette and checked the time on the radio. She didn't know if she was supposed to go in or wait out here. Once, she'd heard that there were two kinds of people: those who waved and smiled and called out to someone they hadn't seen in a long time, and those who held back, shrinking from the emotional reunion. Martha always wished she was the first type, confident enough to be that vulnerable, but knew she was the second, too shy or afraid to let her feelings take over.

She was still trying to decide what to do when the building's front door opened and a young woman came out, carrying a plastic shopping bag, looking this way and that, bewildered, unsure. Martha raised her hand out the window, but the gesture wasn't enough, not even close. She got out of her car, waving, walking across the lot, then running, smiling, calling Izzy's name.

22

TANNER

WINTER AND SPRING 1979

Out in the prison yard, the guards told them not to look up. They were hundreds of miles from the path of totality, but still might go blind if they stared at the eclipse.

Or go ahead and look up, the guards said. What do we care?

He had spent almost two years here in increasing desperation, pulled farther from the phase to the time before the room, before Isabella, back to that life where hope was beyond reach. There were days when he was six again, in that old apartment with that other mother, packing his toy soldiers for the last time. Days when he was back on the school playground, dodging rocks. He had just about given in to his despair when he saw the TV news in the dayroom, the coming of the first total solar eclipse in forty years.

The sky darkened. Men shuffled around the yard, heads bowed like penitents. Some joked and roughhoused, daring each other to raise their eyes. Others fell to their knees and prayed, murmuring into folded hands.

He wondered about Isabella. Was she in her own prison yard, watching others panic as the false sun was devoured high above? Back during his sentencing, when Tanner learned that the room was intended as an art piece, he hadn't given much thought to the woman who made it. But Isabella's attack changed things. She pointed him in that direction. He found a few articles in the prison library, pictures of Jess Shepard and descriptions of her work, first-person recollections of experiences in spaces she had created. He read about a studio transformed into adjoining rooms of different colors; a site in France where the shadows of birds swept into the barn beneath them; a small house deep in the Vermont woods, made to receive the water from a nearby stream. To Tanner they seemed like tentative steps toward the room she was destined to create. He thought of it as *their* room now. They had revealed each other's true purpose.

He imagined her sitting across from him in his cell. The two of them, alone in a room. He wondered what that would be like, if Jess Shepard would feel this connection, if she understood the forces to which she had given shape.

Zero Zone. He liked the name. He repeated it each night as he drifted off to sleep. A refrain or mantra, a summoning.

A sickly dusk fell. The prison yard grew quiet. Tanner felt a pause in the air, the world holding its breath. He looked at the shadows stretching from the basketball hoop, the guard towers. They were all wrong—too long and black, less like shadows than marks or lines drawn.

He wanted to witness the eclipse, lifting his face to the false sun's last moments. But something told him this was not quite the time, not yet. An awareness in the back of his mind.

This wasn't the end, but the end's beginning.

A month later, just before Tanner's scheduled release, the men watched the news of Three Mile Island on the dayroom TV. Shots of the steaming reactor silos, convoys of emergency vehicles, interviews with hysterical neighbors. One of the nuclear reactors was melting down. A man swept a car with a Geiger counter. Hard-helmeted engineers faced a control room gone haywire with flashing lights. Locals gathered in churches, holding hands, begging for deliverance.

Tanner's cellmate Emmett sidled up alongside, his pale gray eyes fixed on the TV. Emmett was spare and compact, with a bushy mustache that looked out of proportion on his small-featured face. He reminded Tanner of a hyena—wily, perpetually amused, always on the verge of an outburst of laughter that sounded like barking. He was dead serious now, though.

What if this is it? Emmett said. What you've been talking about.

A man on TV, one of the churchgoing fearful, said, *This is the end of days.*

Emmett was nearing the end of a lengthy sentence for making bombs. He told Tanner he had planned to mail them to the White House, the Capitol, the Pentagon. Retaliation for the war in Vietnam, which was where Emmett learned to make bombs in the first place.

You should have seen them, Emmett said, whenever the subject came up, which was often. My little babies. So small and light.

The guards let them stay in the dayroom longer than usual, on account of the fact that the world might end. The men stood and paced, restless, watching police cars coming and going on the screen, firefighters in gas masks entering the facility, government officials giving unconvincing statements at a podium, looking green around the gills.

A man in one of the churches pleaded: *Jesus, save us, please.*

But then, slowly, things began to settle, one shot at a time, the temperature on-screen dropping along with a coffee-colored evening outside the dayroom's barred windows. There were fewer sirens and flashing lights, then shots of men in hard hats clapping each other on the back, the churchgoers raising their hands in gratitude.

The news anchor took off his glasses, rubbed his eyes, breathed a sigh of relief.

The dayroom crowd thinned, a disappointed dispersal, like when a football game they had watched was lost in the final minutes. One of the guards switched off the TV. Tanner stared at the black screen. He didn't feel disappointed. He felt that same awareness from the day of the eclipse, the world holding its breath.

Signs, signals, possibilities.

He needed to find Isabella.

23

JESS

SUMMER 1979

The house was deep in Laurel Canyon, a rustic, sun-drenched Crafts-man coming into view as Jess topped a winding wooden staircase. A mutual acquaintance, a gallerist Jess hadn't spoken with since the attack, had given her the address. Voices carried from behind the house, laughter and conversation mingling with the barrelhouse bounce of Neil Young's "Are You Ready for the Country?" A soft summer evening in a beautiful place. Alex and Christine were married somewhere around here. Jess hadn't been invited then, either.

She followed a flagstone walkway to the back of the house. Two dogs bounded out from around a corner, low-bodied collies, circling, licking Jess's fingertips as she reached a large patio. There were maybe fifteen people enjoying cocktails, chatting, nodding to the music. Some of them looked vaguely familiar, from magazines and album covers, maybe, actors and musicians. A long table was set for dinner, decorated with vases of sunflowers and freshly cut lavender.

A handsome, bearded man with a long swoop of dark hair was in the middle of a story, gesturing, pausing for laughs. He looked familiar, too. A movie director, Jess thought. He noticed Jess and nudged a woman in a flowing paisley-print caftan and floppy sun hat. When the woman turned, Jess saw the confusion on her face, then the disbelief, then the fear. Vulnerabilities she hadn't shown two years ago, behind her camera in Jess's studio.

Laura Lehrer excused herself and crossed the patio. The dogs ran to meet her.

"You were there," Jess said. "Inside *Zero Zone*."

"I can't do this right now," Laura said, her voice low, her face tight, suddenly at odds with the breezy ease of her outfit. She stopped in front of Jess, trying to block her from the guests.

There had been moments over the last two years when Jess's fear twisted to anger, with Laura Lehrer as its target. Many times she had reimagined that day in her studio, a new version of events where she pushed back at Laura's questions, standing up for herself and her work. That indignation surged now, validated. Jess refused to hold it in.

"You set me up," she said. "That wasn't an interview, it was an attack."

Over at the gathering, someone picked up a guitar and strummed along with the record.

"It's been two years," Laura said. "I've moved on. I hoped you had moved on, too."

Jess took off her sunglasses. For the first time she wanted someone to see her scar.

Laura pressed her lips together into a thin, tight line.

Jess said, "Does it look like I've moved on?"

"Honey?" the bearded man called over. "Who's your friend?"

"Please," Laura said to Jess. "If you come back tomorrow, we can talk through this."

"Isabella Serrano is missing," Jess said. "Her parents are afraid—*I'm* afraid that she's in trouble. That she's trying to find the other people from *Zero Zone*."

Laura's face fell. She looked like she was going to be sick.

"Laura?" The man was concerned now, taking off his sunglasses, squinting toward Jess.

Laura looked down at the flagstones and called back without turning. "I'll be right there. Can you go in and finish the salad?"

Unconvinced, he took a step toward them, but then there was an eruption of cheers and the party's focus shifted to the open French doors at the back of the house. Someone new had arrived. The man smiled and headed inside, arms open in welcome.

"You were with them in the room," Jess said. "Do you still have the film?"

Laura shook her head. "I destroyed it."

"How?"

"I burned it."

For a second Jess was on the sidewalk outside her front door, standing in Christine's shoes, watching herself lie about the *Zero Zone* photographs. She felt a new respect for Christine now, showing such patience in the face of obvious bullshit. But Jess didn't have that kind of time.

"Laura," she said.

Laura didn't move, as if hoping she could stay still enough for the moment to pass without her. When it didn't, she looked up at Jess and nodded.

Jess said, "Show me."

•

Laura went inside to speak with her husband, then led Jess out to a guesthouse set within a thicket of tall evergreens. It was an airier, neater version of Zack's apartment, with shelves of film canisters and framed posters of recent big-budget hits, each with the same director listed at the bottom, the bearded man from back at the party—his name and face clicked together now in Jess's mind. A flatbed editing table sat in one corner. Jess had seen her filmmaker friends use something similar, looping film around the table's spools and rollers until the image appeared on a small hooded screen at the back of the machine.

Laura moved around the room, pulling the blinds closed. The room darkened a little more with each window covered. Jess stood by the editing deck, a small acidic knot growing in her stomach, a feeling of rising panic as Laura sealed them in.

"Why didn't you tell me?" Jess said.

"I was going to. That's why I wanted to speak to you, to confront you. But you cut off the interview before I got to it. And then we didn't meet again the next day to finish."

"I was otherwise occupied," Jess said.

A burst of laughter carried down from the party.

"Does your husband know about any of this?" Jess asked.

Laura finished with the blinds. She shook her head. "He wouldn't understand."

She looked much older than when Jess last saw her. Dark patches hung under her eyes; a deep furrow ran down the center of her forehead. Jess knew that look: wary, insomniac, wound too tight. The body's instinctive constriction, trying to smother a secret.

"How did you find *Zero Zone*?"

Laura took off her sun hat and set it on a chair by the editing deck. "My boyfriend at the time heard about this hike. Our relationship was cratering, and this was an attempt to save it. I brought my camera and tape recorder. Before the recorder died in the heat, I interviewed some of the people we met along the path. Some were dropouts or college kids walking for the first time, other people, older people, had been coming for years. They had different reasons for their pilgrimage, but they had one thing in common. They all spoke about a room that appeared in the middle of the trail."

Jess thought of her own walk, her inability to engage with anyone she saw along the way. She had stumbled forward alone, looking for something—anything—to help her shake loose from the hole Alex's death had made in her chest. And then she'd found the military base, and the rancher, and that flicker of light that felt like a signal.

"The room was empty when we arrived," Laura said. "My boyfriend was disappointed. He didn't see anything special about it. Neither did I, to be honest. I was hot and bored and thought everyone we had met was simply seeing or feeling what they wanted to. The whole experience felt like a fraud.

"But then," she said, "two men showed up. And then two women. And all of a sudden it was as if these puzzle pieces moved into place. One of the men, Tanner, started talking. I don't know how to describe it. I'm not a religious person. But it was like he was able to see inside me, inside all of us. As if he understood a need I'd never been able to name. And then Isabella started to see things."

"What did she see?"

Laura stared at Jess, considering, then disappeared into the other room. Jess listened for the party, but it had gone silent. She had the strange, illogical feeling that everyone at the main house had left, that she and Laura were alone. That knot in her stomach rose into her chest. She struggled to push it back down.

Laura returned, holding a small cardboard box. She lifted a reel of film from the box and fixed it onto one of the spindles on the editing deck. Carefully, she threaded the film over the rollers, passing it through a small metal gate by the screen, then looping it around an empty take-up reel on the other side. She reached for a switch near the screen, then paused, breathing hard through her nose, as if trying to summon the courage to continue. Jess waited with her.

Finally, Laura flipped the switch. The small screen began to glow.

The dark room and then the light, projected: another dark room. An abstract image, black at the left edge, brightening to a thin stripe of pale orange on the right. The underexposed frame was in frantic motion, swimming with grain. Then another movement, sudden and surprising. A dark figure standing. Isabella. Jess recognized her posture from the gallery attack, slightly rounded, slump-shouldered. Isabella backlit with orange light, moving through the grain as if underwater. Jess heard that bell again, the clean, single-note peal she first heard years ago looking at Agnes Martin's grids. It sounded once in her head and then sustained, slowly fading. The clear tone of recognition. Jess in the Guggenheim; Jess underwater, eleven years old, drowning; Isabella in the last of the day's light, moving toward the center of the room.

Isabella turned and her face caught the light. It was obvious from her expression that she felt she was in the presence of something awesome, fearsome, wondrous. Her eyes widened, her mouth opened. She looked so young. She *was* young, only sixteen. Her skin was smooth, unlined, gleaming with sweat. Her eyes were clear, even through the grain. Slowly, she approached the center of the room, what she saw there, lifting her arms as she approached. She flinched from perceived heat, squinted from a brightness unrecorded on the film. But still she looked bravely into its face, reaching with trembling hands.

There was movement now at the edges of the frame, other bodies following, but Jess couldn't take her eyes from Isabella. The longing in her face, in her body. Jess had never seen such longing before. Had she ever felt it? Isabella stretched forward, arms open, and Jess found her own body mirroring, pulled toward the screen.

But there was a rupture. Whatever Isabella had seen disappeared or turned its back, denying her. She reached after it, dropping to her knees. Her body shook, her face soaked with sweat and tears. She pounded her fists on the concrete floor.

Jess covered her mouth with her hand. She wanted to look away, but she had looked away for too long. She wouldn't allow herself that retreat.

She watched the girl on the screen, her unbearable loss.

"You've shown this to others," Jess said.

"Only a few times. I thought that I could make sense of what happened in there. That if others watched, I wouldn't feel so afraid. But seeing it again only made things worse."

Laura sat on the edge of the editing deck. The only light came from the film's last image, still frozen on the screen: Isabella on her knees, broken and bereft. Laura flipped another switch and the film turned slowly in the other direction, rewinding. Isabella was pulled backward, forced to return again to the beginning of that moment. Trapped in the room.

Jess turned away to the shelves of canisters lining the walls. Her anger at Laura was gone now, evaporated in the face of Isabella's anguish.

"Do you still make films?"

"I haven't touched a camera since I heard about your attack," Laura said. It seemed as if she was going to say more, but then she shook her head. "My husband works enough for both of us."

Jess could see that Laura had run from *Zero Zone*, too; they had simply fled in opposite directions. They had both abandoned their work. But where Jess had shut herself away in her apartment and studio, Laura hoped for protection here, nestled in the canyon with her husband, dinner parties on the patio, friends and noise and light. Different illusions of safety.

The film finished rewinding, spinning alone now, its loose end flapping with each turn. Laura switched the machine off. The screen's light faded slowly, as if falling.

"I should have tried to talk to Isabella, to get her out of there," Laura said. Her voice was lower now, shakier. A confession in the dark. "I could see that Martha was trying to protect her. But something was keeping Martha there, too."

"But you got out."

"My boyfriend dragged me out." Laura's breath quickened. Her fear had returned. "Otherwise I would've stayed, too. He has that power."

"Who?"

"Tanner. The police were wrong. They thought they killed the man in charge. They believed Tanner's story."

Jess remembered the mug shot from Zack's news footage, Tanner Helm's eyes, intense and unapologetic, staring back into the police camera, Zack's TV screen.

"I still have dreams when I'm back there," Laura said. "I hear Tanner's voice. I wake up empty, because I'm here and not in that room. It's like wishing for a sickness. But he makes you believe."

She stood, quickly, as if trying to escape the memory. At each window she pulled the blinds up, desperate for the waning daylight.

"He was using Isabella," Laura said. "She was the key to what he wanted."

She looked back at Jess. Her body shuddered as she spoke.

"You can't let him find her. If he finds her again he won't let her go."

•

Jess stood outside the gallery on Sixth Street, its broad windows lemon yellow in the last of the day's sun. The color was muted, though, darkened through her sunglasses. She took them off. She wanted to see the full color. Her vision crowded with dark floaters and spots, white pinprick bursts. She blinked and shook her head to clear them away and then stopped. Two years of fighting had done nothing. Stop fighting. Just look.

A tall, colorful figure appeared in the window, and then a young woman in a bougainvillea-pink dress pushed through the gallery door, smiling politely at Jess as she passed. The room's breath slipped outside along with her—the slight musty dampness of the concrete floor, the sharp tang of a new coat of paint drying on the walls. Gabe was right. She had forgotten what that smell once promised, the thrill of entering a gallery, the work she might find. She hadn't been inside a gallery since the attack. These rooms and the art within them always gave her the courage to pursue her own work, her own questions. She hadn't realized how much she missed that feeling, how much she had allowed to slip away.

Another young woman sat behind a desk at the other end of the gallery. She looked up and smiled when Jess entered. The paint smell was stronger now. Jess walked to the wall bisecting the room, where she and Anton had stood that night. The walls were bare.

"We haven't hung the show yet," the woman said, her voice echoing in the empty room. "We open Friday, if you'd like to come back."

Jess looked across the gallery floor, through the crowd that once stood there, then to Isabella approaching from the doorway. Jess saw her again now. This wasn't surprising. Laura's film had left her raw and open; receptive, maybe. And this was always one of Zack's assertions, back when he filled his notebooks with branching networks and mazes—that every moment existed simultaneously; that time wasn't a path going forward but a field that stretched in all directions, infinite and equal.

She saw the crowd jostle and part. She saw Isabella holding her metal canister, her wand.

Jess had replayed this moment so many times, wishing for another chance to cover her face or yell for help before Isabella lifted her wand and pulled the trigger. That night it all happened too fast. But here, now, Jess could scream or run or drop to the floor and curl herself into a tight safe ball. She could cover her face, changing history, the sounds of chaos and tumult all around her as Isabella was disarmed and subdued.

"Ma'am?" the woman behind the desk asked. "Is everything all right?"

Jess pressed her hands against the wall at her back. It was still tacky with new paint. She looked at the pads of her fingers, the thin white swirls filling her fingerprints. Even if she could return to that night at the gallery, she would only be able to spare herself. Isabella would remain trapped there, suffering alone.

Jess looked out at the crowd, at Isabella, and felt the familiar fear rushing in. She let it wash over her; she let it pass. Then she stepped out into the room, toward that crowd, turning to stand beside the girl who moved through.

ROOMS

24

Every morning they made breakfast. Pancakes and bacon or Denver omelets, Izzy dicing bell peppers while Martha whisked the eggs. Izzy still wasn't much of an eater, she seemed even thinner than when they'd first met, and Martha thought including her in the ritual might bring her along. Nothing made Martha hungrier than cooking. She hoped the feeling was contagious.

They made breakfast, they made lunch. Martha tried to create patterns of normalcy. They started a garden behind the trailer, working the hard ground. Spades and shovels, the thin shade of a patio umbrella.

"What grows out here?" Izzy asked.

Martha had a gardening book she'd bought at a garage sale in town. *Desert Abundance*. She put Izzy in charge of research, figuring out what they should plant.

"Something colorful," Martha said. "Let's brighten the place up."

That's what they talked about while they worked and cooked—Izzy's discoveries from the book. Martha had so many questions, she wanted to know how Izzy felt about everything that had happened, but she knew she couldn't push.

"*California poppies,*" Izzy said, turning a page. "*Evening primrose.*"

They made lunch, they made dinner. Martha took some time off from work. She called Sam and told him not to come over, not yet. She didn't think Izzy was ready to meet anyone new.

Tanner would be out of prison soon, too, if he wasn't already. Martha felt him somewhere out there, then stopped herself. That wasn't a feeling. That was the madness of the room, phantom pain.

At night Izzy slept restlessly, as if running from danger. Martha wrapped Izzy in her arms, holding her close.

They drove into town for groceries and when Martha turned the corner of the cereal aisle, Izzy was gone. Martha hustled her cart to the end of the aisle and up the next and then left it and ran through the store, frantic, calling Izzy's name. Out on the sidewalk, Martha finally found her in front of the thrift shop next door, looking at something in the window. It was a movie camera, a small black box with a squat little lens and a metal crank.

"You have to let me know if you go somewhere," Martha said, breathing hard, her body heavy with the adrenaline crash.

Izzy took her hand. "I'm sorry," she said. "I've just never seen one like that."

Martha talked the shop's owner down on the price, even got her to throw in a couple of boxes of film. Izzy loaded the camera in the restroom and on the drive home she turned the crank and began shooting out the window. Within seconds she stopped. Martha heard it, too. The sound of the camera whirring was the same as that other woman's camera back in the room. It made her heart rise into her throat. She looked at Izzy, who was a little pale now, swallowing hard. Then Martha popped a cigarette and perched her elbow on the window and said, "Film me driving, like Steve McQueen." She gave her best hard-assed squint out the windshield. Izzy smiled and said, "Ali MacGraw," and started shooting again.

They expanded the garden. The work felt good, solid and physical. Sometimes Martha looked up from digging to see Izzy filming her with the camera or shooting a close-up of a seed dropping into a hole or a bird stepping lightly along the edge of the trailer's roof. At night they sat out on a pair of metal patio chairs and Izzy arranged candles to give enough light for the lens to pick up Martha's face. It seemed Izzy was more comfortable talking from behind the camera. She told Martha about the detention center, about her mother and father, about a friend named Vince, whom Izzy missed. She wondered where he was now, how his life had changed over the past two years. And sometimes they talked about the room, stepping lightly like those birds on the roof.

"I don't know why I did that," Izzy said one night, lowering the camera to her lap. "Why I attacked Miss Shepard. Why I cut her face. I was so angry."

In the unsteady candlelight, Izzy turned the camera's lens, slowly, something to do with her hands. Each turn made a soft click, the lens locking into place and coming loose again.

"I was going to kill her," Izzy said.

"But you didn't."

"But I was going to. I'll never forget that feeling. Like finally falling over an edge. That's what scared me the most."

Martha remembered that feeling when Danny attacked the college boys, her own unleashed desire to see them punished for their intrusion. She knew that edge, but now she understood it was possible to step back.

"You can leave that anger behind," Martha said. She reached over and took Izzy's hand. "I left it back in the room. You don't have to carry it with you."

"Do you ever think about him?" Izzy asked. "Tanner? I hear him all the time. I turn and can't believe he's not there."

"Look at me." Martha waited for Izzy's eyes. "You're here now. We're here. We're not back there, we are never going back there. When you feel it, just grab something." She squeezed Izzy's hand. "Your camera or me or a handful of dirt."

Izzy squeezed back, nodding, but Martha recognized that familiar wavering in her eyes. Izzy was still partly there, in the room with Tanner, in an art gallery in Los Angeles, a weapon in her hand, Jess Shepard on the floor at her feet. She was scattered across time, and Martha wasn't sure how to help pull her back together.

25

Jess and Vince took the afternoon flight to Vegas, a stubby twin-engine prop that jumped and dipped along the airstream like an overeager salmon. Sitting by the window, Jess looked down at the skin of the earth below, the molten outbreaks of fire at the edges of Los Angeles, then farther south to where the landscape simplified to the single curved line of the horizon. *Zero Zone* was somewhere on that line. She wondered what shape it was in. The rancher had died a year after the raid, and the last Jess heard his property was tangled in litigation between distant family and the county, a fight over a now infamous stretch of land. She had no idea if the structure remained standing, but she still felt it out there, the room and whatever had happened inside. What she once might have called the art of the thing but which she now had no words to describe.

In the seat beside her, Vince took a shaky breath. He looked a little blanched. A thin film of sweat glistened on his forehead.

"Sorry," he said, closing his eyes. "I've never flown before."

Jess took his clammy hand and squeezed, holding on through the last half hour of the flight, until the plane's wheels bumped along the runway.

They checked into a small motel a half mile from the Strip, neighboring rooms on the second floor. Jess came back from the vending machine with a couple of Cokes and found Vince out on the walkway, leaning against the metal railing. Two families were down at the courtyard pool, the parents in lawn chairs drinking cans of Coors, an adolescent girl and a pair of boys splashing around in the deep end.

Jess handed Vince his Coke. More than ever he seemed like a child playing cowboy. Costume, gesture, frame of mind.

He looked out over the railing, the pool and the long horizon beyond, the uppermost peaks of the hotels and casinos.

"What if Martha Reed's not here?" he said. "Or works at a different place? Look at all of them."

"We'll find her," Jess said. She hoped she sounded more confident than she felt. It had been two years since *Zero Zone*. Martha could be anywhere.

The sun dipped below the horizon in a final orange bloom. Down at the pool one of the boys lit a sparkler, dancing along the concrete patio, waving the stick, the cascade at its tip like a shimmering white dandelion head.

Vince said, "Why did you build that room?"

The sky's color slipped away, the new twilight creating a monochrome world, grayscale, a living newspaper photograph. Jess heard another sparkler light, a fizzy flare-up and then the phosphorescent hiss. It was the girl this time, tracing oversize letters in the air that faded as soon as they were drawn.

"I lost someone," Jess said. "And I wanted to make something that spoke to that loss. Or maybe I was looking for a place to put it, as if I could contain it out in the desert."

"I never should have let Izzy leave," Vince said. "Or I should have gone with her. I can't stop thinking about her in that room with those people. I should have been in there with her."

Jess turned to him. In the new night his face was scarred with shadows and dark lines, and she saw now what all of this had done to him, the love and worry and regret.

A pulsing glow sprang up over the rooftops a few blocks away, the lights of the casinos jumping to life.

"Let's go find Martha," Jess said.

26

I t was the high heat of the day, the three o'clock desert broil. They had worked outside all afternoon. The garden now circled the trailer and ran along the sides of the driveway, planted with seeds that should bloom in the fall, cornflowers and poppies and primroses. Izzy washed her hands in the kitchen sink, digging at dirt under her nails, while Martha appraised the contents of the fridge. She was starving and bone-tired and thought they might both be exhausted enough to finally get a good night's sleep. On the radio by the toaster, Dolly Parton sang about losing her mind over a man.

Izzy went back to the bathroom closet for a clean towel. Martha carried a head of lettuce to the sink. She looked out the window and saw the pickup at the other end of the driveway. The truck must have stopped just a moment before; a long cape of dust flowed forward from its backside, stretching past the doors and hood. The driver's door opened, and someone stepped out of the truck. She knew who it was before the dust had cleared.

She called for Izzy to go into the bathroom and lock the door. Izzy said, *What?* and Martha heard her coming forward through the trailer so she yelled again to go into the goddamn bathroom and lock the door and not come out for any reason. *Please, honey.*

Martha watched him walk up the driveway. He wore long sleeves, safari pants, and a wide-brimmed fishing hat that shaded his face and neck. About halfway to the trailer he turned, his attention caught by the cry of a hawk high overhead, and Martha saw the unmistakable topography of his profile. Tanner turned back, looking to her window, and when he lifted his hand to tip his hat she felt that undeniable pull, as if there was something in her body that belonged to him, that he could call forward with the slightest gesture.

She heard the bathroom door close, the delicate click of the feeble lock.

There was another man in the truck's passenger seat. He was smoking, looking out the dust-caked windshield. She saw his teeth under a shaggy mustache, bared in a wide smile as if someone just told him a dirty joke.

She ran to the bedroom and opened the drawer. The gun was there, inevitable, but still surprising somehow. She slid it into the waistband of her jeans at the small of her back, blousing her shirt over the top like the man at the gun shop had showed her.

The radio deejay said that caller number nine would win a fifty-dollar spending spree at any Alpha Beta supermarket.

Martha went outside, posting herself in front of the screen door. As Tanner approached, she folded her arms across her chest and then unfolded them, shifting her weight from one hip to the other as if she had never stood before another person in her life. He looked at her and then took in the entire trailer and she had a sharp, scorching vision of him inside, all of them together again, the trailer a furnace, the heat and wicked intensity, another room.

"Miss Martha," he said. "It's been a long time."

She couldn't meet his eyes. They felt like hands in her clothes. She looked down at her tennis shoes, trying to find something solid, a line of ants marching through the dust.

He started talking as if he hadn't stopped since their time in the room. He told her about prison, the things he'd seen there. The eclipse, the near-miss at Three Mile Island. Signs, he said, pointing in one direction. He told her about a man he'd met, Emmett, nodding back toward the pickup.

"He's like us," Tanner said. "He believes what we believe."

Martha wanted to argue that there was no *we*, but the lie wouldn't leave her throat.

The afternoon was breezeless, the heat like a stalled wave. Tanner took off his hat and Martha realized that his hair was gone; he'd shaved his head. He ran his hand over the stubble.

"What a day," he said. He looked at Martha, then to the trailer. "I would love a glass of water."

Martha hesitated. She didn't want to move from the door, but also couldn't arouse his suspicion. She went into the kitchen, filling a glass at the sink and staring at Tanner through the window, as if she could will him to stay outside. She glanced toward the bathroom. The door was still closed. She made a silent wish for Izzy to stay quiet.

The water was overflowing. Martha turned off the faucet and pressed her cool wet hand to her cheek. She imagined lifting the phone from the wall and calling Sam. He wouldn't be home, he would be out at work, but she thought that if she simply whispered into the receiver he might hear her from the top of a telephone pole miles away, her appeal carrying through the line to his ear.

When she looked up from the sink Tanner was in the doorway on the other side of the screen.

She moved quickly, carrying the water, keeping the screen between them. "Just what I needed," he said, before she offered anything. Then she opened the screen and handed him the glass. Reaction, action. She was slipping. In some future he was already inside, had already turned this place into another room. That new man was here, taking Danny's place, and Izzy, rising from the corner toward the center, what she saw there, what called to her.

Caller number nine, the radio deejay said. *You're on the air.*

The gun pressed hard against Martha's back. She thought of pulling it out. She thought of firing a bullet into Tanner's chest, watching him stagger and drop as Danny had staggered and dropped. She thought of turning and sitting at the kitchen table, waiting for Tanner to join her inside.

Tanner tilted his head back and drank the glass dry, then let his shoulders drop, refreshed.

"Isabella's free again, too," he said. "A nice surprise. I wasn't expecting her for another year."

"I didn't know." Martha's voice was an arid croak, pinched and unconvincing.

Out in the truck, the man in the passenger seat laughed at something. Martha couldn't hear him, only saw his head thrown back, a wild, savage baying.

"We were so close," Tanner said. "But we were missing something. Emmett is that missing piece. He has a very particular skill. Once we're all back together, he'll push us the rest of the way through."

Tanner stared at her for a long moment, as if waiting for her to speak. Martha focused on the glass in his hand, a single drop of water sliding down its side.

He set the glass on the windowsill beside the door, his eyes never leaving hers.

"Martha," he said. "May I use your bathroom?"

"You need to leave."

Tanner sighed, disappointed.

He pulled the screen and she yanked back but he'd opened it just enough to push his boot into the gap. He threw the door open and grabbed her wrist, his grip so hard she felt the tiny bones bending.

"I haven't forgotten how you betrayed us," he said, his face nearly touching hers. "Screaming for the police."

She tried to move her free hand, to reach around to her back, but she was fixed in place, his grip on her wrist shutting her whole body down.

He moved his other hand up to her neck, slowly, his fingers surrounding, his palm pushing at her windpipe.

"Judas hung himself, Martha," he said. "Maybe you should follow his example."

Tanner squeezed harder. Martha couldn't breathe. She gagged, her vision dimming, and then she felt something at the small of her back, a momentary touch just above the gun.

Izzy stepped around and placed her hand on Tanner's.

"You found me," Izzy said.

Tanner looked at Izzy and his face shifted, wrath melting to a slow smile.

"I never lost you."

Izzy moved Tanner's hand from Martha's throat and set it down at his side.

"Don't do that," she said.

"Forgive me. I got carried away." Tanner sounded apologetic, but his eyes were still hungry, as if imagining his hand had never left Martha's neck.

"She should stay here," Izzy said.

"No. We all need to be together."

"But she was never really one of us."

"You're not going with him," Martha said. Her throat felt like it was filled with broken glass.

Izzy turned and took Martha's wrists, gently, her fingertips warm on the place Tanner had nearly snapped.

"It's all right," Izzy said. She seemed calm, resolved. Martha tried to read her eyes but couldn't tell if Izzy was doing this to protect her, or if she really wanted to leave with Tanner.

"Izzy, please."

"You've left it behind," Izzy said, "but I can't. I'm sorry."

She lifted Martha's hand and kissed the back of her wrist. Martha wanted to grab Izzy, but her body wouldn't respond. Tanner turned away. Izzy let go of Martha's hand and followed him up the driveway toward the pickup. Tanner opened the door and Izzy climbed in, sliding over next to the other man. Tanner got behind the wheel and closed the door. He started the engine, creating another dust storm as they drove away.

Only then was Martha able to move again. She felt her bruised wrist, then her neck. The rough squeeze of a noose there, or Tanner's hand, tightening.

27

Jess sat at one of the Tahitian's bamboo tiki bars with a beer and a cigarette, using a tin ashtray identical to the one Chloe had shown her
back in L.A. Grass-skirted waitresses worked the room, balancing
trays as they steered through the slots and card tables. As each woman
passed Jess glanced at her name tag, smiling and looking away whenever
she was caught.

Vince was out looking around the casino floor. They'd been there for
an hour or so, though it was hard to tell. There were no clocks; no one
wore a watch. It felt like these rooms moved outside of measured time.

Jess had been to Vegas before, dragged along by friends for a weekend
or birthday celebration, but always felt so depressed by the greed and bad
taste that she failed to contemplate the place itself. She had never been
alone here, sitting quietly in this strange disconnect.

She could make something here. Jess felt the first surge of possibility, the beginnings of an idea. For the past two years she had tamped those feelings down, but she let this one run for a moment, testing the space like a toddler allowed to roam for the first time. Jess watched the idea grow and detour, expanding into questions and possibilities, until she finally caught herself and pulled it back. It didn't vanish completely, though. She still felt it, a thin bright remnant alight in the back of her mind.

She tried to remember the words of that old manifesto, the dialogue with Gabe she wrote down and hung in the bathroom of her first studio. She needed the reminder then, when every morning she awoke filled with criticism and doubt—her own and that of what seemed like so many others. She couldn't remember all of Gabe's questions so she focused only on her answers, the list forming her own koan or incantation, a long string of defiant negations and then that final, single yes, which always felt like an opening she could step through, past the lines that had been drawn.

The bartender came by and she ordered another beer. When he returned with the bottle, Jess asked if Martha still worked there.

He scratched his ear and gave a quizzical look and said he didn't know who that was.

Jess turned on her stool, facing the playing floor again, the waitresses out taking orders. She would have to go to each one until she found someone who knew.

"Martha Reed?"

A young waitress stood beside her now, bottle-blond, runaway thin.

"Is she here?" Jess asked.

"She moved a while back. Out of town."

"Do you know where?"

The girl squinted. "Somewhere out in the desert. Near Twentynine Palms, I think she said. She sold me all her stuff before she left."

28

Every time Martha looked out her bedroom window, she saw the dust cloud from Tanner's truck still hanging in the air at the end of the driveway. She knew that was impossible; they'd left hours ago. It was a trick of the light or a trick of her mind. But even after night fell she saw it there, swirling slowly, glowing in the moonlight.

How could she have let Izzy go? She should have fought tooth and nail. But she'd never kept Izzy safe. Martha was the one who had taken her along the desert trail and into the room. Then she hadn't pulled Izzy out, even when every cell in her body screamed for escape. Martha was responsible for all of it. If she had only ignored those girls that night at the casino and dealt with her own grief instead of dragging Izzy into it, none of this would have happened. And now she had served Izzy up to Tanner again.

Every horrific scene possible played out in her mind: Izzy with the men in their truck, alone with them inside *Zero Zone*.

She couldn't call the police. She knew where that would lead. News footage of another siege, tear gas, and then bullets stabbing through the room. She couldn't call Sam. She refused to involve him in her disaster. Their time together now seemed like desperate playacting. Driving out to his place to make dinner, watching old movies on TV, slow dancing to Loretta Lynn on the kitchen radio. A bullshit fantasy, falling away like flower petals, or clothes shed, leaving Martha exposed again.

The night and another whole day passed. Her throat throbbed; she still felt Tanner's hand there, squeezing. She closed her eyes and was back in the room. The hunger and thirst, the oven-like heat. Tanner was there, and Danny, and this new man who laughed like an animal, each in a corner watching Isabella move toward the center, the new sun unfolding.

This would never end.

She tried to imagine Misty there with her, sitting on the love seat in the living room. She needed her sister's strength, to see that look on Misty's face when she wanted Martha to get on with it and make the hard choice, whether it was getting back on a diet or breaking up with a shitty guy Martha met at the casino. The sculpted arches of Misty's eyebrows raised, her mouth screwed into an irritated line.

Martha opened her eyes to the empty trailer. Misty wasn't in the living room. Misty was dead. If Martha really wanted to join her, there was only one way. Maybe the answer had been that simple all along.

She heard something outside, a crunching sound disarranging the night's silence. Martha went to the window, listening from behind the curtain. Tires on dirt, coming down her driveway. An engine approached, then idled and cut out. One car door opened, then another.

29

In Vegas Jess and Vince rented a tan four-door Plymouth Fury, which the man at the lot said was the fastest car he had. They crossed back into California, reaching Twentynine Palms just after midnight. A handful of bars were open along the main street. They checked each of them, coming up short until the bartender at a country-and-western joint told them Martha worked there but had taken some time off. He asked how they knew her, and Jess said Martha was an old friend. The bartender nodded to a side door. Martha lived down that back road about a mile, he said, the trailer at the very end.

It was an overcast night. Ragged scraps of cloud covered the moon and soon they were out of reach of the streetlights. Jess drove slowly, high beams on, braking when little roadrunners dashed across their path. They passed a couple of trailers and then nothing for a while but open land, broken occasionally by dry puffs of chaparral in the headlights.

The silence was almost as complete as the darkness; the gravel crunching under their tires sounded like shouting. They weren't trying to surprise Martha, but this noise was too much, an alarm announcing their arrival. Jess slowed the car further but that only seemed to make it worse, louder and more distinct.

After about a mile, the road gave out. Jess thought that they had gone too far, but then Vince tapped the windshield and Jess saw a lone single-wide at the edges of the high beams. The trailer's windows were dark. Jess pulled into the driveway beside an orange hatchback. They got out of the car and Jess told Vince to stay put. She walked down to the trailer and knocked on the screen door. Her knuckles on the metal made a tinny racket. Vince paced impatiently in front of the Fury's square headlights, agitating the dusty beams.

Jess went to knock again, then stopped herself. She felt a presence on the other side of the door.

"Martha," Jess said, keeping her voice low. Then, hopeful, "Isabella?"

The inner door opened, slowly, the headlights revealing a woman behind the screen. She had cut and darkened her hair, maybe recovered some lost weight, but Jess still recognized Martha from the TV news.

Vince stopped pacing. Martha dropped her hand from the door. Her arms hung at her sides. Her whole body hung, as if something essential had been removed. She looked at Jess and then Vince. She didn't seem surprised by the strangers at her door. They weren't strangers; somehow Martha knew who they were.

"She's gone," Martha said. "He took her."

Jess and Vince sat at the kitchen table while Martha spooned mounds of Taster's Choice into mugs. The overhead light was on, too bright for this time of night, but the rest of the trailer remained dark, just the hint of other rooms stretching back in a straight, narrow line.

Martha tucked her hair behind her ears. She looked like she hadn't slept in a while; gray puffs like little thunderclouds hung under her eyes. Meeting Martha didn't feel as strange as Jess had thought it would. She was younger than Jess but older than Isabella, and watching her make coffee Jess couldn't help thinking of Martha as a long-lost middle sister. Maybe it wasn't as ridiculous as it seemed. For two years, Jess had seen herself and Isabella as opposing poles, but she had been wrong. There were three of them who had been transformed by *Zero Zone*.

Martha poured steaming water into each mug. When she turned, Jess noticed dark bruises on either side of her neck.

"I don't know if Izzy wanted to leave with them," Martha said, "or if she was trying to protect me."

"Where are they going?" Vince said.

Martha set mugs down in front of Vince and Jess, then leaned back against the counter. "Back to the room."

Jess felt her stomach tumble. "What do they think will happen there?"

"They think they're going to pass through."

"Through to where?"

"Another place. A better place. I know it sounds crazy. But Tanner has a way of making you believe."

Laura Lehrer had told Jess the same thing. But while Laura spoke about Tanner with pure terror, Martha's fear seemed threaded with something stronger, a hard braid of anger.

"What does that mean?" Vince said. "How will they 'pass through'?"

"I don't know," Martha said. "Nothing makes sense until you're in there with him."

Vince turned to Jess. "It's time to call the police."

"No," Martha said. "We know what the police will do."

"Then we have to go. We have to get her out."

Martha stared off into the dark trailer. To Jess it seemed as if she was listening, then receiving confirmation of some kind, the answer to a difficult question. After a moment she met Jess's eyes.

"You made that place," she said. "Tanner would feel you had authority there. And Izzy talked about you a lot—how sorry she was for what she did. If we go, there's a chance they'll listen to you."

At first light they drove back through town, stopping at a gas station on the eastern outskirts. There was no line of waiting cars this early, just a handwritten sign in the station's window: *Due To Gas Shortage Pay 2X What Pump Reads.* Vince got out of the Fury's back seat and went inside to pay and grab some water and food for the drive while Jess filled the tank. Martha stayed in the passenger seat, a black leather purse in her lap, tapping an unlit cigarette against her bottom teeth.

Jess listened to the pump tick up with each gallon and watched Vince through the windows of the station. He moved down the short aisles, deliberate and determined, a kid entrusted with an important task. He *was* a kid. She couldn't imagine taking him into *Zero Zone,* the kind of threat he would pose to those men if he came along. There would be no chance of ending this without more violence, of everyone walking away whole.

She finished pumping and got back in the driver's seat, letting the open door's warning chime ding in steady procession. Martha pushed the dashboard lighter in with her thumb.

"Izzy misses Vince," Martha said.

"Then I have to make sure he's still around when we get her out."

Martha looked at Jess, her head tilted in surprise.

"Won't he follow us?"

"He'll find his way back to your place," Jess said. "He'll get your car running and drive straight through. But he'll be a few hours behind. Hopefully that's enough."

Jess shut her door, silencing the chime. She looked out to the gas station, where Vince stood at the counter, uncrumpling bills from the pocket of his jeans. Then she started the car and pulled out of the lot, heading for the highway.

Martha had bought the purse back in Vegas just after Misty died, during one of those dead-end days where she sleepwalked through her shifts and then wandered the city, drifting in and out of different stores and restaurants, any place that would change her surroundings, this interminable movie's backdrop, even for a moment.

She saw the purse at Driscoll's, hung over the shoulder of a faceless mannequin, black leather with a long strap and a two-inch fringe along the flap. It was a little flashy, more Misty's style than her own. She bought it anyway. The purchase felt obligatory, like she couldn't leave something Misty might have once wanted sitting alone in a store. When she and Izzy drove down to the desert trail Martha brought it along to carry her wallet and sunglasses and when they left her car by the entrance she took what she needed and locked the empty purse inside. Later, after everything, a police officer drove her from the hospital back to her car. She popped the hatchback and stared at the purse, which seemed so strange sitting there, a relic from a past life.

The purse sat in her lap now, as they barreled east in Jess's rental. Martha ran her fingers along the soft leather, the places where thin strips had pulled away, leaving gaps in the fringe. She had told Jess that they could talk to Tanner. This was true. Tanner could talk forever. He would talk until his voice was in their heads, until Martha felt his words in her mouth. They could talk, but Martha knew how that ended.

Jess rolled down her window to light a cigarette and Martha moved her purse to the floor, feeling the weight inside shift and then settle, the gun hard against her foot.

30

A tall fence surrounded the old base. Izzy recognized some of the signs from the last time she had been there: *No Trespassing. Violators Will Be Shot.* It didn't seem like the warnings were very effective. They drove through a giant hole, following other tire tracks onto a potholed road, passing what Tanner said were once the barracks, concrete buildings spread long and low as if lying down in the heat. Graffiti covered the walls, half-legible names and dates and then a series of circles, each split with a diagonal line. At first Izzy thought these were more warnings, like the symbols on *No Smoking* signs. Then she heard Emmet whispering under his breath, the same word each time they came upon one.

Zero, zero, zero.

It was a trail of zeros, one or two on each wall, leading to where the road took a sharp right turn. The building at that corner was marked with a single sentence in black spray paint. Emmett read it aloud:

You are on sacred ground.

The truck slowed. Izzy looked at Tanner behind the wheel, the hint of a smile on his face.

They had been in this configuration the whole night, Tanner driving, Emmett on the passenger side of the bench seat, Izzy squished in the middle. Emmett kept his thigh hard against Izzy's. Whenever he shifted he made sure to push his weight against her, a step away from rolling on top.

The road led to the center of the base, an empty intersection with dilapidated buildings on each corner. They got out of the truck and Emmett shuffled over to the side of one of the buildings to relieve himself. The road continued on for another hundred feet or so and then crumbled back to dust. The room was out there, not too far. Izzy couldn't see it in the unshaded glare, but she felt it, waiting.

"This time will be different," Tanner said. He had come up beside her. "We'll have everything we need."

He was talking about whatever was in the back of the truck, tied down under a blue tarp. Izzy had spent the whole drive with the question in her mind but hadn't asked. Part of it was fear but another part was exactly what Tanner said. Whatever was under the tarp needed to be there.

Emmett zipped himself and Tanner told him to make sure no one was shacking up in any of the buildings. They watched him move from corner to corner, disappearing inside each doorway and reappearing a few minutes later. Finally he came out of the building on their left, what looked like a small school with a rusted swing set sinking into the tall weeds. He carried a case of beer, shaking the box to rattle the empty cans.

"Looks like somebody's been partying." He smiled, showing that long row of top teeth. "I found a mattress, some rubbers…"

"How long ago?" Tanner said.

"There's ashes from a couple fires but they're old. Nobody's been here for a while." Emmett looked at Tanner and Izzy and shook the box again, trying to stir interest, then gave a disappointed snort and dropped it to the dirt.

Tanner nodded toward the school. "You should get some sleep," he said to Izzy. "We'll go up and prepare the room."

"I can help," Izzy said. She wanted to go. She needed to see it again.

"You'll need all of your strength," Tanner said. "We'll come get you when it's ready."

There were four classrooms in the school, each about the same size, with a few broken desks and bookcases, the books gone soft with mold, curled inward, like giant snails sleeping on the shelves. The chalkboards had fallen off the walls, the slate broken in pieces on the floor, leaving just the empty wooden frames hanging.

The classroom at the end of the hall didn't smell as rotten as the first few. Izzy sat at a desk and put her head down. Someone had painted a word or phrase on the windows, a single large letter in white paint on each broken or cracked pane. The paint was long-dried, the drips hardened in skinny streaks that made it look like the letters were melting or crying. Izzy couldn't make out what it said—the letters were painted from the outside. It felt like being inside a mirror, trying to decipher the world in reverse.

A few of the windows were broken and wore plywood coverings that looked like eye patches. They reminded her of Vince. Back when they were eight or nine he'd fallen out of the live oak in their front yard, scratching his eye on the way down. His father took him to the doctor and when she saw him the next day his eye was covered with a square of gauze.

She was too anxious to sleep. It felt so natural to be here again, as if the last two years had been a mistake, a scratch on the record. Here again but not quite, just down the path from the room itself. Like sitting outside a doctor's office, waiting for someone to call your name.

She heard footsteps coming down the hall. Lonely, echoing. Izzy stood, worried it was Emmett, but then Tanner appeared in the doorway.

They were heading into town, he said. Emmett needed a few more things. But she should stay and rest.

She didn't know exactly what Emmett was making in the room. She knew but didn't know. Acknowledging it created a fresh shock of fear and she needed to keep that away. She needed to move beyond fear. Use Tanner's word instead. Emmett's preparing. Think of it like a man setting a table, placing forks and knives and plates.

She heard the truck pull away, the sound of its engine fading. She thought of Vince again, imagined him walking in the classroom door. Taking his hand and leaving this place.

The heat outside was even worse than inside the school. Izzy felt her face burning, sweat prickling the crown of her head. She walked through the intersection, following the pavement until it crumbled into the dirt trail. She wished Martha was here but was glad she wasn't. Martha didn't really want to pass through. There was so much Martha still loved—making meals, digging in the garden, driving fast with the windows down. During those few days at Martha's, Izzy saw how she might grow to love those things, too. Planting seeds, chopping carrots and onions, each satisfying *clop* of the knife edge striking the wooden board. But then Tanner arrived. The only surprise was that it had taken him so long. And Izzy remembered the other times she'd fooled herself into believing there was something here for her. Thinking she could just exist in this body, in this place, with Ford or Chloe or Vince or Martha. But that was a lie. No matter who Izzy was with, she could never escape herself. She was stuck in her body, in her head, screaming, accusing, mocking. There was only one way out, and it was here, waiting.

Up ahead she saw that other fence, taller chain-link topped with barbed wire. And then the room appeared, rising from the horizon. She walked closer and it grew; or it grew, pulling her closer.

Two years ago she had despaired here, dragging her canister, digging desperately in the dirt. Now there was a hole in the fence, and she squeezed through, careful not to snag herself on the ragged ends of the cut metal. Beer cans littered the ground, cigarette packs and butts, an empty backpack. Someone had spray-painted on the room's side, a date in vivid sky blue, two tilted slashes separating month, day, and year. It took her a moment. It was the day the police stormed the room, the day Danny died. She stared at it, not sure what she felt, then walked to the open doorway. She couldn't see past, the doorway was a black mouth, but she began to make out subtleties, faint bars of light hanging in the darkness, the yellow glow of those openings in the walls. She followed them inside. She heard a mouse or lizard skittering, the crinkling of paper under her shoes, what sounded like candy wrappers or potato chip bags. She let her body submerge into the space. The darkness surrounded her; the outside world faded. She saw the walls now, blackened by campfires. A stained mattress, small piles of trash blown into corners from the wind.

What had she once felt here? The fact that she had to ask was terrifying, as if she'd forgotten some fundamental part of herself. She tried to slow her breathing, calm herself down. Let the room take over. Izzy closed her eyes, wishing, then opened them again. A dark room full of trash. She wasn't trying hard enough or she was trying too hard. Always so stupid, impatient, needy. The room was different, or she was different. Something had changed; something was missing. Tanner, of course, but she wasn't sure even he would be enough.

A flash in the dark caught her attention. It blinked again, a tiny red light. She walked closer, making out more of its shape. A package, maybe a foot high, the kind of thing someone might leave on a doorstep. Two thick rectangular blocks covered in heavy paper, wrapped together with duct tape. A pair of thin wires led from the ends of the blocks to a small device on top, what looked like a calculator.

Then that flash again, insistent, the little red light like a small hole opening, showing a glimpse of what waited on the other side.

ALL THINGS BRIGHT AND BEAUTIFUL

31

Martha watched the fences running along the highway, diamond-link or just barbed wire strung between wooden posts. That's how it seemed, that the fences were keeping pace with their speeding car. Fields and pastures beyond, cows sometimes, horses, or nothing, just open space that someone thought needed to be contained.

Neither she nor Jess wore a watch. It could be nine thirty, or almost noon. The morning brightened the vast surrounding country. She had never thought of time this way, as light filling a day. Then she corrected herself. She'd had this experience before. That was how time moved through *Zero Zone*.

Jess said, "I want to know what happened in there, but I don't know how to ask."

Martha smiled and said, "I think you just did."

She was surprised by how much she liked Jess. Until Izzy's attack,

Martha hadn't thought much about the artist who made the room. She thought she'd feel angry, sitting in a car with the woman who created *Zero Zone*. Or intimidated. Jess reminded her of Misty's old Vegas friends, other designers and costumers, the confident, creative women working backstage, away from the lights and applause. Martha had envied and admired that sisterhood, their commitment, their ambivalence toward the city's playground nonsense. They were there to work; they had a vocation, an art. Martha always felt ashamed when she served them drinks, working the casino floor with a grass skirt and as much cleavage as she could mobilize.

But Jess didn't act superior or judgmental. Since the moment Martha opened the trailer's front door, Jess had treated Martha as an equal, with respect, even a little fear. Martha could tell that Jess thought of her as more than a gullible waitress who'd gotten herself into a shitload of trouble. She was the woman who had survived *Zero Zone*. She was the woman who might get them out of it again.

And now Martha understood that Jess had been with them all along. She had created that place, and some part of her was there during those eight days. Part of her was still there. The room wouldn't let Jess go, either.

As Martha spoke she looked at the fences, or over to Jess's profile, the thin white scar running down her cheek. It felt different from when she had told Sam. That was sharing. This was letting go, leaving the story on the road as they sped east. It reminded her of a car she'd once seen on the highway, boxes and suitcases flying from its roof because a strap had come loose. She told Jess of the walk along the trail, meeting Tanner, entering the room. More suitcases, more boxes. She spoke about those final few hours inside, trapped and terrified, yet still hoping for a sign from Misty.

Jess glanced at Martha, then back out at the road ahead.

"Did you ever feel her in there?" she asked. "Your sister?"

Martha wondered what answer Jess wanted to hear. Maybe it would give her some peace of mind to believe Martha had experienced a final moment with Misty's spirit, a last goodbye. But Martha only wanted the truth now. The fantasies had cost her—cost them all—too much.

"No," she said. It felt good to hear the word in her own voice, denying the illusion. She imagined shooting that word into Tanner's chest.

Jess wanted to know about Tanner. It was as if Martha's thought triggered the question.

"He's like the room," Martha said. "Both of them suck you in. Black holes."

Martha turned the radio knob, sliding between stations, stopping on one static-fuzzed song or another. Neither of them spoke about it, but they both understood she was searching for news. Whenever Martha heard a newscaster's self-serious baritone, she paused on the dial. They listened in silence, the air in the car pitched high and tight. A shootout, a siege—they waited for the familiar words. But it was just traffic and weather, a weekend carnival in Flagstaff, a gas leak in Albuquerque.

They stopped quickly for gas, cigarettes, to use the restroom. Each time they half expected Vince to streak by in Martha's hatchback, but there was still no sign of him. They took turns driving. Whoever sat in the passenger seat did most of the talking. It felt easier there, with the driver looking ahead most of time. They could speak without feeling watched.

"Did you know who she was that night," Martha asked, "when Izzy came into the gallery?"

For the last few miles they'd been stuck behind a long tanker truck, but now the passing lane was clear and Martha gunned the rental alongside.

Jess wasn't sure how to answer. No one had ever asked, and she didn't know how to explain. That moment with Isabella didn't make sense on its own. Maybe that had been her mistake all this time—trying to keep that night quarantined from the rest of her life.

Once she started talking, she couldn't stop. Martha had unburdened herself of everything, and Jess felt the freeing pull of that honesty. She told Martha about her parents' accident, Aunt Ruth, Zack, Alex and his photographs, building *Zero Zone*. Finally she paused, back at the gallery, Isabella coming toward her through the crowd.

"I hadn't watched the news," Jess said, "but I still knew who she was."

"What did you do?"

"I just stood there."

"Even though she had that thing?" Martha asked. "That canister. You didn't yell or run?"

"No."

"Why not?"

"Because I thought I deserved whatever she had come to do."

The tank was half full, but they still pulled into line at a gas station in Tucumcari. They were close now. This would be their last stop and they both wanted a full tank for whatever happened next.

The line wasn't long, and after she filled up Jess parked by a pair of phone booths at the edge of the lot. She walked to the restroom behind the station, moving slowly, feeling a hesitancy to barrel ahead that fought with the need to get to *Zero Zone* as quickly as possible, obliterating second thoughts. When Jess came out Martha was crossing the lot toward the restroom, moving in that same measured way. As they passed, Martha placed her hand on Jess's back. After all the hours in the car it was the first time they had touched. She moved her hand up toward Jess's shoulder, rubbing briskly, as if trying to rouse them both awake.

The first phone booth Jess tried was dead, but the second booth's receiver held a distant tone, so she fed enough dimes into the slot for a call to L.A. The air inside the booth was hot and stuffy. She left the folding door open, partly due to the heat but mostly because she wasn't yet ready to close herself inside a confined space. That might come soon enough.

She dialed Zack's latest number and waited through the electronic purr of the long-distance ring. But either he wasn't answering or she had the wrong number again. She was about to hang up when the line clicked and caught, opening up to Zack's wary, *Hello?*

Jess said she was just checking in, but she couldn't mask the uncertainty in her voice. Zack must have heard it, too.

"Where are you?" he asked. The line was bad, coming in and out.

"At a pay phone."

"Where?"

"Out of town."

"Jess," he said. "What are you doing?"

Over at the pump, the line of cars was growing. A long green station wagon with fake wood paneling idled in the middle of the pack. In the back seat, a young girl pressed her check to the window, trying to get a good look at the front of the line. Jess watched her through the phone booth's smeared glass.

"I'll be back in a couple of days."

"Listen to me. You saw what those people did. And what that girl did to you. Let the police handle it."

"They can't, Zack. I have to get her out."

"Out of what? Jess, don't. You don't know this girl."

He was wrong, but Jess didn't want to fight, and didn't have time to explain. "I'll be home soon," she said. "And then let's watch a movie. Not on the phone. At your place. Or let's go to a theater, sit in front of the big screen. When was the last time we went to the movies together? Maybe even tomorrow night. I could be back by then."

Martha appeared from around the corner of the gas station, heading back to the car.

Jess said, "I have to go."

"Wait. Just—"

Silence on the line. Jess thought the call had cut out, but then Zack's voice returned.

"I want you to know something."

Martha stopped beside the rental's passenger door, raised her arms over her head, shaking blood flow back into her hands.

"A couple of years ago," Zack said, "I flew out to Vermont to meet a client, a professor in Burlington."

The connection worsened, splintering his voice with tiny blank spaces. Jess didn't know where this was going. Another story about a hunt for a lost movie? Maybe he was stalling for time, trying to keep her from hanging up.

"Zack," she said, "I really have to—"

"I knew you had a piece there, a place you'd made in the woods. That little house."

"*Waterfall*," Jess said, very confused now. *Waterfall* had been her first major commission. She and Zack had only spoken of it once, right before she left for Vermont to start building. She had been so excited and proud, and she'd wanted Zack to feel the same, but he was dismissive, wondering aloud who would bother to go looking for an art installation in the middle of nowhere.

"I drove out there," he said. "To your piece. I spent most of the day inside."

The line stuttered. Jess felt its struggling pulse in her chest.

She said, "You never told me."

"I've never been able to tell you any of it." Zack's voice was halting, stopping and starting, but he pushed forward. He had to get it out. "I was angry, you know? I've always been so angry. I wanted to be the one to do those things."

Jess leaned against the phone, the receiver warm on her ear.

"I can't describe what I felt in there," he said. "I still can't. But I want you to know that I think about it all the time."

Jess didn't know what to say. She wanted to tell him that he was the reason she'd first considered making anything. That he had pointed the way. And that they'd been wrong all along, dug into the belief that there was only a single spot for one of them to occupy. There had always been room for them both.

But Martha was in the driver's seat now, ready to go, so instead Jess said, "I love you." She couldn't remember when she had last told him. Not since they were little kids, when it was so much easier to admit.

More silence on the line, then a drop down to a deeper silence, airless and complete, the call gone dead. Jess wondered if he had heard, wondered when she'd get another chance to say it. She hung up the receiver, listening to her dimes falling through the machine.

Martha started the car. The line at the pump inched forward. The girl in the station wagon pressed her lips to her window, blowing a kiss, then leaned back to admire the mark she'd left on the glass.

From *Light + Space*

(1977; 16mm film, sound; 82 minutes;
Laura Lehrer, dir.; unreleased)

J ess sits in the chair, listening. The studio is bright; a white glow sur-
rounds her in the frame. The light bleeds over the edges of her body
at times, an arrhythmic pulse owing to an imperfection in the camera's shutter or lens.

It's early in the interview. Jess has just told Laura about seeing Agnes
Martin's grids for the first time.

- Have you ever entered a space you created after it was finished?

- Of course. There's often something that needs to be adjusted, or
fixed, or cleaned.

- I mean as a visitor. Entering a piece purely for whatever experience
you might have.

Jess crosses her legs, considering. She smiles a little as the answer
comes.

- I guess I haven't.

- Why not?

- My experience is noticing the possibility in the first place, and then making the piece. When that's done, something disappears. All I see then is the physical structure, and the imperfections and mistakes, things I should have done differently. I don't experience it as something new or surprising.

The camera whirs. Jess is still holding the question. She isn't finished with it yet. The light behind her pulses, blurring the edges.

Laura speaks again.

- Can you imagine a piece you could enter in that way? That might have that depth of mystery for you, so that you could enter as a visitor?

Jess looks up into the lens, still surrounded by the question. She turns to the window, squinting in the light.

- No. I don't think I can.

32

ere is the ghost town, the abandoned military base crumbling into the flat, sunburned waste. Scrub brush, bare trees reaching. Here is the base's center, the single intersection: the PX, a gas station, a small office building.

Here is the squat brick school, its front doors knocked from their hinges. Someone has painted CLEAR DAY across the remaining windows, a single letter on each intact pane. Overhead the sky is wide and flat, reddening with the spill of sunset to the west.

They had parked the car outside the front gate and now walked through what remained of the base. Jess felt like she was in a warped version of Alex's photos. The remembered structures were still here, the crossroads, but it was all disfigured. Tire tracks gouged the ground, low mounds of trash surrounded the buildings. And every wall was marked, claimed with paint.

Zero, zero, zero.

You are on sacred ground.

This was what her grief over Alex had become.

What little Jess had eaten over the last few hours rose into her throat. But Martha was right behind her, and Jess tried to imagine the strength it took for Martha to return to this place. Maybe she could draw from some of that courage. Maybe it would be enough for both of them.

They turned the corner in front of the school to find a brown pickup parked in the middle of the road.

Martha said, "They're here."

Martha carried her purse on her shoulder, its weight brushing her hip as she walked. She remembered the man at the shooting range back in Vegas, his body too close, his voice in her ear. *Plant your feet; hold your breath.* She repeated the phrase in her head, a chant to clear away the fear and doubt.

With each sound of a bird or lizard in the brush, Jess turned, sure someone was rushing toward them. Martha didn't seem spooked at all. She walked steadily, focused on the trail north, so Jess tried to follow her certainty. She felt someone here, though, just off-frame. Alex leaning over Jess's shoulder back in her apartment, looking at the photos, asking her to give the place a name. She remembered speaking the words for the first time, those twin *z*'s like bees between her teeth.

Martha stopped and Jess came alongside. There was another high fence up ahead, with a hole torn into its side. And through the hole the low cinder-block room, *Zero Zone*, standing silent, waiting.

The room was prepared. Tanner tried to stay patient. It wasn't easy. He felt his composure fraying, its threads loose, hanging in the air.

The sunset filled the space, a deep, smoky red. Isabella sat against the north wall, staring toward the center, where Emmett's device waited, blinking like a blood spot, there and gone.

Emmett fidgeted in a corner, an annoyance now. Tanner ignored him, refocusing on Isabella. Soon he would see that bright, beautiful moment in her face. She would walk toward Emmett's device, toward the new sun. Tanner would join her, and they would finally pass through.

He heard footsteps outside and moved to the western opening, expecting the police. Instead, two women approached on the trail. Tanner couldn't believe who it was. But then he felt the room shift around him, moving into place, like a lock turning open. They had been unbalanced all along. He'd never realized.

One of them had always been missing, but now they were complete.

The long, thin opening in the wall was dark, but Jess felt eyes watching her from within the room.

Martha passed her, walking doggedly around the outside of *Zero Zone* toward the doorway on the opposite end. Then she stopped, taken aback, looking up at the southern wall. Jess joined her to find an enormous date spray-painted across the room's exterior. Each number had to be seven feet high. Jess felt dizzy, dwarfed by that memorialized moment. It hadn't passed, though. The date was a signal. The moment was still there, caught in the dusk. Jess saw the siege happening all around her, spotlights searching the walls, police storming the room. Spots and floaters streaked her vision in the same way Zack's news footage had crackled with static. Martha took Jess's hand, and they moved through the flickering chaos to the doorway. Jess looked down, sure she would see Danny Aguado's body. They would have to step over him to enter the room. It seemed as if Martha saw him, too, or some other horror, because she squeezed Jess's hand. For support, maybe, or to make sure Jess didn't run. Jess wanted to run. She had no idea what she would do or say once they were inside.

There was no body in the doorway, but Jess still stepped over as they entered, leaving the last of the day's light.

•

Izzy felt nothing. She and Tanner and Emmett had been here an hour, waiting for sunset. This was always the time of day when the rupture appeared, but now she only saw Emmett's device, blinking in the growing dark. Tanner was going to use it, one way or the other, convinced it would push them through.

She wiped her cheeks. She couldn't remember the last time she had cried. Yes, she could. It was here, back when she felt she was so close to the new sun, when the police burst in, when Danny died. She tried to focus. She was so tired. She wanted this—she had always wanted this, to leave her body. But now she couldn't stop thinking of the world outside this place, of Martha and Vince, so she continued wiping the tears that blurred her vision, turning the room into a swirl of gold and red.

When Martha appeared, Izzy thought she was seeing things. For a moment she felt such relief. Even if this was a dream it was a beautiful one. Martha had come to take her home. Then Emmett's device blinked and Izzy woke again. She had to get Martha out of here. She started to call out, to shout for Martha to leave but lost her voice when Jess Shepard came through the doorway.

Martha couldn't breathe. The room was filled with stifling red light. She gripped her purse and Jess's hand. Tanner stood by the southern opening, that fucking smile on his face. The other man, Emmett, sat in a far corner, his legs straight out in front of him. Izzy was by the north wall, her face turned to Martha and Jess in the doorway. She looked scared and confused.

Martha knew she should do it right now, before Tanner said a word. Reach into her purse and do it, grab Izzy and go. But then Emmett said, "What are they doing here?" and Tanner said, "They've come to pass through."

Just his voice in the room. All the coiled energy drained from Martha's limbs, her courage and anger pooling on the floor. She let go of Jess's hand and then her purse, her foolish plan, dropping everything.

Jess's eyes wouldn't adjust. The light was almost tangible, a deep red fog. She had never imagined it could be this intense. Tanner walked toward them, appearing and disappearing in its folds.

"Miss Shepard," he said. "Jess. Welcome home."

She couldn't pull her attention from his face. It wasn't the growths or tumors; it was his presence, his voice. Warm, confident, generous. Not the monster she had expected.

"I didn't think I'd ever get the chance to meet you," Tanner said. He smiled at Jess. He looked like a child, full of uncomplicated joy. "But of course you've come. You need to be here, too."

Izzy didn't understand. She never thought she'd see Jess Shepard again. This woman must be so angry about what Izzy had done. Izzy shrank from the memory. Slashing Jess with that wand, the wet red gash opening on her cheek.

Jess didn't seem angry, though. She seemed stunned, overcome by the room. Izzy wanted to go to her and apologize, ask for forgiveness. But she wasn't brave enough. Not yet. She hoped to be stronger on the other side.

Jess knew she should be afraid but couldn't get any safeguards to take hold. It was like striking matches that refused to ignite. The light was overwhelming. She felt its heat on her face and hands, in her chest. Breathing it in. She remembered the color, the weight of the color, from Alex's studio, that first discovery, painting and replacing his darkroom bulbs furnace red. That color had remained here, in *Zero Zone*, waiting, growing. She tried to speak, to recall what she had come to say, but her body was heavy with the light, like water in her lungs.

She saw Isabella against the wall, another man sitting in the corner. Figures from a dream. They looked like prisoners, trapped in the room she had made.

"I'm sorry," Jess said. She remembered now. She was here to apologize for the pain she'd caused. They were all suffering, and in her own selfish despair she had created a place that amplified their anguish.

"There's nothing to be sorry for," Tanner said. His voice seemed part of the room, another fold of the light. "I know about your work. You understand the sickness of this world. Your whole life you've tried to find a way out. And you finally did."

She wanted him to stop talking but was having trouble speaking again. The pain here was physical. It came off each of them in waves, as if it was the source of the light. Jess couldn't think clearly. She needed to shake herself from this fog, concentrate on the tangible space, the art piece she had made, the measurements and material: rebar, concrete, paint. But she couldn't hold on to the facts. They dissolved in the light. This place no longer made sense in those terms. It wasn't hers anymore. It was something new.

She closed her eyes, hoping for relief. And for the first time since the attack, she found she wasn't afraid of this darkness. There was something else here, below the pain, or past it. Another glistening, deeper in. The truth swirling in the room. She'd chased it her whole life, but always pulled back, never giving herself over completely. She made her art and walked away, watching from what she thought was a safe distance. Only Alex went all the way in. She felt him now, lifting his camera to his eye. He was so close. What would it take to join him in that moment?

"You've given us this beautiful gift," Tanner said. "The exit. We're almost free."

She had passed a test, returning here to the heart of her fear and doubt. She had never imagined this grace waiting inside.

Someone gripped her arms then, and Jess opened her eyes to a riot of floaters swarming in the bloodshot fog. Tanner was there, close, his hands wrapped above her elbows as if she were a prized possession. Beside her, Martha whispered, "No," speaking to herself, or maybe to Jess, trying to summon courage or clarity. Her voice came like an alarm from outside the fog, muffled but urgent. Jess tightened at Tanner's touch and a new storm of spots rose in her vision, obscuring his face. For once she welcomed the confusion they created, making space between her and the room, an inch in which to breathe.

She tried to pull free, but Tanner squeezed her arms, holding her in place. The pressure from his hands pulsed, and the light throbbed along with it, narrowing to a small red point in the center of the room.

"What's that?" Martha said, her voice shot through with fear, merging with Jess's own, a cold wind blowing a hole in the fog.

"That's the final piece," Tanner said. He let go of Jess's arms and walked toward the blinking light. "Our beautiful little machine. Like a rocket." The way he said the word made him a boy again, reverent, exhilarated.

The other man stirred, standing in his corner. Jess had forgotten he was there. He moved to where Tanner stood before the dark rectangle, that small box veined with wires.

A bomb in the room.

Jess's body rang with that alarm now, jarring her mind clear.

This wasn't grace. This was obliteration.

"Don't do this," she said, panic taking over. "Please. Turn it off."

"That's just fear talking," Tanner said. "Resist it. Let it go."

When Tanner walked away, Martha was able to move again. She didn't listen to Tanner's voice. She refused to listen. Instead she crouched to the floor, feeling for her purse in the hideous light.

Izzy wanted Emmett to turn it off, too. But was that just more fear, like Tanner said? She was so sick of being afraid.

Jess turned to Isabella, standing frozen against the far wall.

"You don't have to go through with this," Jess said.

Martha crawled on the floor, breathing hard, her heart thrashing, fingers searching the rough concrete.

Isabella's face looked swollen. She'd been crying or was crying now. It was so hard for Jess to see.

"Martha came for you," Jess said. "Vince is on his way."

"Vince?" Izzy asked.

"*Stop.*" Tanner's voice cracked through, loud and sharp. A command.

Martha's fingers brushed across sand or dirt, scraps of paper, little bits of broken glass that stuck into her skin. Then she found a single thin softness, a strand of leather fringe. She pulled it toward her.

"Izzy," Jess said, the nickname she'd heard from Vince and Martha, so full of affection.

"*I said stop.*" Tanner turned to Jess. She felt the force of his anger, a blow from across the room.

"You don't understand any of this, do you?" he said. "Isabella was right to cut you down. You have no idea what you've made."

Martha stood, pulling the gun from her purse.

Jess saw movement to her left, another shadow, the other man rushing at her.

Izzy screamed, "*Don't touch her!*"

Martha planted her feet. She held her breath. She squeezed the trigger and the gun bucked in her hand with a deafening crack. The room filled with the sound. Emmett dropped as if his legs were kicked out from under him.

Jess's hands flew to her ears, reflexively, too late.

Emmett struggled to stand, stumbling, woozy. Martha pulled the trigger again. Another blast from the gun. Emmett toppled to his side. He coughed, twice, then lay motionless, like a heap of clothes on the floor.

Martha stared at him, what was left of him. She wanted to scream at what she'd done.

Tanner said, "Give me the gun."

Martha pointed it at Tanner. He came and went in the shifting light. Those tiny pieces of glass pressed into her fingers.

"You won't," Tanner said. "I know you, Martha."

The room smelled of the smoke seeping from the gun's barrel. Martha wanted to drop it. She wanted Tanner to come and take the gun away.

Slowly, Izzy walked toward Martha. She saw Martha's jaw flexing, the hand holding the gun trying to squeeze, but it was stunted movement. Martha couldn't go any further. Izzy put one hand on Martha's back, the other over the handle of the gun. Martha's eyes were still on Tanner. Her nostrils flared as if she was going to scream or cry. Izzy eased the gun from her hand. Martha's arm fell to her side.

Tanner said, "Bring it to me."

Martha's hair covered her face and Izzy brushed it back, gently, behind her ears. There were two dark spots on Martha's neck. Izzy remembered Tanner's hand there, back at Martha's home, what Izzy thought might become her home until Tanner had arrived. He never should have touched Martha, never should have left those marks.

Tanner said, "Isabella."

She turned to him and the air split open, a blinding line of light expanding, swelling, filling the room. Her breath caught in her chest.

Tanner said, "Is it here?"

The room fell away. She felt the new sun's heat, stronger than ever, searing through every pore. That glorious, terrible beauty. Like crossing the school hallway, her feet leaving the floor, her body rising. Like stepping off the edge of the La Loma bridge, the flock of blue-winged birds rushing beneath. Like starving herself, day after day, pressing skin against bone, aching to be weightless and free.

It was here, finally, the fulfillment of all those promises.

Tanner moved toward the bomb.

To Jess, it looked like another loop of Laura Lehrer's film, Izzy drawn to a presence only she could see. That unbearable longing. But Jess understood it now. She had been consumed by it since Alex's death. It had led her to this place, this room. All this time Jess had been trapped here, too.

"Izzy," Jess said. "We don't need to stay here anymore. We've both been here too long."

Jess's voice splintered Izzy's concentration, disturbing the sun, a fluttering around its edges.

Jess said, "Will you leave with me?"

That fluttering was another pull, a different opening. Something past what Izzy imagined was possible. Martha was here, and Jess said Vince was on his way. Izzy wanted to believe that was true. She thought of working in Martha's garden—*their* garden. Those lovely, fragile afternoons when it seemed they healed a little more with each seed planted. She thought of driving with Vince, some day still to come, a camera to her eye, his face in the frame while she filmed. Maybe she could learn to live in those days, those possibilities.

Izzy couldn't see Tanner through the blazing sun, only his rippling silhouette, like a dancing shadow.

"Don't do it," she said.

"You're afraid," Tanner said. "You have to trust me."

Izzy bent forward, her free hand on her knee. The sun's heat was burning her alive. "I can't," she said. "Please let us go."

"This is what we've always wanted. We're finally here. Don't you feel it?"

Izzy nodded, sweat streaming from her nose and chin.

"Then let's go through."

"Stop," she said.

Tanner moved closer. He wasn't going to stop.

Izzy forced herself upright again, lifting her arm, pointing the gun. She'd never held a gun before. It was small and strangely heavy. Not unlike that other weapon, her horrible canister and wand.

She said, "I want to leave."

"That's right," Tanner said. "We're all leaving." He took another step toward the bomb.

Izzy squeezed the gun and the blast sounded again and Tanner jerked back, twisting at the waist, then down to one knee.

He put his hands on his stomach. They came away dark and wet. He looked at Izzy in disbelief.

The new sun blazed, a final offer. Izzy took a breath, holding its heat for a moment, a last inhalation of that promise. Then she turned away, dropping the gun. She reached out and Martha grabbed her hand, pulling her from the bomb, and then Jess pushed them both out the open doorway.

Tanner watched them run. He couldn't feel his legs. He was kneeling, but there was nothing underneath. It felt like floating. Everything was leaking from his stomach. Once when he was a kid he'd stabbed a pencil into a milk carton and watched the entire half gallon pump out onto the kitchen counter. So much liquid through such a tiny hole. His mother was upset at the waste and mess.

He looked to Emmett, slumped on his side, then turned back to the center of the room, the darkness there, the empty space. He never saw what Izzy saw, was never granted that gift. He was still stuck in the phase.

Stand in the after-work crowd in Pershing Square, the simmering onset of a summer evening. Friends, strangers, lovers, families. Realize that you could shout and no one would look at you. You could sing, you could scream. You could explode.

The answer had been there all along. So much time wasted, searching. There was only one way to pass through.

The device blinked, a small red promise. Tanner reached for it.

The blast threw Jess from her feet. Her vision went black and then the sound of the explosion caught up to her, knocking away all other sound. She was flying, then falling, dragged deeper by the undertow. She was back beneath the waves, that first day at the beach, tossed forward, drowning again in silent darkness. An incredible pressure in her head. She reached for her mother's hand, desperate, straining for that touch, but Barbara wasn't there. Jess was alone, flailing. Then she hit something solid, bouncing, the wind knocked from her lungs. She was out of air, moving too fast, rolling, unable to grab hold, her hands dragging through dirt, her body spinning, and then the ground was gone again. Launched into the emptiness. She hung for a moment, suspended. She was going to fall; she had tumbled over the edge. Her stomach rose in expectation of the sickening drop. She knew there was no bottom. That plunge would never end.

A hand pulled her then, hard, and she could see, could breathe, gasping, her lungs and eyes and nostrils burning. She coughed out what she thought was water, but it was smoke. She was lying in the dust, a rain of ash and rock falling, pieces of the room. A hot orange glow from somewhere behind. Her hearing faded back, a growing roar in her ears, like rushing wind. The sound of a fire. Izzy was there, too, on the ground. They were face-to-face. They had been here before, that night in the gallery. Izzy coughed, blinking away ash. She held Jess's hand tightly in her own, as if unwilling to let Jess fall backward. Izzy reached out with her other hand and touched Jess's cheek, her fingertips gentle on the scar she had made. Jess saw such tenderness in Izzy's face. That tenderness was what she had missed, that night at the gallery. It was buried so deeply, beneath the pain and rage.

Izzy said something Jess couldn't hear. More concrete fell from the sky, larger chunks now, crashing on the ground around them, into the back of Jess's neck, her hip and shoulder. Izzy pulled Jess to her feet and they ran, Jess's vision shaking, ash in her eyes. She saw Martha running ahead. They followed her into a dense cloud, Jess holding her breath in the ash and smoke and burning embers, a field of scalding orange points of light, and then they passed through and she inhaled, breathing again, out the other side.

Izzy stumbled and Jess pulled her forward, surfacing.

Waterfall

(1972; in situ installation; northern Vermont)

The dirt road leads to a flat, open field, the tall grass green and gold in the morning light. You park your car on the shoulder, behind the guide's car, the arranged meeting place. The guide leads you down a trail that crosses the field beside a clear, rocky brook. The air is warm, draped in mist, full with the sound of insects, a single shared note, rising.

Slowly, through the mist, a distant wall of trees comes into view, the border of the forest. The trail continues along inside. The guide stops, motioning for you to continue on alone.

Deeper into the woods, the sunlight flickers through the towering trees, majestic maples and bluish evergreens. Their piney scent is heavy in the humid air. You hear animal sounds in the distance, birdsong and a deer's fleet-footed steps through the tall grass.

After a half hour of walking you see a small structure farther down the trail. It is a house hidden in the woods, square and wooden and roughly made. Inside is a small, bright room, with a bench where you can sit and rest. There are windows on three walls, pulling sunlight from different angles. In front of you is a sheet of falling water that runs from one end of the room to the other, in effect creating the room's final wall. The water falls from a thin slit in the ceiling down to an identical slit in the floor. It makes the slightest sound, a clear, glittering ring. The light from the windows catches in the water, turning, blurring, bending. There is nothing else in the room.

Time passes. You watch the water, the shifting patterns and colors. Sometimes it shows a string of rainbow light; at other times it takes on the autumnal blend of the flame at a match head, orange and yellow and white.

An hour has passed, maybe longer. You have begun to lose interest in the water. You have begun to lose interest in the entire experience. Stray thoughts arrive. The memory of a recent argument, a list of tasks needing completion. You are annoyed by these thoughts, in this place. You were expecting something deeper and more meaningful. You try to push the thoughts away, but they return again and again.

You watch the water. Your thoughts slowly begin to lose their resonance. They begin to pull apart, like cotton gently tugged. The thoughts lose most of their meaning. You feel that they are coming from some external place, maybe the woods outside. They drift in on the light through the windows and swirl in the room, then are washed away in the water. You have less and less control over these thoughts. Memories, fantasies. They are not always pleasant. You remember shameful acts, fearful moments. You are grateful that the water carries these thoughts away. Other thoughts are calming, pleasurable, arousing. But they, too, are taken by the water.

You are hungry and thirsty, but these needs flow away. You remember something particularly painful. You remember something particularly embarrassing. You feel a past loss, a past hope, something you might have done differently, choices and mistakes. The sun moves, changing the angle of light through the windows. The water sparkles. You are crying, possibly. Or you are smiling—beaming, really. Laughing. At times you cover your face and then remember that you are alone in the room, free to feel any way imaginable, in ways you've never allowed before. The sun moves, the light shifts. Sometimes you see your reflection in the water, every emotion playing there, raw and unrestrained. It's frightening, seeing yourself this way. It's freeing. You stand and walk around the bench, to each corner of the small space. You walk up to the wall of water. It smells clear and clean. No one told you not to touch the water, but you do not touch the water. You wonder what is on the other side. You sit on the bench. Thoughts and memories and dreams flow through. You are no longer the central figure in your own life; you are a bridge from one place to the next. You feel as open to the unknown as you have ever felt, open in a way so entirely new that it must be the closest you can feel to being born. There are moments when you cannot catch your breath. Moments of panic, of elation. This is what a baby feels. You know this now. Or you remember. This is what the world feels like when everything is new. You are sitting on the floor, your face as close to the water as it can be without touching. If you touch the water, you will be washed away. Maybe you want to be washed away.

The sun moves. The light shifts. You see someone on the other side of the water. A woman, sitting on a bench just like your bench. There is another room there, or the other half of this room. A perfect reflection. Even the woman is a perfect reflection. You no longer have any idea what you look like, so you must look like her. She is sitting on the bench, crying. In pain or joy, it's impossible to tell. The light shifts. She stops crying and looks at you. You do not speak. You sit and watch, every new part of you going out to her. She is the first person you have seen in this new place. This must be what babies feel when they are placed on their mother's breast, head to heart. This unspoken connection: pelagic and blood deep.

She feels this, too. You can see it in her face. Love and relief. You are here together, at the beginning.

Sunset blazes the water orange and red, a wall of fire. You are frightened again, but the sight of the woman on the other side comforts you. Maybe seeing you comforts her as well. Dusk falls in the room. The light seeps out, the water darkens. The woman fades. You want to call out, to reach through the water, but you have no voice, you are unable to move. The woman wanes, and finally the water is a wall again, opaque and impenetrable.

After some time you manage to stand and walk to the door. Your guide is waiting outside with a flashlight. He leads you back down the trail through the woods. You imagine that the woman was led out of another door, back along another trail. You feel such an emptiness that you almost ask to be carried. Your body stumbles with loss. You do not know how to explain what has happened.

It is not until weeks later, filling a glass in the kitchen, watching the water pour from tap to drain, that you realize: it was not a loss, it was a gift. The entire day in that room, the waiting and terror and shame, the elation, the flow, the rebirth. Watching the water, as you will now always see it, as the sound and sight of running water will now always move through you, cleansing, brightening. You can't see her face, but she is there. Though you will never meet again, though you never need meet again, you know that there is someone who understands.

ACKNOWLEDGMENTS

Thank you to the O'Connor and Anderson families for their love and support.

Yishai Seidman read every draft, sketch, and half-baked idea. Our partnership is one of the true joys of this experience.

Dan Smetanka took a chance on this book, encouraged me to blow it up, then helped put the pieces back together. Dan Lopez and Chandra Wohleber kept their eyes on the details when it felt like I'd lost sight of the entire picture. Megan Fishmann, Lena Moses-Schmitt, Katie Boland, Samm Saxby, Rachel Fershleiser, Miyako Singer, and Dustin Kurtz got the book out into the world. I'm thankful for their enthusiasm, expertise, and hard work. Jaya Miceli, Nicole Caputo, and Jordan Koluch made it beautiful inside and out.

Thank you to Martin Garcia and Susan Weber, Sabra and Chris Goodman, Ben Leroy, Sean Carswell, Jim Ruland, and Natashia Deón.

Robin Lippincott read an early draft and offered timely encouragement. *Blue Territory*, Robin's book on Joan Mitchell, was a continuing source of inspiration. Chris Daley read a later draft, and I appreciate her insights and challenging questions. Karen Anderson read everything, and her honesty and careful consideration helped shape this book.

Each week I have the privilege of being part of workshops with talented, dedicated, generous writers. I'm thankful for that inspiring community.

I'm grateful to the people who shared their experiences with art, from the healing to the harmful. Some of those stories were this novel's first spark. As to my own experiences, I'm indebted to the work of too many artists to list here, but there are a few whose vision I returned to again and again: Agnes Martin, Vija Celmins, James Turrell, Olafur Eliasson, Mary Holt, Helen Pashgian, Chris Burden, Chantal Akerman, Marina Abramovic, Bas Jan Ader, and Lee Lozano.

And to Karen and Oscar: all the love in the world.

© Kathryn Mueller

SCOTT O'CONNOR is the author of *A Perfect Universe: Ten Stories* and the novels *Half World* and *Untouchable*, which was named the 2011 Barnes & Noble Discover Great New Writers winner in fiction. His stories have been short-listed for the Sunday Times/EFG Story Prize and cited as Distinguished in *The Best American Short Stories*. Additional work has appeared in *The New York Times Magazine*, ZYZZYVA, *The Rattling Wall*, and *The Los Angeles Review of Books*. He teaches creative writing at Cal State Channel Islands. Find out more at scott-oconnor.com.